I0641317

A Portion of the Eternal

Maurice Jovan Billington

A Portion of the Eternal
Maurice Jovan Billington

Copyright © Maurice Jovan Billington 2013
Images Copyright © Courtney Literary 2013
Cover Art by Samantha Nipps
Cover Design by Greg Harvey
Author Photo by Gregory Pruden with a special thanks
to Kris Misveski

ISBN- 10:1-945812-16-8
ISBN- 13:978-1-945812-16-3

2nd Edition 2017
Published by Richter Publishing LLC www.richterpublishing.com
All rights reserved. No part of this book may be reproduced in any form by any
electronic or mechanical means (including photocopying, recording or information
storage and retrieval) without permission in writing from the author or publisher.
To purchase copies wholesale or for libraries and bookstores you can contact the
publisher at 727-940-7647 or email: rpublishingadmin@icloud.com.

All characters appearing in this work are fictitious. Any resemblance to real persons,
living or dead, is purely coincidental. The opinions and writings in this book is that
of the author and not the publisher.

My first book is dedicated to my first born,
Jovanna Dejenueve,
without whom I would not have known the words to
express an unconditional love.

I would like to give special thanks to the following people without whose assistance, support or friendship during the process of writing this novel would have made it almost impossible.

Mark Elliot
Taylor Fleury
Shelly Lyon Harrison
Melanie Neal
Robin O'Dell of The Proofreading Boutique
Kelly Oris
and
Sheila Tekavec Magendantz

There are more and I will thank you each individually

Sodomizing Dragonflies

I am the particle that drifts through the air, unseen, until the light from an apathetic sun pulls my existence into your view. I will be forever changed. Once I have been betrayed by a random refraction of light, I will never be able to hide from you again. And you will never allow me to remain what I was, when I floated along, hidden in the safety of the shadows.

His was a bedroom I imagine to be like that of any other boy his age. Posters of girls they could never have, electronic items they could not afford and clothing littering a floor they hoped someone else would clean. Oh yes, and there is the football in the corner.

If you listen closely you can hear his breathing. I know I can...

The only difference, the defining difference between the hypothetical rooms of boys I speak of and this particular boy of eighteen's room is he could have those girls, he could afford the electronic items and there was someone who would come clean his room. Why? I've already told you, because of that football in the corner.

I still hear him breathing. I will never be able to forget the sound and, subsequently, I don't think I will ever breathe the same again.

Every girl dreams of the first time she makes love. How will it be? Who will it be with? Will she like it? Will it hurt? And will she know what to do? There are a thousand questions, but the truth is, none of them can ever be answered until the moment it actually occurs. So we are left with our imagination. Imagination and time... Oh, and circumstance. Circumstance may not ask questions like the things we imagine do, but it can become the primary giver of answers.

He's getting up now. I'll return to what I was saying in a moment.

Do you think he's handsome? The golden-blond hair? The athletic body? The face untouched by concern? Is that what we are born to desire? Is that why some are born to be hurt? Is that why others are born *to* hurt?

He's gone now. He's in the bathroom. What was I saying? Yes, I remember now... One thing you don't imagine about your first time, your first sexual encounter, is that it will be with someone you don't love. Someone you don't even like. And you definitely don't think the proper term for it will be *rape*.

He's back. I have to stop thinking or I believe he will hurt me...

I'm getting dressed. I have to go. I have to go now. I don't belong here. I never did. And I don't want to be in this room anymore. Though I think there is a part of me—a portion—that will always remain.

"You are so hot," he says. But I don't feel hot. I feel cold. My insides are a sun that was frightened by the sudden appearance of night and now can't remember what its purpose was. And as I walk out his bedroom door I am left to wonder if I will ever remember my purpose or if I will ever feel anything again.

I begin down the spiral staircase and the cruelty of the degree of a circle forces me to look at where I have just left, again, again and again. I close my eyes and hope that my feet will understand and compensate. I touch the downstairs floor. I am not out of the house, but I will look at that particular door no more.

Is he behind me? I ask myself this as I feel for the front door in the darkness of the house, in my shame. Please don't be behind me. Again.

I have now opened the door. Light from the moon pours in but seems to go past me. Am I too dark for illumination?

I step outside and I close the door behind me. It is ninety degrees at night. Desert towns are so hot. Hot... I remember what he said. There's that cold feeling again.

My name is Liv. I am seventeen years old though as of five minutes ago I can no longer remember what the innocence and hope of that age feels like. My hair is dark. Almost black. There is a hint of light to my hair but that is an illusion created by the intensity of the color of my eyes. My eyes are green. I have bangs that rest just above my eyes like shades that are too short for the window. The remainder of my hair is long, like curtains that ache for the floor. I have a smile strangers tell me is beautiful. Be wary of strangers that comment on your smile.

In the last picture I took of myself I was lying on my bed. I was on my belly as if the weight of the day were on my back and holding me down. There is a collage of pictures on the wall in the background. That is what the weight on my back feels like now, not the day, but a collage of every moment in my life that might have warned me of this. My arm is stretched out, obscuring half my face and hiding most of my smile. You can see just the corner of my mouth, but you can still tell I am smiling. It was taken over a year ago, but when I look at it now, it makes me wonder if that's all the smile I need, a portion? And if so, why was I born with so much? Wolves prefer sheep that smile, don't they? Nothing runs fast when it's smiling. I feel like I was born with too much smile, but I feel that is no longer going to be a problem.

My body is a girl's body, not a woman's. I have just enough curves to make me want more, and just enough to make others want me. My body is a lot like my smile. And like my smile it will never fully belong to me again.

My skin is white. There is a hint of dark to it. I sometimes wish there were more.

If you wonder how I dress, if you want insight into my soul from the fabric that drapes me, then you are fortunate for you have never been raped. I am naked now, and I feel that I will forever be. Clothing, like the light in my hair, is now too an illusion. I am a bird that has had its wings torn from its body and is suspended from the sky by a thread.

I am everything I am and I am nothing that is I. I am the girl that you will hold close and never be able to touch. I am the girl you will touch but never be able to hold close. But I will compel you to try. And try. And try.

I am the dragonfly you will never be able to sodomize. You can't sodomize dragonflies. Dragonflies never remain still. My body will never be in the same place as my mind. My eyes will never be looking in the same direction as my stare. I exist in a state of perpetual motion where who I now am will constantly collide with who I could have been.

I want to scream, but I can feel him watching me from the window as I walk away. For now, I think it best that I remain silent.

Desert Promises

We are sheltered beneath a sun-bleached sky surrounded by a blanket of white sand. We are riding in a 1965 powder-blue Ford Mustang. It is a convertible and the top is down, allowing the sun to bathe us as the wind deflects its heat. We are kids riding on the edge of the threat of becoming adults. Sometimes you arrive before you know you are there.

His name is Brandon. Other than my father, he is the most important male in my life. His smile is the sun-bleached sky. His arms are the white sands that surround me. And his heart is a '65 Ford Mustang racing toward me at all times.

Everything about his features is dark except his spirit and soul. From the jet-black strands of hair that hang just below his smile, to the brown of his eyes that go deeper than the color should allow. He is the gentle night in which I fold myself away from the harsh realities of the light of day.

There we sat, quiet as the desert sand that our bodies sank beneath. It was there that I told him. We had been together three years. We were going to college together. We were going to get married. We were going to have children. Are there two sadder words when put together than *we were?*

I purposely made him drive me out to the desert before I told him. That way, if he were so mad that he wanted to do something, something crazy, something regretful, he would have an hour's drive to think about it. All he wanted to do was hold me. And that was all that I needed.

> *"In the highest of places they watch*
> *Some almost fall with their anger*
> *This is why they are needed*
> *This is why they are here*
> *But in your arms their existence is unnecessary*
> *And angels get caught as they stare."*

They say it never rains in the desert. It did that day. Little drops of water falling from the sky like holy water redeeming our bodies.

Night eventually falls and the sky now seems to purposely conceal us as we whisper secrets and promises...

"You only have six more months of school," Brandon says to me.

"I can't go back," I say.

"You have to," he says, attempting to reassure me with his voice in the same way his arms did as they held me. "It's your last year," he continues. "You have to graduate to get your degree so you can become a teacher. Then we can get married."

I look at him. Why is he still talking about our future as if it had not been irreparably damaged? Had I not been damaged in his eyes?

"Nothing's changed. I'm still going to wait for you to join me at college," he says. Brandon is one year older than I, a freshman already enrolled in our city college.

"But things *are* different," I tell him. "I wanted you to be my first. I wanted to give you something no one else had."

"That doesn't matter," he replies softly, even as he can see in my eyes that it matters to me. "I don't love you any less. I couldn't."

"How could you not?" I ask, wanting it desperately to be so.

"You haven't changed. I love you. And it doesn't matter whether or not I'm your first. I want to be your last."

"I'm sorry."

"Sorry for what?"

"I shouldn't have been there. I—" Tears interrupt me. "I tried to leave. He stopped me. Then—" Tears again.

"It's OK. It's over. Everything's going to be fine."

"I was so scared."

"I know," Brandon whispers in my ear. "I know."

Brandon brings me around so that I can look into his eyes as he speaks. "Do you trust me?"

"You know I do," I say to Brandon, shocked that he would even ask me such a thing.

"You need to go to the police."

I say no before he has even completed his sentence.

"I can't."

"Yes you can, Liv. And you should. He needs to pay for what he did."

"No. You don't understand. He won't. He won't pay. You know this town. You know his family."

"We'll force the town to listen."

"No, Brandon, no," I plead. I am so close to him that he can feel the shaking of my body and I think that speaks for me even more. "You don't understand what he did to me, what he made me do. I don't think I can repeat it. Not in front of a roomful of strangers, not in front of my—" I stop. Brandon knows who I was going to name. He pulls me back into his arms—I won't allow him to let me go so easily this time.

"It's OK. It's OK. I understand."

"I'm sorry," I tell him.

"No. You don't have to be sorry. I am."

"Why?"

"For letting someone hurt you. For not being there to protect you."

"Don't think that way, Brandon. Please. It makes me afraid."

"Afraid of what?"

"Of what you will do. If something were to happen to you, too…"

"Nothing's going to happen to me."

Why am I afraid again? I turn from within Brandon's arms and slowly remove the heart-shaped pendant that hangs around my neck.

"I wanted to give you this for your birthday. I know it's not for a couple of weeks, but I want to give it to you now."

I place the chain and pendant around Brandon's neck and clasp the lock into place. I look into his eyes as I speak.

"Now you have something no one else has."

"What is that?" Brandon asks.

"My heart."

"I won't ever lose it," he tells me.

I want one thing more from him. "Promise me," I say. "Promise me you won't do anything."

It's very silent in the desert.

"Promise me," I beg.

There is no bargaining with the desert. Brandon takes my hand within his.

"I promise," he recites.

He kisses me. It is moisture upon my lips in a world where water is too fragile to exist.

"I love you," I say. "Eternal."

"I love you," Brandon tells me. "Eternal."

I look into his eyes. I try and commit them to memory. I try to hold on to how they shine even in the night. I try because somehow I know it will be the last time I see them. I pull the over of night over our heads and close my eyes to the rhythm of his breathing. Somehow I know it will be the last time I am to hear it.

Never make promises in the desert. The desert is a barren place. Hostile. Dry. There is not enough of anything in the desert to keep promises alive.

The Beauty of Ruins

I am my father's only daughter. I am my father's only child. My father once told me there are no absolutes in youth; there is no forever nor are there unchanging constants. There can be no unflinching reserves in the physical or the mental world of the young. There was no time for such designs within the ever-shifting realm to which I belonged. There was only time enough for things to die. My father told me this when I was three.

Perhaps my father related this truth to me at such a young age so I would have the time to understand the meaning before I would be forced to watch his relationship with my mother die. Perhaps because, like a pebble disrupting the tranquility of water, the ripple would leave my relationship with my father disrupted, as well.

I don't believe my father ever stopped loving my mother. I don't believe my mother ever stopped loving him. I believe they were both incapable of looking into each other's eyes. She could not look into his without wondering if he was looking back, and he could not look into hers because he knew that he was not.

Don't fall in love with a writer. My father told me this. All writers drink... all *great* writers. To my father every word you wrote should be a temptation, every sentence a sin and every completed work a demon that would haunt you eternally for that about which you chose to write. Those that were not tormented by their words enough to drink were not digging deep enough to excavate the pain from beneath the muddied ground of their soul, or the demons that surfaced with it.

My mother never realized that the reason my father did not look her in the eyes was because he was trying to protect her and therefore could never fully take his eyes away from the demons that he had surrounded himself with.

"He writes so beautifully
But he lives in its ruins
Day to day everything he gives to explain
Only takes away leaving nothing
He could write a smile
It will return to him as rain
My father writes so beautifully
But I've never heard him laugh."

It is Sunday. I always visit my father on Sundays. Sundays are our day. I took it away from God. He had it long enough.

My father was never published as a writer, and I will always think less of the world because of that. He has the ability not to think anything of it. He smiles when I come to visit him and if we decide to stay in, he will make me homemade lemonade and I will pour him a bourbon. Sometimes he will just have lemonade because I do. Whatever he drinks I know that when I get up to leave I will look at the warm wet circle beneath his glass and imagine that, like the circle, we will always be unbroken.

I think today we will talk about amusement parks. Maybe we will go to one. Maybe we will ride the merry-go-round. Ride it as it revolves, like a warm wet circle.

I will not tell you my father's name. His name to me is Father, Dad if I am so inclined, and anything anyone else should call him is neither greater nor more important. I will not tell you his age.

Look at your father. Does he not look like he did the first time your eyes opened up to him? Time cannot alter such an important image. No. I will not tell you any more of my father right now. I need him just to be mine.

Oh, and most importantly… unlike the ever-changing realm of youth, I will not give this day time enough to die.

Kinski

I haven't been to the desert in over a month. I doubt I will ever go again. Even though I feel surrounded by the death that it hides.

> *"Nothing is eternal*
> *Not the daylight.*
> *Nor the night.*
> *Nothing lasts forever except the pain*
> *Knowing I will never see you again."*

I sit beneath this tree trying to be alone. I cannot. The tree is in the middle of an expansive park that is the front of a school. Lago High. It is a small high school campus, some might say the slightest of transitions from a middle school. But it will be on the national map soon. And he will put it there because his football team is undefeated.

"He," the quarterback, has a better record than players at major universities. His destiny is to go to a great Midwestern program, commit to four years, play the requisite three, then draft into the NFL. Superstardom and all that goes with it then waits like a cheerleader sitting in a running car. But first he has one more game to win.

It is November. A breeze blows, a winter's breeze where there is no winter. Snow cannot exist here anymore than joy can reside in me. The breeze blows again, tapping me upon my shoulder. I look up. There stands a stranger. I cannot tell who he is or what he looks like for his face is concealed behind a black motorcycle helmet and shield. He looks at me as if he knows me. I stare back at him in an attempt to see beyond the reflection of his windshield. It is like peering through a two-way mirror, being unable to look into the eyes of those that search your soul. Then an uneasy feeling washes over me. The tilt of his head, the manner of his stand, why is it so familiar?

"Brandon," I say with the hesitation of doubt and disbelief. He does not respond. What was I thinking? Of course it's not Brandon. How could it be? "I'm sorry," I say. Again, he does not respond.

I look back down but I am compelled, compelled by another breeze that blows past me to look up again. He is gone.

"Nothing is eternal
How can it be
When we are not
Because we are
Nothing."

The school bell rings. Students file into the building amidst discarded cigarettes and conversation. I glance at them all. Some I know, some I don't, some I no longer want to know. Sometimes it's hard to tell which student belongs to which feeling.

My father told me that at one time Nastassja Kinski was the most beautiful girl in the movies. He professed his love for her. She, he said, was once photographed naked, covered only by a snake. It was by some famous photographer with a famous last name. Avedon? I looked him up one day. He was known for large portraitures that were said to capture the soul of his subject. He would do that by asking them psychologically probing questions, often making the subject uncomfortable just before snapping the picture. He died of a brain hemorrhage in 2004. I wonder what he asked Nastassja, or if she was able to keep everything so hidden that he was forced to dress her with a snake in place of her soul. My father would like that about her. I hope that I can hide things as well as Nastassja. My father said he is glad she no longer makes movies. That way he can remember her as she was.

Your last year of high school, I think, is the first year you make a conscious choice to remember. It is a year filled with the filigree of passage to help you do just that, from the yearbook to the class ring to the prom leading up to graduation. It is your first true end into your second true beginning.

Can you ever accurately recall your last year of high school? And if you can, will it make you happy when you do from where you are now or will it make you sad? Would it be best left in the graveyard of your youth, never to be celebrated or mourned? Can you remember it as it was, or simply as you wished it to be?

I've never seen any of Nastassja Kinski's movies. I will have to watch one someday. I wonder if when I do I will see what my father saw. I wonder, will I think she is as beautiful as she is in pictures.

> *"Nothing is eternal*
> *Not even nothing*
> *Even though nothing*
> *Remains the same after it is gone."*

I wonder when I'm older and I look in my yearbook if I will remember who any of these people are.

The Wind Is a Mistaken Name

Introductions will be easy. Everyone has the same first class. Everyone, however, is not here. He will enter five minutes after so that everyone sees him, so that everyone knows he is special.

What about the teacher? Why would he allow this? Because he is like almost everyone else in this town; he loves to watch Christian throw a football. That he requires Christian's attendance at all is only a formality for the records.

There. I have said it. That is his name: Christian. Christian, the one that... I think you know.

Sometimes parents look into a child's face searching for a name that his destiny will catch up to. I don't believe in destiny. And I believe sometimes a name is the first mistake parents make regarding their child.

Jai is smiling at me. Jai is always smiling. His bright white teeth the perfect complement to his mocha-colored skin. Mocha is his word. He hates being called Black. I don't blame him. It lacks the descriptive nuances of who he is. Black seems blunt, oppressive, but mocha embodies his essence as much as the afro that he wears from an era he was never a part of.

Jai is orphaned. His parents were killed in a horrific traffic accident when he was two. The town called him a miracle baby because he was in the car but emerged unhurt. It was as if moments before the crash he had been removed from the car and placed back inside afterward, willed out by the love of his parents, who it is said saw the oncoming truck. The wreckage of the car wrapped around Jai's body like a bassinette. His parents died instantly. They probably never knew their love saved their baby.

Murdoc is smiling, too, but Murdoc's smile is like the perceived smile of a shark. It's not a smile at all. And it should be feared. Murdoc is Black… blunt… oppressive. He is the school's star wide receiver. His parents are neither the poorest nor the most privileged in this town, but because of his talent they are hoping to fall into the category of the latter and never have to sympathize with the former.

Russel is Murdoc's best friend. Russel is white. I only point that out because he is not white by race but by trait. He is an albino. Genetics? Or maybe it has something to do with the fact that he has the personality of a vampire so his skin is attempting to accommodate his soul.

The clock on the homeroom wall says it is now five minutes past the hour. The door of homeroom opens. In walks Christian. I think I can say it now. He's the one who raped me.

Christian takes his seat. It is across from me. He looks over and smiles like we are lovers. I look away. I cannot stand the sight of him. My face is not turned away for long, however. There is that breeze again, and this time it compels me to look toward the door.

A stranger walks in.

All heads turn. Christian is supposed to be the last one to enter the room. Who dares command attention when all should have been given already?

A motorcycle helmet no longer conceals the stranger's face. I can see that he is about eighteen. His hair is a desert brown and just as windswept. His eyes. I have no words to describe eyes that are so beyond the color they are supposed to be that they are beyond color. They are a blue in a world where there is nothing but blue and so they are translucent. He wears black jeans and a black pullover hoodie with a white T-shirt beneath. Multiple black bands entwine both his wrists. He wears black motorcycle boots with an *H* embroidered on the sides. It is not the Harley-Davidson *H*. I am unsure what it stands for.

He is beautiful. And I am aware of this even though beauty is currently dead inside me.

The stranger doesn't look at me. He doesn't look at the teacher. He doesn't look at anyone. It is time for roll call. Everyone knows everyone so everyone waits for a name they don't know. His name.

"Gabriel?" the teacher asks.

"Here," he says.

I think he will no longer be a stranger.

Monster Dark

Gabriel rode a Ducati 750 Monster Dark. Which meant with the exception of the engine and certain other points, the motorcycle was completely black. I think it's Italian. I don't know much about bikes, but I know that when I saw it in the school parking lot, I thought it looked like a bird of prey. There was something organic about its design. Something purposeful. Something menacing. Even as the bike sat parked, it was as if it were in motion.

Gabriel is sitting at a table in the school courtyard. It is lunchtime, but he is not eating, just sitting.

Jai steps over and takes a seat beside him. If there was anyone that was going to be the first to welcome the new kid, it was Jai.

"Hi, I'm Jai," he says.

"Gabriel."

"Yeah. I know. Gabriel. That's, like, biblical right?"

"I suppose that depends on if you read the Bible," Gabriel responds.

"No. I don't."

"Why not?"

"My parents died when I was two. My grandmother raised me, but she died three years ago of cancer, after suffering for five years. I took care of her for most of those so there wasn't a lot of time for me to go to church and get to know Him, if you know what I mean."

"In the Bible," Gabriel says, "Gabriel is an angel, referred to as the messenger of God."

"So you bringing us a message?" Jai asks as he smiles.

"I don't believe in telling people things they already know," Gabriel says.

"Well, let me tell you something you might not already know," Jai says as he leans into Gabriel so that no one else might hear. "You see that guy over there … the one with the two guys around him like bodyguards?" Gabriel looks over to where Christian, Murdoc and Russel stand. "That's Christian, Murdoc and Russel. And they don't like you."

"They don't?" Gabriel asks.

"No," Jai answers. "They don't."

"Is that going to be a problem?" Gabriel asks in a manner indicating he remains somewhat unconcerned with the answer.

"Not for me," Jai states.

"What about you?" Gabriel asks. "Do you like me?"

"Yes."

"You do?"

"Yes," Jai repeats.

"Why?" Gabriel asks.

"Because they don't," Jai says.

Gabriel smiles. Gabriel looks in my direction. I know this because I look at him at the same time.

"What about her?"

"That's Liv," Jai answers.

"Do you think she would like me?"

There is a pause before Jai responds.

"The only thing Liv is interested in is that notebook."

"Why? What's in the notebook?"

"Words. Poems," Jai states. "It's all she does since her boyfriend died."

"Boyfriend?"

"Yeah, boyfriend. His name was Brandon."

"Brandon."

"Yeah."

"Did you know him?"

"Not really," Jai responds.

"How did he die?" Gabriel asks.

"Accidental drowning," Jai says. But there is something in his voice, something in the manner in which he says it. Gabriel hears it.

"You don't sound like you believe that's how he died."

Jai looks at Gabriel.

"He was captain of the swim team."

"I guess things happen," Gabriel offers.

"Shit," Jai says. "Shit happens to people. Especially when things are planned by other people."

Jai sees out of the corner of his eye that Murdoc and Russel are standing beside Gabriel's motorcycle. He looks back over to Gabriel.

"Looks like they want to meet you."

Gabriel rises from the table.

"What are you going to do?" Jai wonders.

"Meet them."

Gabriel walks across the courtyard toward his bike. As he passes me, I look up and he smiles at me. I do not smile back. It's nothing personal. I haven't smiled for a long time.

I continue to watch as Gabriel stops in front of Murdoc. He looks at Murdoc's biceps. Murdoc doesn't put a lot of effort into covering them, and it's almost as if they look back at Gabriel.

"This your bike?" Murdoc barks.

"Why? You gonna wash it for me?"

If you could see the look on Murdoc's face. I can and I will never forget it.

"Am I gonna what?" Murdoc asks with the indignation of a disrespected entity.

"He asked if you were gonna wash it for him," Russel needlessly responds.

Murdoc turns and shoots a look at Russel. I doubt I will ever forget that look, either.

"He's right," Gabriel adds, taunting Murdoc. "I asked if you were going to wash it for me."

"Why would I want to wash your bike?" Murdoc asks.

"Because that's your blood on it," Gabriel responds.

Murdoc looks down at the motorcycle. When he looks back up, there is nothing but the tightly wrapped flesh of Gabriel's fist in Murdoc's face. And then, as Gabriel foresaw, there is Murdoc's blood on Gabriel's bike.

For the third time today, as his knees buckle, and he falls to them, Murdoc has given me a look I will never forget. He offers that same look to Christian, who watches from the safety that distance affords him across the courtyard.

Gabriel removes the bandanna hanging from Murdoc's pocket and first wipes the blood from his bike and then from his hands. He then looks over to Russel, who wisely says nothing.

Gabriel walks back in the same direction he came from, smiling at me in the same manner as he did when he walked past the first time. This time, however, I smile back. Sort of.

Gabriel continues back toward the building. Everyone is watching. Why? Because he is about to walk past Christian's table, the one Christian has been sitting at and watching from the entire time. If you ask me, I don't believe anyone in the courtyard thinks Gabriel will stop at Christian's table. No one but me. I don't know why, but I know he will. He does not disappoint me.

Gabriel takes the bloodied bandanna and tosses it onto the cafeteria tray of food that Christian was not yet done eating.

"I think that belongs to you," Gabriel says.

There are four people sitting at Christian's table, waiting for him to respond. As far as I know, to this day, those four people are still waiting.

Gabriel stares at Christian as Christian stares back; then he brushes past Christian. I feel that breeze again before he disappears into the school. I'm not sure, but I think that "sort of" smile is still on my face.

You Wouldn't Want to Make the Same Mistake Twice

I stand before my locker. I have to get the book for my next class. I dial the combination. Why is flesh not this secure? Why is there no combination you must remember to unlock it? Why does it open so easily? I pull down the lock, remove it and open the locker. The book is on the top shelf. I look at the book before removing it. I wish I were that book. I wish I were put on a shelf and locked away from everyone and everything that surrounds me. I wish I were only removed when someone needed me, but if I were that book, I would wish that I were never needed. I would hope that my contents were never sought after. Never required. And if you did need me, if you were to remember the combination to lock, unlock it and take me out, my every word inside the book would tell you to read no further lest you compromise everything you believed in. Everything you thought was good. Everything you thought was true. I would implore you to put me down, close the cover and place me back into the locker. Lock the lock, then spin the dial as if you were turning yourself away from everything you had just read. I would then tell you to lose the combination for the prose would always remain the same. The story would never end happily.

If you listen closely, you can hear his breathing. I can. I don't turn around. I may not be able to escape his presence, but I don't have to look at him this time.

"Aren't you going to say hello?"

No. I am not. And there are few times a person is more smug than when they ask you a question they know you won't answer because they are already aware of what the response would be.

"What about Motorcycle Boy?" Christian asks. "Did you say hello to him?"

Christian's breathing may be the most vile thing I've ever heard in my life. Even more so than the smugness that drips from his every word like saliva drips from a rabid dog's mouth.

"I wouldn't," Christian advises. "As a matter of fact," he continues, "I wouldn't say anything to him."

Christian places his hand upon my shoulder as he leans into my ear. It is the first time he has touched me since the last time, and I feel my body wanting to collapse into my throat before I vomit it back out and onto his shoes.

I hold my breath as he whispers into my ear. His words penetrate my ear like the night he—

"You wouldn't want to make the same mistake twice."

He leans back and looks into my eyes before he turns and walks away.

I have yet to exhale.

Gestures Frail

Five minutes have passed since Christian left. Five minutes that have passed with the difficulty and excruciating slowness of horses pulling promises underwater. I must be alone now. I have to be. I no longer hear his breathing. I don't even hear my own. I finally am able to reach into my locker. I remove my book, and that is when I see that there is another book inside. I reach in. I remove the new book from my locker. I have never seen it before, though I read the title and am made to feel warm, fleetingly so.

Exhale...

Somewhere a Bell Is Ringing

Some students can't wait for the dismissal bell, while some students dread the imminence of its ring. Dread it as if it were a bell tolling the coming of their demise. What a horrible dichotomy then, the sound of a bell. Depending upon what awaits you at the split of an hour, you can either love it or despise it.

Jai is in the halls almost immediately after the bell rings. It is not quick enough. He slams his locker and finds himself with the company of both Murdoc and Russel. Murdoc is wounded, a bandaged nose, but he is no less menacing, maybe even more so, like a dog that's been hit but not beaten into submission.

"Where are you going so fast, Noodle?" Murdoc asks.

"My name isn't Noodle," Jai responds defiantly but still fearful.

Russel responds for both. "Don't worry. It's not you we're interested in, Noodle."

"What do you want?"

Murdoc takes over. "We have a little job for you."

"What kind of job?"

"The kind of job perfect for you, Noodle," Murdoc says with a weird sense of confidence.

"I don't want a job," Jai says. Russel is only inches away from his face when he speaks, or, rather, threatens.

"Did we ask you what you wanted? I didn't hear us ask, so I'm pretty sure we didn't!"

"What do you want?"

"We want you to find out about Motorcycle Boy."

"Who?"

Murdoc now leans in closer to Jai. "The second time I say something it's with my fist!"

"Gabriel," Jai responds, understanding the threat not so hidden within the context of what Murdoc said.

"See, Murdoc," Russel intones, "I told you he would understand if you just asked nicely."

"What is it I'm supposed to find out?" Jai asks.

"Everything," is Murdoc's answer.

"What do you mean, everything?"

Murdoc brings his closed fist up to Jai's face. Jai does not ask him again. Murdoc and Russel leave. Jai turns his head and sees Gabriel standing at the other end of the hall. Jai looks at him as students pass back and forth in front of Gabriel like traffic.

"What was I supposed to do?" Jai yells out. Gabriel does not respond.

Jai looks away. "What was I supposed to do?" Jai asks again, this time under his breath. He turns his head back to where Gabriel stood. Gabriel is gone; only passing students remain.

I myself, I am outside, in the parking lot. I am walking up to my car. Well, what is now my car. Brandon's '65 Mustang. His mother gave me the car after he died. She did not need it and she knew how much it meant to me. I was with him when he picked it out. It is dangerous driving it because sometimes I drift away in thought imagining he is at the wheel and it is only the sound of impending danger that brings me back in time enough to swerve and avoid it.

As I insert the car key into my door, I see a reflection of someone behind me in the glass. I gasp. I turn around. It is not who I was afraid it was.

"Sorry. I didn't mean to frighten you," Gabriel says. He didn't frighten me—his reflection did—but I don't tell him that.

"Do I know you?" I ask, knowing that I don't.

"I wanted to know if you liked the book," he answers.

He is referring to the book that was placed mysteriously in my locker, though now the mystery is solved. It was a book of poetry, not of one author but a collection of works.

"How did you know—" I was going to ask how he knew I liked poetry, but he interrupts me before I can finish the sentence.

"In your most frail gesture," he recites, "are things which enclose me, or which I cannot touch because they are too near." It is a poem from the book he gave me. I know. I have already read them all.

"E. E. Cummings," I say. And for a moment I am lost in the beauty of the words. For a moment I forget that this will only last a moment. For a moment... I forget I have moments that will unfortunately last a lifetime.

"Someone told me you liked poetry," he says.

The book is in my hands. I hand it back to Gabriel. See I told you. The moment is gone.

"I used to like poetry," I tell him.

"What about now?" he asks.

"They're just words, words that trick you into thinking they mean something because they rhyme. Or fool you into believing something because they're so short they don't give you time to think."

I get into the car and start the engine before Gabriel has time to say anything. Or maybe he respects the futility of trying. I roll down the window, partially, and look Gabriel in the eyes.

"But eternity doesn't mean forever. And love never keeps anyone together. So what good are words that lie to you by telling you it does?"

Gabriel watches me as I pull away. I know because I am watching him in the rearview mirror as I do it.

> *"Somewhere a bell is ringing*
> *Somewhere a bride has died*
> *Somewhere a dove escapes*
> *Somewhere a groomsman lied*
> *Somewhere there is cake that shall never melt*
> *Somewhere there is a day that will never be felt."*

The sound of an engine revving grabs Gabriel's attention away from the vanishing me. It is two engines. It is two cars. Muscle cars. Murdoc is inside one of the stallions; Russel is strapped inside the other.

Gabriel tucks the book of poetry inside his jacket and turns to face both cars.

Tires squeal. Rubber burns. Dust flies into the air as both cars speed with a thought-out recklessness toward Gabriel. Gabriel does not move even as both cars race toward him. Students of both apathy and complicity stop as they watch both cars disappear into a cloud of dust agitated by the fury of the tires atop it.

Gabriel vanishes from sight as the dust that builds around him announces the impending steel of both vehicles. Even the birds in the trees look on with concern. After seconds that seem more like minutes, both cars emerge from the cloud of dust and stop. After a few moments more the dust settles around Gabriel like a holy garment, and it can be seen that he stands untouched.

Somewhere a bell must be ringing.

The sound of another car's engine is heard. Gabriel looks down the other end of the student parking lot. This car is not a stallion—this car is a bull. A black Ford F-450 raised high enough to walk beneath without bending over.

Atop this bull sits Christian. He kicks the sides of his bull with no regard, racing the engine until it is compelled to break out of the gate and rush toward Gabriel.

And now I find myself here again, in a moment that includes Christian? I don't know why, but there I am pulling my Mustang into the path of this bull.

"Move, Liv," Gabriel says to me.

"Get in," I say to him.

Somewhere a bell must be ringing.

"Get in!" I command, as if to say I am not a bull to be challenged. Gabriel gets into my car, and it is now my wheels that agitate the ground beneath them as we disappear into the dust.

The Dissipating Dust

I speed down the road with Gabriel in the seat beside me. We pass houses spread so far apart that it is in question whether they can be called neighbors or not. I turn to Gabriel. He sits close to me. Closer than he should be sitting.

"He would have killed you," I tell him.

"No," he says to me. "He wasn't going to hurt anyone."

"How do you know?" I ask.

"People like him are cowards," he says. "The daylight doesn't provide as much cover as the night, where they usually show who they really are."

I am unsure if he is talking about what just happened or what Christian did to me. How could he be talking about me? He couldn't be. He wasn't there. I haven't told him. So why do I feel comforted by his words? And why do I feel they were meant to comfort me?

"I was afraid for you still," I say. He smiles.

"You don't know me, remember?"

"But I know Christian," I tell him. "So I was afraid."

We are coming upon the town's old church. I say old but I should say abandoned. It was the only church the town had until people stopped coming. Now the wood-framed structure is decrepit and splintered, allowing fractured rays of light to penetrate the darkness that resided not around it at night but within.

"You can let me out here," Gabriel says. I slow the car and stop almost directly in front of the church even though it is not my intention to simply leave him here.

"Let me take you home," I say.

"No," he tells me. "I have to go back for my bike."

"Then let me take you back."

"No," he says again. "You can go home now. I'll walk back."

I look out across the expanse of road. It must be at least five miles back.

"Are you sure?" My attention is momentarily held hostage by the sadness I feel looking upon the decay of the church. After hearing no answer I ask again. "I said, are you—" I stop speaking as I turn to the passenger's seat and find that Gabriel is gone. "Sure," I finish softly. I look out the window. I look out every window. He has vanished amid the dust as if he were an echo of a confession from the structure I am parked across from, carried away by the wind.

I glance down to the passenger's seat. The book of poetry he had given me and I had given back is now once again mine. I pick the book up. A page is bookmarked for me. I turn to it.

"Water spills from your eyes
But tears do not wash away pain
They only empty the soul to store more hurt
Rain
I will be your pool
Empty into me
Until I overflow
Then empty again."

A tear explodes onto the page as if it fell into the ocean. The drops of water that rise from the book pull me down with them until I am submerged beneath the waves of memory.

I can see Brandon's casket. It is at the front of the funeral home, and I am standing right before it. It is long. Black. Cold. I wish it looked warmer. Maybe that's all he needs is warmth. Maybe that's all he's waiting for, someone to wrap themselves around his body and hold him until the heat from their body awakens him. I want to climb into the casket and be that person. And if he doesn't awaken, I want them to lower it in the ground with me still inside.

How will his soul be able to escape when they close the lid? Will it be unable to? I look down upon him and hope that his soul has already departed. I hope that it is standing beside me, keeping me from falling. I hope that afterward it leaves and never has to come to this world again. The world doesn't deserve someone like Brandon. It never did. Maybe that's why he's gone. Maybe God woke up and realized he'd made a mistake.

I am outside now. Everyone is. There is a row of black cars that stretch ten miles long. Maybe not ten miles, but I can't see past the limousine that carries Brandon's body to its grave, so even if it is just one car, it may as well be a hundred.

I climb into the limousine. Brandon's parents sit across from me. I look into his stepfather's eyes. There is nothing in them. It is as if he has been hollowed out and all that remains is the shell. A shell so fragile even a soft-spoken word of sympathy would cause a fracture that could crumble him into a million tiny pieces that then blow away, dissipating into nothing. I look at his mother's face. There is none of the temporary sanctuary that hollowness provides. She is carrying the weight of all the grief

God told her she would have to bear in her lifetime in this single moment. Maybe that's what God meant.

They are lowering Brandon's casket into the ground. I stand there dressed in black looking around a clear blue sky for signs of his soul ascending. I see none. I look back down as his casket is completely lowered into the ground.

Ashes to ashes. Dust to dissipating dust.

Carrion of His Absence

"I am the carrion of his absence
I am this that remains
Empty
Do not call my name
Lest the birds know where to feast."

I am opening a door that should not be opened at this time of night. It is the door to the school's indoor pool. It is the pool where Brandon and the rest of the swim team practiced. It is the pool where school administrators found his body the day after he drowned. I have opened it with his key.

Light spills in and then dies as I enter and close the door behind me.

I am now bathed in nothing but the moonlight that washes down around me through the glass roof above my head. It is all the light I need. I don't need even that.

I step onto the diving board fully clothed. I walk out to the edge. I look down into the pool and remember how deep and how brown Brandon's eyes were. I almost feel that he is looking back at me. But I am happy that he is not, because he would not like what I am about to do.

I turn around so that my back is to the pool. I close my eyes and I raise my arms to the side. I take a deep breath and hold it.

This is what emptiness feels like. This is what I wish to forget. I am the carrion of his absence, and I want to drown the pain that is feeding off me.

Splash.

I am beneath the water. Bubbles rise though I do not. They explode with the sound of the word that was the last breath I expelled buried beneath my watery grave.

"Eternal."

I wait for death to reunite us… then… I hear my name. Even beneath the water I can hear my name being called clearly. I open my eyes. I can see a figure, blurred by the motion of the water, standing at the edge of the pool. Brandon? Did he come to save me? I ascend with the quickness of a first kiss until I break the surface and water cascades down my face and hair.

"Brandon!" I cry as I swim to the edge of the pool, where I find that it is Gabriel who waits for me.

"Liv… Are you OK?"

I was before I interrupted a destined sleep because I imagined Brandon. But I do not tell him that.

"I'm fine," I say.

Gabriel helps me from the pool and takes me over to bleachers, where I take a seat. He stands before me.

"You're shivering."

"I know. I'm cold," I say.

Gabriel walks over and takes a towel from the rack beside us. He brings the towel back and gently wraps it around me.

"It's a little late to go for a swim," Gabriel says as I continue shivering. I do not answer this time. "But I suppose you didn't come here to swim," he continues as he stands before me. "Did you?"

"Why are you here?" I ask him.

"Because I knew you would be."

"You couldn't have. How?"

"Liv, you can't conceal mourning. It's always there, even in a smile. Your mourning is so deep nothing can surface to even try and hide it."

"But how did you know here?" I demand.

"I saw your car when I came for my motorcycle," he says.

I look into his eyes. Why don't I believe him? Why do I want to?

"What do you want from me?" I ask.

"Nothing."

"Then why won't you leave me alone?" I ask even though I am unsure if I want him to go.

"Is that what you want?"

I look up at him.

"I want things to be like they were before."

"Before what?"

Tears falling from my eyes are the only answer he receives. He extends his hand out, softly, so as not to frighten me. I don't know why, but he doesn't scare me at all. He gently wipes the tears away from my eyes.

"Come with me," he says as he extends his hand out to mine. I look at it; then I look back to him.

"I can't. I don't know you."

"You know all you need to know about me."

"I do?"

"Yes," he says.

"What is it I know?"

"You know I won't hurt you."

The tears come again. I thought that once before and it cost me everything.

"I can't trust anyone."

Gabriel kneels down to me. We are now face-to-face. I like his face. There is something sanctuary-like about his features. There is something comforting about his stare. And there is something forgiving about his smile.

"If you believe that," he says, "you would have stayed at the bottom of the pool."

I take his hand.

The Abandoned and the Reborn

Both Gabriel and I have driven back to the abandoned church. The one difference is this time we have decided to enter it. I sit in one of the dilapidated pews, looking around at the moonlight pushing its way through the splintered cracks. It is the only light that illuminates us inside.

I look over to the empty pulpit, where once the word of God was spoken. Now it is silent. Is silence as comforting as his word? Is it as strong? I still believe in God, but I'm not interested in what he has to say at the moment, so for me the silence is fine.

I turn to Gabriel. "Do you know what happened to this place?" I ask.

"No. I don't," he says.

"The pastor hung himself after it was discovered he'd fathered a baby with one of the parishioners."

"How sad for him," Gabriel responds.

"He begged for forgiveness," I tell Gabriel, "but no one was willing to give it. He finally had to close the church when no one would come to service anymore."

"Do you believe that's why he killed himself?" Gabriel asks.

"Don't you? I mean, his purpose for being was no more. Gone."

He doesn't answer my question; instead, he asks me another.

"What were you doing in that pool?" I turn away from his and the question. He continues, "It won't bring him back. You do know that, right?"

I turn back to Gabriel.

"Maybe I don't want him to come back. Maybe I just want to be where he is."

"That's not what you want."

"How do you know?"

"No one does. I think you're just afraid," Gabriel says.

"Afraid of what?" I ask.

"That you can't make it without him. That life won't be the same."

"It won't," I say, interrupting so he understands just how strongly I believe that. "It won't be the same. It can't be the same. We were meant to be together and now that can never be. So why stay after my purpose for being is gone?"

"Your purpose simply changed," he continues. "Now it's to remember him and you can't do that if you're afraid you were responsible for his death."

"You don't know anything about his death. Or anything about me!" I say as I rise from the pew, and it quiets him, for a moment.

"I'm sorry," he says.

"It's OK," I say as I sit back down beside him.

"What happened to the mother and child?" Gabriel asks.

"What?" I say, unsure of the question asked.

"The woman that the preacher slept with. What happened to her and her baby?"

"The mother died during childbirth," I tell him. "No one knows what happened to the baby."

Gabriel rises.

"To answer your question, I think the preacher killed himself not because the town couldn't forgive him, but because he couldn't forgive himself."

"What if he didn't deserve forgiveness?" I ask, knowing that he is trying to make a parallel with me.

"Does this church deserve to be repaired?" he asks.

"I don't know," I say. "Does it?"

"There is so much love and comfort even within these splintered walls—to destroy it would be a greater sin than abandoning it."

"What if it can't be repaired?"

He steps closer to me. I want him to.

"Then it can be reborn," he says.

Reborn. Gabriel is right. I do not want to die, but I want to be reborn. I need to be reborn. But I will not tell Gabriel that. I will hold on to the thought for myself and allow myself the false belief that it can happen. Even though I know it cannot, for thinking that it can keeps me warm. And ever since I was raped, I so desperately want to be warm.

The Beach Is No Place for Lovers

I must let my mother know I am home so she doesn't worry. I know where to find my mother. My mother will be where my mother always is at this time of night. My mother will be in the back of the house in her office. The lights will be low and the glow from her computer monitor will illuminate the ever-deepening lines of her face. My mother is an attorney, a prosecutor to be exact, and the world, restless with ill acts, never lets a prosecutor rest.

My mother is very different from my father. I don't know if that is what brought them together, pulled them apart... or both.

The influence of evil is but one of the things that separates them.

My mother is face-to-face with evil almost every day. She cannot easily detach herself from the particles that attach themselves to your skin when you brush up against those who harbor monstrosities. When your skin is bruised by too much contact, it cannot help but inform how you touch the world around you.

My father was able to write about evil in a way I believe my mother envied. He did not have to brush up against evil to understand it. My father had but to smell my mother's skin or others that had already come into contact with it. I think that is what makes great artists great. They need only look where others must touch. They need only to listen where others must speak. And they need only live where others must die to understand the weight of the world can be contained within a single pebble of sand that finds itself beneath your feet.

I haven't told my father that Brandon is dead. I don't want him to have to worry about me any more than he already does. When I told my mother, she took me into her arms and said that everything would be all right. That is the way of her mind. To my mother if one of the aforementioned pebbles that carry the weight of the world gets in our eye, tears will eventually wash it away. Therefore, everything will be all right. That doesn't make my mother uncaring; it just makes her different from my father. My father would know that some pebbles embed themselves so deeply within you that they can never be found by tears, can never be washed away.

I open the door to my mother's office. She smiles.

"Hello, sweetheart," my mother says.

"Good night, Mother."

I close the door and go to my room.

The Fountain That Burns

I watch Jai fumble through his locker, like a child looking for a favorite toy buried inside a chest full of others. I observe this as I walk down the school hallway in his direction.

So focused on this quest is he that not only does he not seem aware of the traffic of people that pass by, but he doesn't notice me even though I now stand right beside him.

"What are you looking for?" I ask.

"Lisa."

"Who's she?"

Jai pulls a CD from between the pages of a folder and holds it up to me. "This is who she is," he proclaims. "Lisa Germano."

"OK," I say. "I still don't know who that is."

Jai looks at me as if I just cursed his very existence.

"You, who constantly bleeds onto the pages of her journal. You, Mr. Mortenson's favorite student in creative writing class. You," Jai continues, "who has taste in music so obscure that some of the artists probably don't even exist. You don't know who Lisa Germano is?"

"No. Who is she?"

Jai cannot wait to tell me.

"Only the most incredible female singer/songwriter ever." He offers me the CD. "It's called *Lullaby for Liquid Pig*. Once you hear it ... Well, just listen. Trust me. It will make you cry."

"I don't want to take your disc," I tell him.

"Don't worry. Burn it to your iPod and then you can give me the disc back," he says.

"OK." I take the CD from his hand and put it in with my other things. "Thank you."

Jai suddenly looks at me in the oddest of ways. It's as if he hasn't seen me in years, almost as if he's looking at a ghost.

"What's wrong?" I ask.

"You're talking."

He's right. I was. And now I'm smiling.

We are in Mr. Mortenson's class, English Lit. This at one time was my favorite class. Though since Brandon died, I don't believe I've said one word in it. His death made me aware of literature's love affair with mortality and now I see him between the spaces of every sentence as if his flesh were the punctuation.

Jai sits behind me. Christian sits across the aisle from me. It feels like Christian is always across from me. There was a time I loved how small our school was. How close everyone was. Now that closeness is suffocating me.

"Death," Mr. Mortenson begins. "Is it really the end? As Shakespeare proclaimed, do we shuffle off this mortal coil only to rest in a dark lonely place?"

Mr. Mortenson walks between the rows of seats as he talks. He has to or most of the boys in the class will quickly lose interest. If Shakespeare had known how to throw a pass or kick a field goal, I would imagine they would not need Mr. Mortenson's imposing presence in order to pay attention. Pity for William that Hamlet was not a wide receiver.

Mr. Mortenson, with his long brown hair pulled back and his storied face, the type of face that acknowledges his forty-eight years without betraying them, was in his youth a football player. It is for this reason and the fact that English Lit is now required that I am forced to endure Christian's presence in a world of eloquent ideas that has no need for the savageness of his existence.

"Was the English poet," Mr. Mortenson asks, "John Dryden correct when he said, 'Like pilgrims to the appointed place we tend; the world's an inn, and death the journey's end'? Or was French novelist Alain-Fournier closer to the truth in describing the complexities of death when he said, 'Perhaps when we come to die, death will provide the meaning and the sequel and the ending of this unsuccessful adventure'?"

"Sequel?" Christian interrupts. "Sounds like he thought life were a movie." No one laughs, especially not Mr. Mortenson.

"Your assignment," Mr. Mortenson continues as he gives Christian what he didn't want, his undivided attention, "was to find a poet or philosopher who best described your own view. And, Mr. McCoy"—that was Christian's last name—"whom did you choose?"

"Shakespeare," Christian mumbles with none of the confidence he has on a football field.

"Ah," Mr. Mortenson intones. "Shakespeare. The path of least resistance. Or the man with the most quotes from which to choose." Mr. Mortenson, unlike Christian, is able to make the class laugh.

"And which pearl of wisdom from dear Will struck within you a philosophical chord?" Mr. Mortenson asks.

"The one where he talks about death, you know, being like an undiscovered country." I loathe having to hear his ugly voice speak of such beautiful things. "Who knows?" Christian posits.

"Was that the wisdom Mr. Shakespeare intended to impart upon us about the great beyond?" Mr. Mortenson asks, seemingly as disgusted by Christian's dim-wittedness as I am.

"Who knows?" Jai shoots out, and laughter erupts from the class. Christian, however, is not laughing.

"What Shakespeare actually said," Gabriel interjects, his voice a rich respite from the desolation of Christian's own emptiness, "was that death was the undiscovered country, from whose bourn no traveler returns."

Everyone looks over to Gabriel. None is more impressed than Mr. Mortenson.

"Is this your view as well?"

Gabriel answers, "I believe he was saying death was the end."

"And you don't believe this to be true?" Mr. Mortenson inquires.

"I don't know. But I would hope it's not."

"And do you know of a philosopher whose ideas more closely support your belief?"

Before he even answers, I know that he does. He cannot tell me who it is soon enough.

"Percy Shelley," he responds, releasing me from limbo.

"Ah," says Mr. Mortenson. "'Adonais.' Superb choice."

"What did he say?" I ask, wanting to know more about the poem and the one who has just introduced me to it. Gabriel looks over to me as he recites.

"He wakes or sleeps with the enduring dead; thou canst not soar where he is sitting now but the pure spirit shall flow."

I know this. I feel this. I cannot wait until he finishes…

"Back to the burning fountain whence it came; a portion of the eternal."

There is silence in the room. I embrace it for it gives me more time to embrace the words I have just heard. A portion of the eternal. There is the warmth rushing over me again. The warmth that I need. The warmth that allows me to remain.

"And what do you think Mr. Shelley was trying to tell us in his eulogy to the young poet Keats?" Mr. Mortenson asks Gabriel.

Gabriel answers as he looks at me. "That if your heart is pure, your spirit will live on." Gabriel then turns to Christian. "That not even death is the end..."

"Go on," Mr. Mortenson encourages. Gabriel looks back to me.

"That maybe... the spirit returns to the place it was first born."

Mr. Mortenson continues for Gabriel. "The burning fountain?"

"Yes," Gabriel says. "The burning fountain."

"Did he mean life?" Jai asks.

"Perhaps, Jai," Mr. Mortenson responds. "Or maybe it is a metaphor for something else." Mr. Mortenson looks at the entire class. "Are there no poets among you? 'The place it was first born.' What could Sir Shelley have been referring to?"

"Love," I say. "Maybe he was saying it returns to its first love."

"Beautiful," Mr. Mortenson offers.

"Does that mean Christian will go back to himself?" Jai inquires, and the classroom shows their appreciation by laughing again. Perhaps it is one too many times.

In high school it seems someone always laughs one too many times.

Do Animals Have Souls They Sell?

I never sit in the school cafeteria. If I'm going to eat, whatever I am going to eat was never alive, and I would prefer not to eat in a place that smells like it was never alive. I am a vegetarian not because I think animals are equal to us but because sometimes I don't believe we are equal to them. So I sit outside watching others who for their own various reasons prefer the hot desert air to cold institutional comfort.

I'm not eating today. I'm just observing. Gabriel is leaning against one of the school walls. I feel like he is watching me even though his eyes do not look my way. I'm unsure why I care if he is or not, but I do. It's a feeling made all the more uneasy because I also feel like it is somehow betraying Brandon that some other boy has gained my attention. I do not think of him in that *way*, Brandon.

I am not the only one that is watching Gabriel. I am not the only one that cares about his presence. Christian glares from over the shoulders of both Murdoc and Russel.

"He's just some punk motherfucker," Murdoc tells Christian, still wearing a bandage on his face from their first encounter.

"He beat you down," Russel adds, perhaps ill-advised.

"He got lucky. You won't be if you don't shut up."

"I don't trust lucky," Christian barks. "And I don't trust him around Noodle or Liv."

"You think Liv is going to say something?" Russel asks. And from the look on Christian's face, there is no doubt that this *was* ill-advised.

"Say something about what?" Christian asks, not expecting an answer. Russel is not that sharp.

"You know."

"No. I don't know," Christian states. "I don't know anything. Why? What do you know?"

Russel finally, luckily, catches on. "Nothing. I don't know nothing."

Christian turns to Murdoc. Murdoc has always been smarter than Russel, but more importantly, Murdoc doesn't fear Christian; he needs him. Christian is his quarterback. Christian is his ticket out of this town.

"The only thing I know is we have a game to win in two weeks."

There's that smile on Christian's face. The smile he gives anytime anyone mentions the "game."

"It's not a game to win—it's a game we will win."

"The first undefeated season," Murdoc adds. The smile grows larger upon Christian's face, then just as quickly fades as he sees Jai approach Gabriel. Christian motions with his eyes so that Murdoc and Russel take notice also.

"You know what the problem is, Murdoc, when you deal with people who you know can't be trusted?" Christian asks.

"No. What?"

"You can't trust them."

All three continue to look on as Gabriel and Jai engage in conversation.

"I don't think your friend appreciated your joke," Gabriel tells Jai.

"Christian is a joke. He's always been. Ever since I first met him in middle school. And he's not my friend."

"He seems like he's everyone's friend."

"That's only because he's rich. Everyone wants something from him."

"You don't?"

"I have everything I need."

"You're a lucky person," Gabriel tells Jai.

"I don't know that I would say that."

"If you don't need anything, no one can buy you. If no one can buy you, then no one can own you. Only thing about that is—" Gabriel stops.

"Is what?" Jai begs.

"Is that you're responsible then for every choice you make."

Jai is silent.

"Looks like your luck has run out," Gabriel says to a still silent Jai.

"Huh?"

"Your friend is coming over," Gabriel says in reference to the fast approaching Christian.

"What's up, Noodle?" Christian asks, now right behind, Jai. Jai turns to Christian.

"My name is not Noodle."

Christian smiles, then turns to Gabriel. "So, Motorcycle Boy-"

"Gabriel," Gabriel immediately corrects. "My name is Gabriel."

There is an uneasy silence as Christian looks at Gabriel and Jai stares at the both of them.

"Gabriel." Christian gives up, defeated.

"See. That wasn't so hard."

"We need to talk, Gabriel."

"I am talking. To Jai."

Christian looks over at Jai. Jai looks away. One day, hopefully Jai will learn that you can't always look away. Christian turns back to Gabriel.

"It's about Liv," he says.

"What about Liv?"

"Why don't you and I go for a walk?" Christian asks.

Gabriel and Christian walk the length of the school's football field. They are isolated.

"You play football?" Christian asks Gabriel.

"I thought you wanted to talk about Liv," Gabriel responds.

"I do. I'm just trying to find out a little bit about you. Get to know you better."

"You don't know me at all."

Christian stops. Gabriel stops. They look at each other, one clearly unsettled, one clearly unconcerned. After a moment, Christian begins walking again.

"Football is my life. I've played it since I can remember. It got me a scholarship out of this dust bowl."

"I don't think this is such a bad place."

"So what does that mean? You're not going to college after you graduate?" Christian asks.

"I think for a lot of people, college is just an extension of their adolescence. A refusal to let go of things."

"I'm not afraid to let go of anything," Christian tosses off.

"Why would you be afraid to let go of anything when you never had to work to get it? Or..."

"Or what?"

Now it is Gabriel who stops first and Christian who follows suit.

"Or you just take it."

"What's that supposed to mean?"

"What do you think it means?"

Christian stares at Gabriel, searching out the meaning of Gabriel's last few words. He will not find them. He has no choice but to change the course of conversation.

"Liv's not looking for a boyfriend," Christian says.

"Neither am I if that's why you brought me out here."

How Christian's eyes burn. How poetic it would be if the fire consumed the rest of him.

"Let me give you some advice, Motorcycle Boy. You want to get along in this school, you need to associate with the right people. Liv and Noodle are not the right people."

"His name is Jai," Gabriel corrects.

"I know what his name is. Let me tell you something else I know about Jai. He's a loser. He walks around this school like he's better than everyone else because his parents died, but the truth is even if they'd lived he'd still be a loser, so dying was probably the best thing that happened to them."

Gabriel turns and begins to walk away. Christian, however, is not done.

"And as for sweet little innocent Liv, she's nothing but a whore," Christian yells. Gabriel stops. Some insensitivity you cannot walk away from or there is the chance that you become it.

"That's why her boyfriend died. He drowned because he was drunk. Drunk because he found out what a lying little slut his girlfriend was."

Gabriel walks back up to Christian. It's a football field and Christian's feet should be used to running on it. They unwisely remain still.

"You seem to know everything about everyone. How is that possible when you know so little about yourself? Or maybe you know exactly who you are and that's why you have to put other people down."

"Thinking you know me," Christian begins, "would be a big mistake."

"Yeah," Gabriel says. "And I wouldn't want to make the same mistake twice."

Christian is frozen by the echo of his own words. Wouldn't it be poetic if he were never allowed to thaw?

Gabriel turns and starts to walk away again. Christian is still not done.

"If you go against me, you're gonna lose," he yells. "You're gonna lose."

Jai is alone in the hallway. In high school it seems someone's always alone in the hallway when they shouldn't be. He sees Murdoc and Russel at the other end and wisely turns around to go the other way. When he does, Christian is standing in front of him.

"What did I ever do to you?" Christian asks.

Jai does not respond. Instead he stands and listens as Murdoc and Russel approach him from behind. Christian continues, "I like you. I think you're smart. But sometimes I think you're too smart for your own good. You know what else I think? And trust me, this is not good… I also think you don't know when to keep your mouth shut."

"I know…" Jai stutters before Christian interrupts.

"No. You don't know," Christian almost growls. "And now I have to show you. Again."

All three boys now surround Jai. He looks down at the end of the hallway and sees Gabriel standing there. Jai's eyes go wide. When you see a messiah, your eyes do this out of respect. Sometimes who you think is a messiah is simply a witness to the retribution. It can be difficult to differentiate between the two. And sometimes there simply isn't enough time. Jai looks as if he is about to say something. Christian brings his own fingers to Jai's lips.

"Shhh."

Christian's fingers become a fist and Jai doubles over when that fist meets his stomach. When Jai straightens back up, he looks back to the far end of the hallway. Gabriel is gone.

I am walking back to class. I think I hear the sound of a baby crying. I think. I follow the faint sound and it brings me around the corner even though I am afraid. As I said, there's always someone alone in the hallway when they shouldn't be. I don't want it to be me.

"Jai," I say as I round the corner and see that he is curled up in a ball on the floor.

Jai raises his head. He looks born of a beating. The crying sounds he was making have ceased though the tears in his eyes remain.

"Jai," I say again. Again he does not respond. I kneel down beside him. He looks at me. My stomach drops as I have seen that desolation reflected back to me in the mirror. "What happened?" I ask, already knowing the answer.

"You think life is easier once you graduate?" Jai asks. Or at least I think it was a question.

"Who did this?" I ask, another question he need not answer, and does not.

"I mean it has to get better?" Jai wonders loudly. "Right? Once you get old enough, once you're not a kid anymore."

I know Jai is lost in a wilderness of pain, but I am unsure if it is safe to try and guide him out of it. It may only cause more.

"We're not kids anymore, Jai."

I sit there and watch as Jai begins to emerge from the wilderness and see the world as it actually is. I think how every now and again in the course of conversation someone says something in a manner, in a way, with a certain intonation that you never have to question its truth.

Jai wipes away the tears from his eyes and looks at me. "I hate high school," he says.

I do, too.

The Echo of Rocks

So calm is the water. So soothing. How it makes me feel clean again even if for only the time that I swim beneath it. Part of me doesn't ever want to come up. I feel that dirty.

The clock on the school wall said five when I first entered. I look at the clock again; it is now eight. One more dive. One more purification. I climb atop the diving board and look upon the crystal blue surface, knowing beneath it lies the sanctuary of a different sort of baptism.

I dive. Breaking the surface feels as if I'm entering a womb though I will not ask to be born. I could live here within these liquid walls. Could I not feed off the sustenance tranquility provides? It makes me wonder why we are forced to be born. Is there no safer place than when you are in the belly of the one that would birth you? Does her body not provide the perfect shield against the horrors of the outside world? Why then are we forced to breathe? Because breathe we must, and so I surface and he is standing at the edge of the pool.

"Christian."

The school is closed. The lights shut down. I didn't bother to turn them on as it was daylight when I entered. Now it is night and the only source of light is from the illumination of the pool.

Christian is shadowed, nothing but the outline of the menace he is filled with. He reminds me of the shapes you see at night when your room is dark and you are certain that the monsters were waiting until your parents have fallen asleep.

"Touch me and I'll scream."

Christian smiles, and his smile I am able to see even in the dark, even though the smile is dark. "You're still waiting for someone to hear the last time you screamed," he says.

I exit the pool. Suddenly I don't feel very safe in the water.

"I'm not going to hurt you," Christian tells me.

"You already have," I say.

"Why? Because I liked you?" Christian's voice and his question echo in the dark. "Because I wanted to be with you?"

I want to spit in his face. I can't. It is not who I am. Though I get lost for a moment imagining that it is.

"No! Because you raped me!" I scream.

"That's not how I remember it," he says with the calmness that should only accompany the truth.

"Then you have a lack of memory to go along with your lack of self-control."

Christian raises his hand. Amazing how threats can be seen so easily in the dark. I recoil even though my mind tells me to stand strong. My mind does not feel the pain though; it only has to recall it. My feet inch towards the edge of the pool, but I am afraid if I go in, this time I will never reemerge.

Christian slowly lowers his hand without ever striking me.

"See. You're wrong," he gloats. "I do have self-control."

I almost wish he had hit me. I imagine the pool is on fire and Christian stands with his back to the water. I imagine pushing him in and looking him in the eye as he falls into the flames. Then I imagine watching his body blister away as the fire even burns itself to make sure he is gone.

The flames of the pool that consume quickly die out in my head. I cannot imagine this. This is not who I am.

"You're wrong about being raped, too. You came to my house. You came up to my room."

"I trusted you, Christian. You were my friend."

"Remember when we were kids and went on that field trip to the city?"

I don't want to remember. But I do.

"We were nine," he continues. "We went to the museum and you wanted one of the rocks from an exhibit and I tried to give it to you."

"I remember," I say. "The teacher said you couldn't give it to me and made you put it back."

"Do you remember I took it anyway and gave it to you on your birthday?"

Another memory I would rather have not remembered.

"Yes. I remember. I remember that you wanted me to give you a kiss, and when I didn't you got mad. I also remember thinking later that I should have given it back."

"I didn't want it back," Christian tells me.

Why am I having this conversation with him? Why am I not compelled to run away? Maybe I am tired from running away from him, from him and his shadow. Or maybe, unlike that night, this time I want to be heard.

"Well now you've taken something from me, Christian, and I want it back, but I can't get it back. Ever. So what am I supposed to do? How am I supposed to be whole again?"

"I want you to go out with me," Christian says as if I have just told him I think flowers are pretty.

"What?"

"I want you to go out with me," he clarifies. "Like on a date."

"Never!"

"You know I always get what I want."

"And what if you don't? Are you going to try and take it? I'm not a rock in a museum, Christian. I'm flesh and blood."

There's that smile again. Shining brightly in the dark. How long will it torture me?

"I know you are. Remember?"

"You won't ever touch me again."

"We've been here before," Christian states.

"Ever again!" I say. And this time it is my threat that is observed in the darkness.

"I just came here to ask you out," Christian says. "But I can see that you're upset so I'll just leave."

I say nothing. Mercifully he leaves.

I step to the edge of the pool. I look down at it. Even it cannot wash away how dirty I feel at this moment. So I just stare into the shallow abyss and watch the tears that fall from my face explode onto the surface of the water.

Onto Whom Does the Blood from Your Fingers Fall?

I have come back to the church, not to pray, but to see him. Gabriel. I do not know if he will be here, but I know of no other place to find him. His motorcycle is out front so I enter. I push open the door and step in, perhaps more pensively than anyone should when stepping into a holy place. The door closes behind me. I don't close it; it closes of its own will.

I see Gabriel immediately. He is down the aisle, standing before the stage, looking up at the cross that now hangs askew. He speaks without ever turning to me. Without me ever letting him know I am there.

"What's wrong?" he asks.

"I'm scared."

"Why?" he inquires, still with his back to me.

I feel as if I am at confession, but I have nothing to confess, only that I have come into contact with those who do.

"I keep having nightmares," I say.

"Nightmares?"

"They follow me around, even in the day."

Now Gabriel turns around. The hood from his pullover is over his head and shadows half his face. But I know it's him. Like a threat that protects you, I can see his eyes, even in the dark.

"What's in your nightmares, Liv?"

"A monster."

"Just one?" Gabriel asks.

"Isn't that enough?"

"Yes." Gabriel steps closer to me. "What are you looking for, Liv?"

"You."

"Why, Liv?"

"I told you. Because I was scared."

"You don't have to be scared anymore."

"I'm not," I tell him. "Not right now."

"How did you know I would be here?" he asks.

"I didn't. Why are you here?"

"I'm not sure. I think it's because the story you told me made me sad," he says. "I was thinking, maybe the town could help rebuild the church."

"Everyone goes to another church," I say. "This one is going to be torn down."

"Then maybe those who burned it should rebuild it."

"No one knows who burned it. No one will admit to it. It's as if it were like this from the beginning. Even when people were coming to it."

"Maybe not the church. Maybe the people inside."

"I don't know. It burned a year before I was born."

"Shame," Gabriel says.

"Where do you live?" I ask. "Where are your parents?"

"Is that why you came here? To find out about me? Where I'm from? Where I live?"

"I was just wondering. I'm sorry if—"

Gabriel interrupts me. Somehow, without me knowing how, he is now standing right before me. So enthralled was I with his voice that I never saw him walk towards me.

"It's OK," he says. "Like I told you, I live a few miles from here. I can take you there, show you if you'd like."

"No. I don't think that would be a good idea."

"I thought you wanted to know."

"It's OK. I just wanted to be sure you had somewhere to go."

"Why?" he asks.

I turn away. How much can I tell him? How much is too much? And why would I?

"You don't have to be afraid anymore," he tells me. "Especially of me."

"Can I ask you something?" I say.

"You can ask me anything," he assures me.

I pause. I look at him as if I am looking at him for the first time. That is how I look at him every time. It dawns upon me that my questions are inappropriate. Maybe the questions are even dangerous. I will ask him the question regardless.

"You were there when Jai was attacked, weren't you?"

Gabriel's silence answers my question for me. It takes me a second before I can ask him another.

"If you were there, if you saw what was happening, why didn't you help him?"

"Sometimes people have to learn to defend themselves," he tells me.

"Are you an expert on what people need?" I ask. "They hurt him."

"Maybe that was what he needed."

"What about me? If you know so much why don't you tell me what I need?"

"Do you really want to know?"

"I wouldn't be here if I didn't," I tell Gabriel.

"I think," he begins, "you need to stop feeling guilty about Brandon's death."

"What?" I angrily ask, unsure if he has said what I am sure he has said.

"It's not your fault he drowned."

"He didn't drown," I yell at Gabriel. "I killed him!"

I look beyond Gabriel to the cross hanging askew on the stage. We are in church; this is where you confess, right?

"I killed Brandon!" I yell even louder and then I look back at Gabriel. "That's why you should be afraid. Not me! Because if you're around me long enough, I'll end up doing something stupid and you'll die!"

"I make my own choices. I'm responsible for what happens to me," Gabriel says.

"Why do you do that?" I ask him.

"Do what?"

"Talk like him?"

"I don't know what you mean. Like who?"

"Brandon."

"Maybe because if Brandon were here, he would say the same thing to you I'm saying."

"What are you saying?" I ask.

"That it's not your fault Brandon is dead."

"Well he's not here, is he?" I ask. "So how will we ever know?"

Gabriel does not answer me. I didn't expect him to. How could he?

"I'm sorry."

"Why?" Gabriel asks.

"Because I shouldn't have come here. You can't give me what I need."

I turn and begin walking towards the door, or what remains of it.

"Tell me what that is," Gabriel shouts. "Tell me what you need, Liv?"

I stop and turn back. "To not feel like this church." And with that, I turn away and leave.

The Percussionist Pauses for a Piece of Candy

I sit alone in my room surrounded by shelves filled with books that have all been read more than once. Books that mean something to me by either content or the context in which they were given to me. While there are many works of fiction and more than a few biographies, most are books of poems, of which my most cherished is the first book of poetry my father ever gave me. It is a collection of poems by Charles Bukowski. It is called *Play the Piano Drunk Like a Percussion Instrument until the Fingers Begin to Bleed a Bit*. My father gave it to me when I was five. I'm not sure I could even read then, but I am certain Mr. Bukowski was not writing thoughts suitable for a five-year-old mind, not even when he was five. I think my father had faith in two things: one, that I would eventually learn to read, and two, once I did, I would fall in love with the manner in which Charles Bukowski used his pen. My father was right about both. Have you ever read Bukowski? He wrote beautifully, even though what he wrote about was often ugly. I think he used his pen like a percussion instrument and the words were the blood from his fingers. How perversely beautiful... a hand that drips blood because bleeding is the only method in which to paint. I am not reading Bukowski at the moment, however. I am appreciating a different artist. I have my iPod on and headphones over my ears and I am listening to the music given to me by Jai. It is the CD *Geek the Girl* by Lisa

Germano. I try not to take offense by thinking Jai thought I would like it because the title in some way represented me. As I listen to it, it is impossible to be offended. I happen upon track five, "Cry Wolf." As I listen I wonder if Jai remembered that particular track was on there. I wonder if he remembered what Lisa Germano was singing about. I wonder if he knew I would listen to it over and over and over again until my ears started to bleed a bit. I don't think he would have given it to me if he did. Lisa Germano has a beautiful voice. Soft like a lullaby. Sweet like a piece of candy. Sad like when you outgrow both lullabies and candy. "You shoulda known better," she sings. "You shoulda known better. You shoulda known… it's all your fault."

I think Charles Bukowski would have liked her.

Riches

Friday. One more day of school. This day cannot be done with fast enough. Neither can Saturday. All I can think about is Sunday, my father and what we will do. Hopefully he will take me somewhere that doesn't reek of dust. My nostrils burn from all the dust that surrounds me, and it is difficult to smell anything that reminds me I am alive.

The school courtyard is full. The bell has not yet rung. I walk with my head down. I don't want to have to look at or say anything to anyone. Every person I pass could be the next person I am about to pass; that's how anonymous they are to me. It makes me sad that I feel this way. People should not be particles of dust I don't want to inhale.

I am about to walk past Jai. I know this not because I look up, but I hear his voice. You can always hear Jai's voice. He is standing beside Gabriel. I don't hear Gabriel's voice. I know he is there because I can feel it. It is hard to continue walking towards them, but I do. I don't want to hear any of Gabriel's words; I don't want to see Jai's smile. I've already told you this. I only want to hear and see my father. I walk past both and into the school without ever acknowledging either.

"What happened between you two?" Jai asks Gabriel.

"There is no us two," Gabriel states.

"I didn't mean anything by it," Jai offers.

"I know."

"She just seems different since you showed up."

"Well I don't think she likes me too much right now."

"You know how girls are," Jai says.

Gabriel does not respond. He is too busy looking across the courtyard at Christian, who is looking back at both Jai and him. Jai follows Gabriel's eyes to where Christian and Russel stand.

"Asshole," Jai offers, still displaying bruises from the subject of his last word. "One day he's going to get what's coming to him."

"What's that?" Gabriel asks.

Jai pauses before he replies. Hesitation fills his eyes.

"Nothing," he says. There is another pause by Jai. "What have you heard about me?" he asks Gabriel.

Gabriel looks at Jai. "I don't listen to what people say about other people. I think it's better to watch what people do and judge for yourself."

"Maybe sometimes people do things they don't want to do," Jai replies.

"Then that tells you even more about them."

Jai laughs. "That sounds like something Brandon would say."

"I thought you told me you didn't know him."

Again, that same hesitation fills Jai's eyes and this time spills over into his voice as he replies.

"He was my best friend."

"Why didn't you tell me that before?"

Jai's hesitation becomes refusal. Gabriel looks over to Christian, then back to Jai.

"How did he die?" Gabriel asks.

"I told you—he drowned." Jai answers.

"You also told me you didn't know him."

"He drowned. That's what it said on his death certificate, so what does it matter what I say?"

Gabriel does not answer.

"Why do you care anyway?" Jai asks. "It doesn't make any difference what you or anyone else knows, thinks or believes. Brandon's dead and nothing's going to change that."

"If he didn't drown, then someone should be told," Gabriel says.

"Someone was told," is Jai's reply.

"And what did they say?"

Jai now looks over to Christian, then turns his attention back to Gabriel.

"You play football?" Jai asks.

"No," is Gabriel's response.

"Are you rich?" Jai then asks.

"No."

"Then the only thing you have going for you in this town is that you're white. And that ain't worth all that much by itself anymore. And if you don't believe me, just ask Brandon."

Jai walks away, leaving Gabriel standing alone. Gabriel turns to see that Christian is still watching him. Gabriel walks away.

Christian turns to Russel as he leans up against his truck, caressing it as if it were his girlfriend.

"What do you think they were talking about?"

"I don't know," Russel answers.

Christian continues as he walks to the back of his truck and removes a football from the bed. "Well do you think we need to worry?"

"I don't think we have time to worry. We got a game to play. A championship game."

"I know we have a championship game to play," Christian says. "I'm the reason we're playing it. Or did you forget?"

"No. I didn't forget."

"Good." Christian then begins tossing the football up and down as he thinks. That's how Christian always thought. As if the football were his brain being jostled for a thought of worth. "Take care of it."

"Take care of what?"

"Take care of the problem before it becomes a bigger problem. Understand?"

"Yeah," Russel answers.

"Good," says Christian. "Because if it becomes a bigger problem, then you're going to have a problem. With me."

"What am I supposed to do?" Russel asks.

"Fear can be a good thing," Christian explains, "for those smart enough to be afraid."

"What are you going to do?"

Christian tosses the football back into the bed of his truck, opens the driver's door and steps in before answering Russel's question.

"I'm going to throw a few footballs around. I have a championship game to win."

The Rabbit, the Lion and the Wind

A red light glows, even in the glare of a desert sun. Gabriel is at the light, waiting, as the engine of his motorcycle roars with impatience. The streets otherwise are silent at the moment. Gabriel's is the only vehicle on the road, leaving the wind as his only traveling companion. It is a wind that blows ferocious and intense, displacing dust that coats the road with indifference.

Gabriel looks up at the stoplight. The light is still red, but he then hears another sound, another vehicle. He glances in his side-view mirror. Either the image of the other vehicle is too large to fit within the confines of the glass or the vehicle is uncomfortably close. The only thing visible is a silver grill, the teeth, if you will, of some massive behemoth waiting to strike.

Gabriel looks back up at the light. It is now green. The Monster Dark takes off and is immediately pursued by a monster of a different type, a monstrosity of glistening black and steel.

They roar down the highway, a rabbit being chased by a lion, both racing into an unforgiving wind.

The pursuit reaches speeds in excess of one hundred miles an hour as the Hummer continues to come perilously close to pouncing upon its prey. Is Gabriel worried? It is impossible to tell as the reflective tint of the helmet's visor conceals his fear or lack thereof.

Why is it that the road is never patrolled by those whose job it is to intervene in such situations when such situations need intervention? Like a guardian angel that only guards over you when you sleep, those that guard the roads seem only to be there when you don't need them. It does not matter now. Gabriel finds an opportunity and takes his bike off the highway and into the vast escape of the desert's openness. He glances behind him as the Hummer also makes the transition from concrete to unstable terrain with little problem.

Gabriel struggles to keep his motorcycle upright on the soft surface as he makes a sharp turn to his immediate left and heads to the center of the plains, where he stops.

The Hummer stays on the outer perimeter where Gabriel now waits. It circles Gabriel and his motorcycle, certain that the kill is now only moments away.

Gabriel revs the engine of his bike and watches as the Hummer kicks up dirt into the air that quickly surrounds him, trapping him in a dense, cloudlike purgatory.

Christian steps out of his truck onto the patchy soil of a grass-covered field. Green surrounds him. He slams the door of his pickup and immediately makes his way to the back. The tailgate comes down. Footballs spill from the bed of the truck onto the ground like candy. Fifty, maybe a hundred, fall down at Christian's feet. Christian leans down and picks one up. He rolls the football in his hands, then rocks the arm holding the football back and forth like a pivot. He steps from behind the truck. Christian looks out into the open field, locks his arm back and then thrusts it forward as the ball is released. The ball spirals like a bullet, dividing the wind with the unassailable force of its momentum.

Russel grins like a maniacal cat as he continues circling Gabriel's bike. Why would a lion smile at trapping a rabbit? Wouldn't the rabbit be proud that such a ferocious beast would focus his attention upon a meal so insignificant? The visor on Gabriel's helmet comes up. Yes. The rabbit is smiling. Russel circles one last time, then stops, spinning his Hummer around so that it now faces Gabriel.

Russel revs the engine of his Hummer, waiting for the dust around Gabriel to settle and present his meal to him. The dust obliges. Russel's eyes go wide. Gabriel is not there. He has vanished, disappeared, as if he and his motorcycle became a part of the dust and escaped with the wind. The grin from Russel's face is now gone, as well.

Another football is thrown by Christian, then another, then another and another. Christian throws each ball with the precision you give hate when it is in a word or a group of words and directed at someone specific.

Russel remains inside the presumed safety of his Hummer, watching, waiting and wondering. Where did Gabriel go? His answer appears like answers often appear, without warning.

The sound of Gabriel's motorcycle engine, first faint, then louder than the speed at which sound should travel, echoes, then falls upon Russel's ears. Russel leans forward, peering through his windshield for a better view. He can see nothing. There is nothing to see. Russel leans back. And then, unexpectedly, as retribution often comes, Gabriel's bike slams down onto the hood and then roof of the Hummer.

Glass from the windshield shatters, sprinkling down like a cold desert snow. Gabriel's motorcycle rolls over the hood of Russel's SUV and lands on the ground behind it. Gabriel kicks out the kickstand, dismounts the bike and walks toward the Hummer.

Christian picks up another football, releases the ball and watches as it spirals through the air before falling to the ground. Hard.

Gabriel opens the SUV door and pulls Russel from the driver's seat. Russel falls to the ground. Hard. Gabriel takes a few steps back so that he stands within full view of Russel, who looks up at him. The wind picks up and dust seems to swirl around but not upon Gabriel as they speak.

"Who are you?" Russel asks with terror in his voice.

"You know who I am. I am Gabriel."

"No," Russel says. "That's not who you are."

"Then who am I?" Gabriel asks.

Russel stares up at Gabriel from the ground. Russel shakes as if a cold wind blows over his body. But the desert is hot and still. There is no cold. There is no wind.

"I don't know," Russel says.

"Do you know who Gabriel was in the Bible?"

"No," Russel says somewhat fearfully.

"He was an Archangel," Gabriel says. "Some people believe he was the messenger of God."

"Is that who you are?"

Gabriel laughs. "No. I'm just a high school student. I don't have any message." Gabriel leans down so that he is just about eye to eye with Russel. "But maybe you do?"

"Do what?" Russel asks as he looks into Gabriel's eyes.

"Maybe you have a message for me," Gabriel tells him.

"I don't know what you mean," Russel says.

"Are you sure? There's nothing you want to tell me?"

"Yeah, I'm sure," says Russel. "I have nothing to tell you."

"Why did you kill him?" Gabriel asks.

"What?" Russel responds. Gabriel repeats the question, this time slower and leaning in closer to Russel.

"Why did you kill him?"

Russel stares into Gabriel's eyes as his own fill with a strange awareness.

"Who are you?" Russel asks again, though this time it is not with terror but disbelief.

Gabriel does not answer Russel. Instead Gabriel holds his hand out. "Take my hand," he says.

Fear glistens upon Russel's face like desert sweat. He doesn't move.

"Take it!" Gabriel commands without ever raising his voice.

Russel takes Gabriel's hand. His eyes flash with an epiphany that his mouth cannot speak.

"Close your eyes," Gabriel tells him. Russel's eyes slowly close. As they do, the wind stops as if his eyelids were the open windows to the desert.

"How long can you hold your breath?" Gabriel asks.

"I can't," Russel says.

"What do you mean, you can't?" Gabriel asks. "Everyone can. I want to see how long you can hold your breath."

"No," Russel cries with his eyes still shut. "Don't make me."

"This is your message," Gabriel begins.

"I can't breathe. I can't breathe," Russel says. Gabriel leans in and whispers into Russel's ear. Russel does not move as he listens. When he is done, Gabriel releases Russel's hand and stands. Russel slides back beneath the surface of the sand like a snake. His breath is panicked, labored, as if he had been suffocating moments earlier.

"Will you remember what I have told you? Will you remember who to tell it to?" Gabriel asks as Russel still struggles to regain his breath. "Will you?"

Russel answers Gabriel's question with a question. The same question he has already asked.

"Who are you?"

Gabriel kneels down again so that he and Russel are eye to eye. A breeze picks up and blows Gabriel's hair back so that Russel sees his entire face.

"I am the wind that remembers. And you are the leaf swept up by its vengeance."

Whores

Sometimes the conversation you wish to have is so vile in its necessity, so disgusting in its arrogance, that the only person you can have it with, the only person that will listen, the only one who will care, is you.

There is one football left in the cab of Christian's pickup. He picks it up. He looks out into the distance. His future is out there somewhere. Waiting. All Christian must do is throw the ball straight into that direction. He must hope the wind carries it far enough. He must hope that it is caught. His future is out there somewhere, waiting.

Christian takes the last football and releases it into the air. The football sails effortlessly through the air as if all it needed to propel it to its proper destiny was Christian's touch. Christian watches as it disappears down the field. Every yard the football travels represents more future riches.

Listen… You do not hear the sound of the football hitting the ground. That is because it never does. The football is caught… by Christian, who also stands at the other end of the field. Sometimes the conversation you wish to have, you can only have with yourself.

Christian Imagined throws the ball back to Christian. It falls directly into Christian's hands. "Good catch," Christian Imagined tells him.

"I know," is the reply from Christian.

The ball is now tossed back and forth as Christian, standing beside his pickup truck, and Christian Imagined, yards down the field, continue their conversation. It is a conversation originating in Christian's head but visualized in front of him.

"Nice to know that if you ever have to play wide receiver you can," Christian Imagined's compliment is interrupted by Christian.

"I won't. I'm a quarterback."

"I know what you are. You're the best. That doesn't mean you don't have to expect the unexpected."

"Nothing is unexpected," Christian tells Christian Imagined, "when you're the best. That's what makes you the best."

"Really?" Christian Imagined asks.

"Yeah. Really."

"Then you expected Gabriel to show up?"

Christian throws the ball back to Christian Imagined. Hard. He catches the ball.

"No," Christian says. "But I think I'm handling the situation just fine."

"It would be a shame if everything you worked for, everything that's supposed to be yours were taken away because some stranger started asking questions about things that were none of his business."

The ball is thrown back to Christian from Christian Imagined. After Christian catches it, he holds it for a moment instead of throwing it back.

"He can ask all the questions he wants," Christian says. "Who cares?"

"You should care."

"Why? You know as well as I do that nothing happened. You do know who I am, right?" Christian asks.

"Yeah. I know," Christian Imagined responds.

"I'm the most popular kid in this entire town. I'm the golden child. I'm rich, good-looking and destined for greatness. Why would I have to force myself on some school whore when I could have any girl I want? I could have sex with the coach's daughter in front of the coach and he wouldn't say a word about it as long as he knew I was going to put up over fifty points on the board during the championship game."

"Yeah," Christian Imagined says. "But the coach's daughter *is* a whore ... Liv isn't."

"They're all whores," Christian says as he finally decides to throw the ball one last time. "They all are."

Pools of You

"The sky is a pool of blue
Clouds crash like waves
I am told
When you look up
And rain cascades
To dive into you."

All my dreams have become nightmares. This is the nightmare from which I will never awake. There are two deserts, separated by day and night. The two deserts are both beneath the ceiling of a surreal sky, separated by sunlight and clouds. The sunlight burns down upon my head. It is oppressive, like an unwanted embrace. I do not want your warmth, not when Brandon is right before me, clothed in shivers, showered upon by a rain that will not cease until he is drowned in its sorrow. All my dreams have become nightmares.

Brandon looks at me. There is a deluge of sadness in his stare. I cannot tell if the moisture in his eyes is tears or rain. I know that tears fall from my eyes. But the heat of the sun burns them away before they can be read; therefore I don't know if he knows how sad I am.

There are two deserts… separated by dreams and reality, and I watch helplessly as one desert fills with rain and the water slowly rises around Brandon. From this I will never awake.

"What did you do?" I ask.

"What you asked me not to," he replies softly.

"Brandon…"

"I'm sorry, Liv."

"Don't be."

"But we wouldn't be apart if I had listened to you."

"No. We wouldn't be apart if I hadn't told you what I did."

Silence.

There are two deserts… separated by truth and consequence. I try and reach through to his desert, but my hand cannot escape mine even though I am a victim of his consequence. It doesn't seem fair.

"Can you make the rain stop?" I ask out of desperation.

"I can't do anything," he tells me, "but look at you."

I bang upon the invisible plane that divides his world and mine, but it will not give. Dreams often give; nightmares never do. It doesn't seem fair.

"You won't be able to free me," Brandon says.

"I'm not trying to free you," I tell him. "I'm trying to join you."

"No," he pleads. Why should he be the one to plead? Can he not even find peace in death? It doesn't seem fair.

I want to reach above me and pull myself over that which divides us, but you cannot climb the sky no matter how hard you try. I will say this one last time. It doesn't seem fair.

"Liv, don't."

I look at Brandon. The water is now above his waist. It looks as if he could take a step forward and he would be out of the rain and into my arms. I know this is a nightmare so I know that he can't. I know that there will always be a desert that separates us. It doesn't seem fair. I know... I lied.

"Close your eyes," Brandon tells me. "I don't want you to see me drown."

> *"The sky is a pool of blue*
> *Clouds crash like waves*
> *I am told*
> *When you look up*
> *And rain cascades*
> *To dive into you."*

Accidental Gestures

That is what Brandon's eyes were, pools of brown. And that is the name of the poem I have just written for him. "Pools of Blue." It makes me smile because the words keep him alive to me. I can no longer hold him, but I can hold on to words that placed beside each other are as warm to me as his embrace. I cannot kiss him except when I say those words that are as soft on my mouth as his kiss. I cannot speak to him, but I hope he can hear the echo of the words. The poem also makes me sad—sad because is there anything that is suffocated by its own futility more than a poem written for someone who will never read it?

"And rain cascades…"

I close my journal and place the book down beside my folding chair. I am at home, out back, by my pool and beneath the sun. It had been the pool that inspired the verse. That and the nightmare I had the night before.

I pick up the book of poetry that I came out to read and begin absorbing myself in it. It is the book of poetry given to me by Gabriel. Moments in though, the sun becomes too hot and I am tired from writing. I fold the book across my chest, lean back in the chair and close my eyes.

"Hi," I hear.

Why does Brandon's ghost still haunt me? Why am I hearing him say hi? Did my poem awaken his spirit? If it did, then I will write until there are no more words and he is alive again.

"Am I disturbing you?"

That can't be Brandon's voice I am imagining. Brandon would never ask that. He would know it could never be true. I open my eyes. I have not been dreaming Brandon's voice—Gabriel is standing outside the pool gate.

"No," I say, surprised to see him. "I was just laying out."

"Can I come in?" he asks.

"What if I say no?"

"Then I will leave," he says.

"Too bad," I reply.

"Why?"

I smile at him, sort of. "You'll figure it out. Yes, you can come in."

Gabriel opens the gate and enters. He walks over to me and stands before me, blocking the sun from my eyes, as if even his accidental gestures cannot help but be kind.

"I felt bad," Gabriel says, "about the way we left the last time we talked. I don't have any right to tell you how you should feel."

I move my book from my chest and ask him if he wants to sit down. He sits in the chair beside me, but he turns to me, and, again, blocks the sun from my eyes. I have to begin to wonder if his kindness is an accident after all.

"I'm sorry if I seemed angry with you," I tell him. "You didn't deserve that. You were only trying to help me."

"That's what a friend should do."

"Friends? You hardly know me," I tell him.

"Really?" he asks.

"Yes, really," I say. He smiles. "Why are you smiling?" I ask.

"I knew where to find you," he answers. " And I knew you would be reading the book of poetry I gave you."

"Really?" And now I smile.

"Yes," he responds. "Really." There is something so strange about him but so familiar. And there is also something unsettling about his presence. I feel safe around him, but I don't feel as if he is safe. I don't know why.

"What poem were you reading?" he asks me.

"You mean you don't know?" I ask back. Gabriel pauses as if he is gathering an answer he should not have.

"The minute I heard my first love story," he begins, "I started looking for you not knowing how blind that was. Lovers don't finally meet somewhere. They're in each other all along."

I am stunned. There is that feeling again. Familiarity. And fear... for him. People who know things they shouldn't know are often places they shouldn't be. And someone eventually finds them.

"I believe the author is Rumi," he states. "He died in 1273."

"How did you know?" I ask.

"I read it somewhere," he says.

"No. How did you know that was the poem I had been reading?"

And now he turns my words back on me.

"You'll figure it out."

"You know a lot of writers," I say.

"Poets mainly," he responds.

"Why poems?"

"I'm not sure," he answers.

"Brandon liked—" I stop myself. I am not sure why. "I'm sorry."

"It's OK," Gabriel reassures me.

"I feel like every time I'm around you I bring up Brandon. I don't know why that's so hard for me to control."

"Probably because you loved him."

I look away. Is that something he should know? Is that something we should share? But he is so familiar to me.

"Do you think he knew how much?" Gabriel asks.

"I don't know," I tell him. "I wanted to be with him forever. How do you tell someone that so that they can truly comprehend how you feel? Is it even possible?"

"Maybe that's why I like poems," he says.

"Why?"

"Because poems allow words to convey thoughts which are impossible to say with just words."

I smile inside. Was what he just said to me a poem in its own way? Does that make him right? Because suddenly I understand why I like poems so much.

"Do you want to go swimming?" I ask.

"I don't have anything to swim in."

"I promise not to look," I tell him.

"You want me to swim naked?"

"No. You can leave on your shorts," I reply. "It's hot and I want to swim."

"I don't know," he says, and it's a hesitance I have not seen in him before this.

"You're not afraid of the water, are you?"

"No. It's OK. I'm not afraid."

We both rise from the chairs. He removes his motorcycle jacket and then I take his white T-shirt and begin to pull it over his head. There it is. The familiarity again. Gabriel stops me. I step back as he pulls his shirt completely down.

"What's wrong?"

"Nothing," he lies.

"Are you shy?" I ask.

"No. It's OK."

"You say everything is OK."

"Because it is," he says.

"Then you shouldn't be bothered by this…" And with those words my hands come into contact with his body for the first time. But it is a push, not a touch, and it sends him back and into the pool. As he sinks to the bottom I immediately regret it. The first time you touch someone it should never be a push.

I wait for Gabriel to rise, but for some reason he seems unable to. I watch as the thrashing of his body beneath the water in the deep end only pulls him deeper. What have I done? He didn't tell me he couldn't swim. Is that what it is? I dive in and in the fear of a moment I am beneath the water and beside Gabriel. For the second time I touch his body, but this time it is a pull not a push. I bring him to the shallow end and back him up against the wall so that he may catch his breath. Water almost immediately begins to expel itself from his lungs.

"I'm so sorry," I say.

He looks at me and somehow manages to smile. How do some people always manage to smile?

"I'm OK," he says. I smile even though I still feel bad. I am the somehow now.

I brush the hair from his eyes. His hair feels soft, like silk. So soft is his hair that my hand has slipped from it to his face. His skin feels oddly cold to me. It is colder than the temperature of the water we stand in. Even so, it has a magnetic pull like the grin of a child. He looks into my eyes because I am looking into his. He looks at my lips because my eyes tell him to. I look away because my heart is not ready.

"Did I do something wrong?" he asks.

"No," I say while still looking away. "You didn't do anything."

"Why did you look away?"

What was it I said to you before? That people that know what they shouldn't know are often places they shouldn't be. He is asking me a question that will put him in a place that he shouldn't be. But as I also said, there is something so familiar… and when you feel vulnerable, familiar is a calming embrace.

"I was raped," I tell him. "It happened two months ago."

"You don't have to explain," he begins.

I step out of the pool and go to my chair. I sit with my back to Gabriel. I can feel the hot sun burning down on my mostly bare skin. It feels as if the sun is burning away my flesh, and then, it is gone. Gabriel must be standing behind me. There it is again, that accidental gesture. I turn to him.

"I want to tell you. I need to. I need to tell someone. Anyone. I feel like there's a virus inside me and it's killing me because I won't let it out because I don't want anyone to know I have it."

Gabriel kneels.

"Rape is not a virus. And more importantly, it's not your fault. It is never the victim's fault."

"But I should have known better," I tell him. "It happened because of choices I made."

"The devil makes choices," Gabriel tells me. "That doesn't make him the devil. It's the intent behind his choice that does."

"I feel like he's inside me."

"The devil?" Gabriel asks.

"No," I say. "One of his choices."

Gabriel rises and extends his hand out to me.

"Take my hand," he says. I do and he leads me back into the pool. In the shallow depths we stand.

"Come with me," he says. He wants to take me deeper into the water.

"But I thought you couldn't swim," I tell him.

"It's OK," he says.

"Aren't you afraid?"

"No. I'm not afraid," Gabriel tells me. "I know you won't let anything happen to me."

Did I tell you that when you're vulnerable familiarity is a warm embrace? I feel as if I am wrapped within his arms at the moment.

"I won't," I say. I follow him farther out into the water and we stop. He takes one hand and places it on my back. He then turns to me.

"Everything inside you that you wish to forget, this water washes away. All that you want to remember, this water soaks into your soul."

He leans me back until I am submerged beneath the water. I want to be held like this forever and be allowed to breathe through his touch.

He brings me up. Water cascades from my face down my body like baptismal tears. I turn to him. I don't know why, but my heart is ready to begin beating again. It has not since I lost Brandon.

"Kiss me," I tell him as I stand shivering with the desire for his lips to be pressed against mine.

"I can't," he says to me.

"It's OK," I say. Though I am unsure if I actually say it or the look in my eyes whisper it to him. Such is the confusion of impulse.

I can feel his hand on the small of my back even from beneath the water. Gabriel pulls me in closer. The water makes it feel as if I am floating towards him. I begin to close my eyes and it's like the shades being drawn for privacy. I can feel his breath, hot but not dry like the air that surrounds us. My lips burn still, waiting for his.

"Liv…"

I think I am just hearing things at first, but then I hear it again.

"Liv."

My eyes suddenly open and my body is quickly pulled away from Gabriel's by the threat of discovery. The voice is my mother's. I turn towards the house.

"Yes, Mom?" I yell back.

"Mrs. Green is here," she says. Mrs. Green. That is Brandon's mother.

"OK," I tell her. "I'll be right in."

I do not want my mother to meet Gabriel. I do not want Brandon's mother to, either. I hear the sound of the sliding glass door sliding back. My mother or Mrs. Green or both are about to step out onto the back patio. I turn to Gabriel to tell him to go. He is already gone.

Happy Fracture

I have not seen Brandon's mother since the funeral. When I received Brandon's car, it was his stepfather that delivered it to me though it was Brandon's mother who made the decision that I should have it. I think the reason she no longer wanted to look upon the car was the same reason she could not see me. I don't know if she is wrong or right—I do know that I don't blame her because it is not my son and it is not for me to tell her how to grieve. It is not for me to tell her that she should hold on to everything and everyone her son held dear. Perhaps in time she will be able to. Perhaps in time that will be the right thing to do, but right now I know how she feels. It would be holding on to a ribbon with a balloon at the end that has lost its air. Easier to let the ribbon slip from your hand. Easier to try and forget there was ever a balloon on the end of the ribbon. I don't judge Mrs. Green because I know she will never be able to forget that balloon. The air from within was sucked inside her when she was told her son had died. She is still holding that breath, for fear that if she breathes and allows it to escape, it will be as if the balloon never held air at all.

She told me she had to see me. What she wanted to give me this time was more personal than a car and needed to be given in person. We talked for over an hour, remembering Brandon while consciously trying to avoid words that spoke of him in a remembrance way.

Before she left, Brandon's mother gave me a letter that she found while going through the things in Brandon's room. Brandon has been dead for more than two months, but yesterday was the first day Mrs. Green told me that she went into his room. Yesterday, she said, was the first day she could. Then she started to cry because she said all that she has of her son now is yesterdays. There is the remembrance. There is the hand holding on to only the ribbon that remains.

One of the things Mrs. Green asked me was what I missed most about Brandon. I told her that I missed me most. I missed the person Brandon made me because he was with me. She tried to assure me that I would fall in love again. You're so young, she said. I don't think she understood that even if I were to fall in love again, even if I were happy, it would not be the same me that I was with her son. The happy me has been eternally fractured. I can never be happy as a whole again because now there is a hole.

Mrs. Green said she didn't read the letter because it was in a sealed envelope and addressed to me. She also said that it was strange where it was because it was almost impossible to find. It was as if, she said, Brandon had put the letter where he did on purpose because it was always going to be his intent to have someone else give it to me. It did not seem, to her, as if he ever intended to give it to me himself.

I put the letter on the nightstand beside my bed and every now and again I will pick it up and hold it in my hands. I haven't read the letter yet because I feel like it's the last conversation I will ever have with Brandon and I want to be able to look forward to it a little while longer.

Resurrection

Russel's house is not unlike any of the other lower-income homes of our town. It is a modest, well-maintained dwelling designated lower income only by its size and not necessarily its appearance. Lower income only because of its neighborhood and not necessarily its neighbors. Sometimes, how rich you are is determined not by how much you have, but by how much the others around you possess.

Russel lives with both of his parents. I don't really know his parents, but I have seen them both at all Russel's football games. They cheer him on with the ferocity of someone cheering a truck full of money being backed up to their lower-income home. Russel has two younger brothers. They sit beside their parents at every game. I have noticed on occasion that they don't seem to get much cheering of any type, but then again, they don't play football yet. I ran into his littlest brother at the second game of the year. I think his name is Ricky. I think that he is six. He was near the line for peanuts. I don't think he wanted to buy any. I don't think he had the money to; he just wanted to be near them. I bought him a bag. I remember that when I handed him the bag, the first thing he did was extend it back to me, offering me one of the peanuts. I think he showed greater generosity than me. I think it is good his parents don't pay much attention to him if they are the reason Russel is how he is.

Russel's dad maintains the grounds at the town cemetery. He has since before I was born. People say around town that Russel's father is tired of the dead, that his father feels like he is one of them. They say his son's future is his resurrection … Or was.

It's the time of day when the sun prepares itself to descend, and it throws across the sky a reddish hue as if the sky has been cut and is bleeding. Russel sits in a chair in his room, staring out at the wounded sky.

A creak signals that his bedroom door is slowly being opened. Then there is the sound of something being repeatedly tossed and caught. Without turning around, Russel knows it is Christian. Perhaps, even, he was expecting him.

"How was practice?" Russel asks quietly.

"Practice was great," Christian responds.

"Good," says Russel. "You guys will need all the practice you can get."

"No," Christian corrects. "What we need is for every member of the team to show up for practice."

"Every member did," Russel says, still staring out into the increasing darkness.

"You know your mother is out there in tears. She could barely speak," Christian states.

"I know. She's been crying since yesterday. Since I told her."

"What about your father?" Christian asks.

"What do you think? He won't even talk to me. I'm surprised you are because I guess you know now, too?" Russel asks, keeping his back to Christian.

"I don't know anything. I know the coach said you quit the team and football, but I also know that can't be true. So why were you not at practice?"

Russel now turns around. "Because it is true," he says.

"We have one more game, the championship game, and we end with a perfect season. We can write our own ticket in life. We can have anything. Anything we want. Don't you want something better than this?" Christian says as he gestures to Russel's dwelling.

"All of a sudden my house is not good enough for you?"

"That's not what I'm saying," Christian argues weakly. "I'm just trying to get you to see that there's better out there for you. And for your parents. Hell, there's better out there for me! You can't quit the team any more than I could. Football is in our blood."

"Blood?" Russel asks.

"Yeah," Christian nods.

"Our blood is poisoned," Russel responds.

"What?"

"Poisoned because of what we did," Russel continues.

"What are you talking about?"

Russel rises. Christian takes a step back, somewhat startled by this sudden movement and Russel's overall demeanor.

"Do you believe in ghosts?" Russel asks as Christian's face goes blank at the question.

"Ghosts? What are you talking about?"

"Ghosts. Do you believe in ghosts?" Russel repeats.

"No. I don't," Christian answers. "But say I did. What the hell does that have to do with anything?"

"If you were dead," Russel begins, "and you came back as a ghost, what would be the reason?"

"There is no reason," Christian states. "People don't come back from the dead."

"What if they did?"

"They don't!" Christian exclaims.

"But what if they do?" Russel yells even louder than Christian. "Why would they come back?"

"I don't know." Christian surrenders. "Why would they?"

"There's only one reason to come back," Russel says. "Revenge."

"What the hell happened out there with Motorcycle Boy?" Christian asks.

"I'm not talking about him."

"Then who?" Christian demands. "Who are you talking about?"

Russel turns away, back to staring at the sky whose hue seems as angry as Christian.

"You know who."

"No. I don't. Who?"

"Brandon."

Christian laughs. It is a release of tension that quickly empties him out so that he can refill himself with rage. He shoves the football into Russel's chest.

"I told you to never say his name!"

"What are you going to do, Christian? Kill me? Huh?" Christian does not respond. "It doesn't matter what you do. I'm already damned."

"What happened out there? What did he say to you?"

"He said he's coming for you." Christian's rage drains as quickly as his laughter did moments before, and this time he is filled with fear. "And I'm not your left tackle anymore. So I can't protect you."

Christian steps closer to Russel, shoving his face at his former friend in the same manner in which he shoved his precious football into Russel's chest.

"I don't need you," Christian says. "I'm the quarterback."

"How far can you throw, Christian?" Russel asks. "Can you throw past the things you've done?"

The Momentum of Sons

I remember sitting outside a coffee shop one day. One of those chain coffee shops that emerge from a small town when the small town is ready to emerge. I think it was a Sunday afternoon. I had my laptop with me. It was sitting on the table and I was listening to new music trying to find something to download. I remember watching this father and son across the street. I can't remember exactly why I started watching them. No, wait... now I remember... I had just come back from visiting my dad, and as I watched the father and son, I wondered if fathers related to sons differently than they did daughters. I wondered if the emotions were different, if the expectations were different, if the disappointments were different. Were daughters so fragile to fathers that they would never open up the world fully to girls like they would a boy? Was this good or bad for the girl? And if the reverse were true, how did that affect boys? Should fathers raise boys with more caution? Should boys be more cautious of fathers?

The boy across the street was around seven. He had curly blond hair that looked windswept even though the air was still. He wore shorts and sneakers. Chuck Taylor sneakers. They were cute on him. He was cute. I don't know that I could properly describe his father. His head was hidden beneath the hood of his red truck, which had broken down on the side of the road. It was a type of truck that looked like it was always breaking down on the side of the road. From its condition, and the tattered nature of the father's jeans, it didn't look like he had much. But from the smile on his son's face, it looked like whatever the father had, he gave to him.

Traffic on the road was light, but there was a steady stream of cars that drove past as the father worked on the engine of the truck. The boy bounced a yellow rubber ball against the curb just beside his father. Bounce, then catch. Bounce, then catch. Bounce, then catch. Bounce, then... the ball is over his head, and this is where everything slowed down. I watch the boy's head arc as his eyes follow the ball. He is looking back out at the street where the ball is rolling. For a moment I think he even looks over at me and smiles. I want to smile back, but I know what he's about to do and I have already seen the delivery truck that is headed towards him.

I am trying to get out of the wrought iron chair I am sitting in to run to him, but the momentum of the moment is like a magnet that won't allow me to rise.

What's wrong with the father's truck? Why did it break down? Why did it have to break down along the side of the road? And why isn't he watching his son?

The boy steps out into the street. His eyes are on the ball as if it were the only object in the world. His world. He leans down, his tiny fingers outstretched, and grabs a hold of the ball. I am about to yell because the truck is about to strike him, but then a hand, his father's hand, yanks the boy back and into the protection of his arms as the delivery truck speeds past, unaware he has just crushed a yellow ball beneath his tires.

I fall back into the chair. I watch as the father embraces the boy with both anger and relief. And I look over at the little yellow rubber ball that is now flat. Removed of the air that gave it life.

Is that what a parent's life consists of, pulling their children out of harm's way? How many times has that father had to save his son? How many times will he have to be there for the boy until he becomes a man? How deep and strong must a father's love for his son be and how could anything ever come between that love?

I forget why I started talking about this. No... Wait... Now I remember. Russel's father shot Russel in the head today... He then turned the gun on himself. I suppose now he'll never get out of that cemetery.

Feigning Corpse

The last time I was at Mercy Hospital it was because I was told Brandon was there. I was actually told that he was dead, but I came anyway, hoping that once I got there I would be told that there was a mistake. It's weird, but when I walked in tonight, I almost expected to see him walking out towards me. He is not.

I go upstairs to the intensive care unit. ICU. If you're fortunate in life, you will never see those three letters together. The ICU is where Russel is. He doesn't know it though. He's been in a coma since his father shot him. The hallway is lined with friends and family. I find it odd though that no one from the football team is here. I thought they were both friend and family. No one says anything to me. I'm the girl whose boyfriend drowned in this town. I'm the girl who Christian said was a whore. I'm the girl who knows the truth, and some people never want to get too close to the truth.

I arrive at his room, having survived the tunnel of grief that I have just walked through. I stand at the window into the room and now I have a front-row seat. I look at Russel lying in his hospital bed. His skin is almost as white as the sheets. It's odd, the way it looks, and the way he looks, as if he were born prepared to be dead. I continue to watch as his mother holds his lifeless hand. His hand is bigger than hers, almost twice the size, but there is her hand, supporting the weight of his. As it is fathers that often pull their sons away from harm, I think that mothers may be there to hold their hands when the father fails. I also think that I don't ever want children.

Even from outside the room I can hear the rhythm of Russel's breathing. It sounds like the mechanical breaths of a respirator whose heart is being powered by the cord that snakes along a cold clinical floor. I think back to when Christian raped me and I wonder what was breathing for me, because I remember specifically not wanting to. Is God your respirator when you want to give up? Or is it the devil? So he may torture you some more? Where does that cord snake to? Heaven or Hell?

Suddenly I feel sick to my stomach. It is as if my intentions for coming sank from my head into the emptiness of my belly and infected it with my guilt. I came because I wanted to look at Russel and feel good. I wanted to feel vindicated. I wanted to look at his feigning corpse and for it to give me back my smile, if even for a moment. Instead I am watching another mother mourning her son, and even though I see a murderer, there is sadness knowing we are looking at the same person.

Whose Deaths Become Revenge
by Mourning

"It's not him."

That's the first thing I hear when I exit the hospital. The doors have not yet even closed behind me. The next thing I know I am being pulled over to the side, but I will only let him pull me so far. He seems to always be pulling or pushing me. That "he" is Christian. I knew it was him before he even spoke. I knew he would be waiting for me before I exited the hospital. I don't know how or why, but I knew. Maybe because a hospital is where the dead or dying belong.

"Let go of me," I tell Christian. He does. "What do you want?"

"I want you to know, it's not him," he repeats.

"It's not who?" I ask.

"Brandon."

I'm unsure what Christian's talking about, and I certainly don't like hearing Brandon's name come from his mouth, but there is something in Christian's eyes I have never seen before. I think it's fear, but it is dark and I can't be certain.

"Who's not Brandon?" I ask him.

"Gabriel," he says.

"I never said he was."

"Maybe you didn't, but I know your friend Motorcycle Boy did. That's why Russel quit the team. Because Gabriel got him to believe that Brandon sent him here to get revenge."

"Revenge for what?" I ask, knowing Christian won't answer. He does not. I smile, sort of.

"You know that's why Russel's father shot him, right? Because of what your friend said?"

"No," I respond as I shake my head. "Russel's father shot him because Russel's father was sick. Almost everyone in this town is sick about football, about winning, about just about everything. And you know what else is sick?"

"What?" he asks with a tone that makes it obvious he does not at all care what the answer is.

"The fact that you are down here with me talking about someone you don't even know instead of being upstairs with someone you call a friend."

"You don't have any idea who my friends are," Christian says to me.

"Neither do you," I respond. Christian steps closer to me. Police walk past us and into the hospital. They are unaware of what Christian should be charged with and, from the look in his eyes, could be charged with moments from now. I say nothing; instead I am curious as to what Christian wants to say to me. And if he does hurt me this time, at least I will not have far to go.

"Russel was my friend," Christian begins, "until he walked out on me and the team. I don't really care what his reasons are—he should have finished what he started. Maybe one day when he gets out of here he can find me and come up to me and apologize. But until that happens, he doesn't deserve me to be there for him."

The doors to the hospital open, and I hear a wailing that almost deafens me. It is as if the hospital itself expresses grief at the incredible lack of humanity in the words Christian has just spoken. I want to wail like that, but I am no longer capable of being shocked by Christian's lack of humanity. In a way, it makes me feel dead, and I hate him for that.

"There's one other thing," Christian tells me, ignoring the wailing like an unwanted baby's cry. "Tell your friend to stay away from me and anyone else on my team. I'm not like Russel. I'm not afraid. And if he tries to scare me, he'll be the one seeing ghosts."

Christian turns to walk away. I will not allow him to. Not without responding even though I want him to be gone.

"Why don't you tell him yourself?" Christian stops and turns back to me. "Or are you afraid to?" One, two, three steps and he is now standing as close to me as he was before. "What if Russel was right? What if someone you wronged did send someone back for revenge? How many ghosts would you have to hide from? One? A hundred? Can you even remember how many?"

Christian doesn't respond, though the look in his eyes whispers what I already know. "That's the scary thing about ghosts, Christian," I finish. "They always remember."

Christian finally looks as if he is about to respond, but before he can the hospital doors open once more. We both look over because the wailing that was once a faint and distant echo now rushes towards us. It is the cry of Russel's mother as she is all but carried from the hospital. Russel no longer feigns death. Death no longer waits for Russel to stop pretending.

I turn back to Christian.

"Looks like you're going to have to go to Russel to get his apology."

Strawberry Intentions

Rain creates a shifting portrait of a desert deluge as it pours down my bedroom window. It doesn't rain that often in the desert. The desert is a face born without the ability to cry. Only every so often does it hurt enough that tears are able to fall. By that time, the sun has scorched it to near death. Maybe that is why it cries.

I am sitting on my bed listening to the desert weep. Its burns must have been bad. The last letter Brandon wrote to me is in my hands. It is still unopened. My teeth ache, wanting to rip open the envelope. My fingertips pulse, wanting to hold the letter inside. And my eyes tear like the unrelenting sky. What if Russel was right? What if Gabriel was sent by Brandon? How would I know? Maybe that's what's inside the letter, Brandon informing me that if something were to happen to him that he would send someone to protect me. Someone to watch over me until he could make it back. Or maybe the letter is going to tell me that he himself would come back. Is that what I am holding in my hand? Is it Brandon's promise to return? One of Brandon's favorite writers was the English poet Andrew Motion. I cannot recall the title of the specific poem I am thinking about now, but I remember one of the lines. I believe it was, "Whose deaths become revenge by mourning." "Deaths," plural. The death of my love. The death of our future. The death of me.

I laugh to myself. I wish I could be that naive. I wish that somehow I could believe that is what the contents of the letter read. No amount of mourning brings back the dead. If it did, I would cry until the desert was an ocean.

I put the letter back on the stand beside my bed. I am not ready for the truth of it. I will let the desert cry alone. I will not intrude upon its melancholy with the addition of my tears.

Brandon's favorite color was black. I never understood that about him because he had the brightest soul. It was a soul so incandescent it was as if light from God accidentally remained in him during his creation.

The first time I saw Brandon he was wearing black jeans, a black T-shirt and black boots. His boots were Harley-Davidson brand boots. He did not have a Harley or a motorcycle, nor did he know how to ride, but it was his intent, and it was buried with him along with all his other intentions. Is that the measure of a well-lived life, the lack of intentions that are buried with you in your coffin? If so, Brandon did not live well at all. His coffin overflowed with intentions, so much so that it was almost impossible to close.

I met Brandon at a festival concert in Austin, Texas. It was a concert I was only able to attend because my father took me. Somehow our tastes in music had crossed generations twice. What he had loved before me I also loved, and what I began to love as I grew older he found value in, as well. Though, as if guided by fate, at one particular moment when two bands played at the same time, one on the larger stage, and one on the smaller, we parted, led by the particulars of our individual tastes.

I cannot remember who my father chose to see; I only remember that as I made my way to the smaller stage I missed him, thinking no one would share my love for the artist I was about to watch perform live. Martin Grech. He was a British artist, barely appreciated in his homeland let alone known in my tiny desert town.

That is the beauty of music, that sometimes it finds you. That is the impact of music, that sometimes it allows you to find someone.

I found Brandon.

Brandon was standing at the front of the stage. I could see him because he was the only one standing at the front of the stage, in the precise spot that I had hoped to be standing. I had no choice but to stand next to him.

Different people believe different things about love. Some do not believe in love at all, and for some, they have no reason to. I do not believe in love at first sight. But I do believe that you can be in love with someone without ever having met them or even knowing they exist. "Lovers don't finally meet somewhere, they're in each other all along." I think this is what the poet Rumi was saying. I believe that what you will love in a person is often predetermined before you ever come across them. That person is in you already, born within because of everything that has made you who you are up until that point. And then … after falling in love, you meet.

Both my parents predetermined I would love Brandon. My father predetermined it by having the soul of a writer and the heart of a rebel. My mother predetermined it by falling in love with my father. My mother sealed this predetermination by not letting my father destroy her, even though his heart tried. That she stayed with him as long as she did. That she did not cry until she was so badly scorched by my father that she needed the wetness of the tears to soothe her burning skin. This allowed me time to love my father and anyone that would possess those same qualities my mother fought so hard to love, as well.

I have to stop thinking about the first time we met. It is too painful. And every unknown intention that was born of it is now six feet under. It is too difficult to dig in the rain, so I will not try. No. I don't want to think about what Brandon's first words were to me any more than I want to open up the envelope and read his last. Instead I open up the window. I do not care that rain splashes from the windowsill onto my skin. It feels good. Respite. From what, I do not care. I look out into the darkness. The night is accompanied by clouds, forced to be darker than it has to be, perhaps than it wants to be. I know how the night feels. I have felt this way for months now. But I do not feel this way tonight. Why? Because Christian was afraid. Christian was afraid of Brandon. And therefore there is no night in me now.

From the window I see Brandon coming to me in the rain. He is holding a box of chocolate-covered strawberries because I love chocolate-covered strawberries. It's hard to get fresh fruit in the desert. It's not hard to get chocolate. Everything melts in the desert, like chocolate. Hurry, Brandon. Hurry, before you melt away, too.

I turn away from the window and there is Brandon, sitting on my bed. He smiles. Brandon was always smiling. That night, the night I am remembering, he was smiling because he had made the decision to go to Lago University even though he was accepted elsewhere. Elsewhere were colleges quite bigger and more prestigious than Lago University. Elsewhere was where he had intended on going before he met me. Brandon was smiling because he knew that news would make me smile. That was Brandon, happy because he could make someone else happy. Brandon was wrong.

I told Brandon to get out of Lago. He was a musician, a great musician, and he needed to attend a university that would allow him to become greater in a city that would allow him to play more. Brandon wanted to wait for me. He figured he would attain his degree in language just in case no one wanted to hear his songs. That was impossible to me, the thought that no one would want to hear his songs. Brandon thought it was impossible that we both lived in the same town but met each other outside of it. And because of that, he always wanted to be prepared for the impossible. So he was going to get his degree. He was going to go to Lago University. He was going to be near me, too near, otherwise I would have never have... and he would still be...

"If only"... Is there a sadder combination of two words? I don't think so.

I remember sitting down on the bed beside Brandon. He pulls a chocolate-covered strawberry from the box of five he has brought me. I can taste the strawberry and the chocolate as Brandon places it into my mouth. What feels better upon my lips though is the end of Brandon's fingertips. They are not soft; he is a guitarist and the strings have removed that element from them. But what a guitar replaces in a musician's fingertips is a sensitivity that is soft not because of texture but intent. His fingertips touch my lips as if they were going to play him the most beautiful song in the world. Oh my God, his touch is sweeter than the chocolate that coats my tongue. I want to bite down upon his hand, but I must show restraint. The instrument may not hurt the one who knows how to play it properly. Brandon brought five chocolate-covered strawberries that night and I take every one from his hand to my mouth, and I try to make each one last as if it were the last. Each time his fingertips touch my lip, I take hold of his hand and kiss it. His hand must taste like strawberries. I know my heart is melting like chocolate.

"Open Heart Zoo" was our favorite Martin Grech song. I whisper the words to the song as I sit upon my bed, the taste of the chocolate-covered strawberries and the memory of Brandon sitting beside me both vanishing.

"Suffocate your thoughts, empty my head, fill this full of light... and open up."

I am starting to feel night inside me again.

All of a sudden I remember! I spring from my bed and race from my room into the kitchen. It has to be there still—I know it does! I fling open the door to the freezer and my melting heart immediately begins to ice over not only from the frosty mist that pours out and all around me but because I cannot immediately see it and am now unsure if it is even still there. I pull items from inside the freezer with a reckless disregard befitting something that is frozen and cannot therefore be harmed. Onto the counter beside the refrigerator each item goes or is thrown. It has to be here. If not, I will never open this freezer again. I have just about emptied the freezer's contents when I see not it, but something. I still cannot be sure. My trembling hand reaches into the coldness and grabs the small item protectively wrapped in freezer paper like an edible gift. I remove it, close the freezer door and race back to my room and back onto my bed.

Slowly I open the gift, not wanting my heart to break quickly if the content is not what I believe it to be or is no longer the same. It is. There within the protective wrapping is the last chocolate-covered strawberry from that night. I remember that I had saved it for a time when I was missing Brandon… missing the touch of his fingertips. I remove it from its wrapping and count the moments in between the thaw. I wonder if someone could say the same about me…

Enough time.

I bring the chocolate-covered strawberry to my lips. The anticipation of sweetness kisses them. I take a bite… and the night disappears from within me.

His Eye Was the Pen of His Saddest Work

I often wonder, what is the rain's release? What does it wash away, if anything? What does it empty out for God? When you are a child, you are sometimes told that rain is God's tears. I was told this. Now, while I know there is much for God to cry about, I never believed someone as powerful as him would allow you to know he hurt. That was before I saw my dad cry. I only saw him weep once, but some things you only need to see once. And sometimes you wish you had never seen them at all. Either way you will never be able to forget it.

The first time I saw my father cry was when my mother found out he had been unfaithful. She suspected such at various times, but this time she had proof. It's not important what the proof was. Proof is like blood; its presence is almost always in the wake of devastation.

I'm unsure why my father was unfaithful to my mother. My father is a strong, decisive man, and if he wants something, he goes after it. I don't know why that trait doesn't carry over into things he doesn't want... or no longer wants. If he did not want my mother anymore, why didn't he simply tell her? Would that not be the strong thing to do? Would that not be decisive? Wouldn't the hurt be less? Again, I do not know why he knew how to get what he wanted but did not know how to let go of what he did not. Maybe he never stopped wanting her. But...

I remember how my mother's eyes quivered, unable to remain still due to the flux of emotions they had to express. That is a mirror no one wants to see themselves reflected in, the mirror of sudden awareness. It is a mirror that strips away everything you tell someone you are and leaves you clothed in nothing, and sometimes not even you are able to recognize yourself amid the remains.

Remains… There is so much sadness to that word that I hope it is never spoken by or to me in my lifetime.

All that remained of my father was the realization that he had hurt his true love. And though he was a poet, he would never be able to arrange words in any order that would make her forgive him. How tragic is a poet that is no longer allowed the use of words? My father's tears were the final poem he would ever write to my mother.

So… If the rain is God's tears, for whom is he crying? What does the rain release? What does it wash away? What does it empty out?

I try and think back to when it rained the night my mother found out my father betrayed her. Did God cry along with my mother? I don't think he did. I don't take it personally. God can't cry when all his children do lest we drown in his misery. I didn't cry when my mother did. I suppose I should have, but somehow I knew my father would never hurt me as deeply and for that I was more happy than sad. I still don't necessarily understand how a daughter is able to love a man that her mother hates. Is that a fault of love? Is another fault of love the fact that my father could do that to my mother, who he loved? And isn't it the final fault of love that even if the rain were God's tears, most of his children would walk beneath them not caring why he was sad? Does that make God sad?

Tomorrow is Sunday. I am going to see my father. I can't cry with you tonight, God.

The Desecration of Thunder

Christian looks at the watch on his wrist. It is midnight by the time and it is midnight inside Christian's head. As he stands within the cemetery gates, as he reads a headstone engraved with the name of my departed, Christian is caught between the promise of a new day and the wreckage of the night before. Because of what he did, it doesn't matter what time it is on the clock; it will always be midnight for Christian.

"Why did you want me to meet you here?" Murdoc asks as walks up and stands beside Christian.

"Russel's dead," Christian says while staring at Brandon's headstone.

"I heard," Murdoc responds. "He got what he deserved."

Christian turns to Murdoc. "Be careful who you say that around." Christian cautions as his eyes motion to the fact that the dead surround the two of them.

"Why?" Murdoc asks.

"Because," Christian begins, "we all have something we deserve."

"Is that why you brought me out here standing in the middle of the rain? We supposed to feel bad for Russel now? He's not even buried yet."

"I could give a damn about Russel," Christian spits out. "It's not him being dead I'm worried about."

"Then who are you worried about?" Murdoc inquires. Christian's eyes now motion to Brandon's headstone. Murdoc looks down upon it. His lips mouth the name. "Brandon?" Christian remains silent, but for the first time thunder roars as the night's storm intensifies. "What are you worried about him for? He's dead, too. Dead and buried."

"Is he?" Christian asks.

"Is he what?"

"Dead and buried?"

Murdoc makes a statement as opposed to answering the question. "Don't be stupid." Christian doesn't acknowledge the statement; instead he waits for an answer. "Yes. He's dead and buried," Murdoc finishes.

"How do you know?" Christian asks again. Murdoc is about to answer when Christian interrupts to caution him once more. "Remember to be careful who you say what around."

Murdoc understands what Christian has just said though maybe not perhaps completely as Christian intended it.

"So I'll ask you again. How do you know he's dead?"

"Because," Murdoc says, "we're standing at his grave."

"Did you go to the funeral?" Christian asks.

"No. I didn't," is Murdoc's response.

"Neither did I."

"So?"

"So how do we know he died? How do we know he's in there?" This time, Christian's eyes motion to the ground. Murdoc's eyes follow.

"I guess we don't."

"That's right!" Christian snaps. "We don't. But we're about to find out."

The silence is now louder than the thunder.

"How?" Murdoc asks, though his eyes don't exactly yearn for the answer. And for the last time Christian motions with his eyes, this time over to his parked truck and specifically to the two shovels sticking out of the bed. There is the answer Murdoc did not want to hear.

"Hell no," Murdoc cries. "I'm not digging up no dead body!"

"That's what we're trying to find out," Christian fires back. "If there even is a dead body."

"Dude, you're crazy," Murdoc says as he turns to walk away. Christian quickly prevents that by grabbing Murdoc's arm and spinning him around.

"No. I'm not crazy," Christian says. "I'm your quarterback and you're gonna help me dig up that body."

How many choices do you have in a cemetery at night? None. If you did you wouldn't be there at all.

Both boys now have shovels in their hands and both stand towering over Brandon's grave. The intensity of the rain appears to increase along with the depravity of their actions. Christian takes his shovel and plunges the spearheaded end into the earth. Thunder roars… and thus begins the rhythm of two shovels, one after the other, waking an eternal sleep.

There is a character in a BBC television series that my father used to watch who once said the word *elbow* was the most sensuous word in the English language; not for its definition, but for how it feels to say it. I think the most vile word may be *desecration*. Go ahead, say it. Desecration. It is an ugly word. It feels like an abomination on the tongue. As if your mouth is vomiting out thunder.

"What if he's not in the coffin?" Murdoc asks. "What are we going to do then? Have you thought about that?"

"Yeah," Christian answers. "I have."

"Well?"

"We'll find him. Before he finds us."

Murdoc breaks the rhythm of the digging by stopping and looking over to Christian. "What if he already knows where we are?"

Now Christian stops. "Then he better hope that I don't hear him coming. Because I won't leave anything for them to bury." Christian takes his shovel and thrusts it one last time into the dirt. What sounds like thunder is actually the sound of metal hitting the top of Brandon's coffin. Both boys throw their shovels out of the hole, then use their hands to begin removing the thin layer of soil that covers the casket. Christian looks over at Murdoc as he takes hold of the handle and readies to lift the lid.

"You think we can go to hell for this?" Murdoc asks.

"I don't believe in hell," Christian answers.

"My father told me once," Murdoc begins, "that it don't matter if you believe in hell, not if hell believes in you."

"What is that supposed to mean?"

"That nobody goes to hell. Depending on your actions, hell comes to you."

Christian looks away from Murdoc and down to the top of the casket. His hand tightens around the handle as he pulls the top open.

The silence is now louder than the thunder.

"See," Murdoc says, breaking the silence. "He's dead," Murdoc continues as they both stare into the deteriorating visage wrought by the decay of death.

Christian and Murdoc look upon Brandon as rain drops stream down his face starting at his eyes as if he is crying... crying for them.

"Close it!" Murdoc screams. "Close it!" Christian closes the casket.

Murdoc climbs from inside the hole back onto solid ground, and he is almost halfway to his car before Christian emerges from the grave.

"Where are you going?" Christian yells. Murdoc turns around as his body is pounded by rain.

"I told you to leave Liv alone."

"What?" Christian asks as he, too, is pounded mercilessly by the rain.

"Remember? I said you could have any girl you wanted, why did you want to go after some nobody that didn't want anything to do with you?"

"So?"

"So? So? Don't you get it?" Murdoc asks as he takes two steps closer to Christian with the shovel still clenched tightly in his hands.

"Get what?" Christian responds. "You better start making sense before I start digging a grave for you."

"There are some people who are just different. Special. Not because of who they are but what they do and what they mean to other people. They may not even know they are special, but they are. They're like a mother's favorite child."

"And?" Christian wonders.

"And when you do something to them, God doesn't wait until Judgment Day to make you answer for it. He wants his revenge now."

"Bullshit," Christian says. Murdoc turns and begins walking back to where their vehicles are parked. "Is that what you believe?" Christian yells. Murdoc does not stop or answer. "Is that what you believe?"

Murdoc makes it to Christian's truck and tosses the shovel back into the bed. Murdoc then turns to Christian. "I thought you understood what my father was saying. It doesn't matter if I think she's special, it only matters if the person that wants revenge does."

The silence is now louder than the thunder.

"I wouldn't bother putting the dirt back on him," Murdoc says as he opens the door to his vehicle.

"Why?"

"Something tells me he won't stay that way." Murdoc gets in his car and drives off into the night.

Christian looks down at the mound of dirt before him and moments later stabs at it with the shovel as if the earth needed to be put out of its misery. Lightning strikes and, with it, the inevitable sound of thunder. Christian looks up as the dark is temporarily lit. Someone or something stands off in the distance, framed by trees whose branches bend at the mercy of the wind.

Who is it? Gabriel? Why would he be out here and what does he want? Christian strains to see. Is it Brandon? It can't be...

"Who's there?" he yells. There is no response. Whoever it is just stands there, letting the rain pound his body.

"Who are you?" Christian yells. Lightning strikes again, as if simultaneously punctuating his question with an exclamation point and giving him more illumination by which to see. The flash is too brief. Whose face was that? Brandon? No. It can't be.

"You're dead!" Christian screams into the dark.

The silence is now louder than the thunder for the last time.

Christian takes a step closer. Whoever is near the trees doesn't move. Christian picks up the football that was a few feet away from him. Remember I told you, he is always holding a football. He spirals the ball into the dark; it crashes through the trees and to the ground. There is no one there.

Christian spins completely around, looking for whoever it was he saw to be there but he's alone, alone with the other dead bodies.

He looks back to the grave. It is untouched, the ground around it undisturbed. How can that be? Christian looks at his watch again. It is still midnight.

It will always be midnight for Christian.

Bourbon and Caramel

"What lies beneath a Sunday sky?
The weeping of a child, his lullaby?
Wake Mother, breakfast is dying on the table."

That is the opening to a poem my father wrote. It is one of my favorite poems of his, especially now that I only get to see him on Sundays. Today is the day I picked for us to go horseback riding. I always get to pick where we go or what we do. I'm his daughter, his only child. That is something I didn't get to pick, but I am happy to exploit it.

We are riding two Appaloosas. There is nothing fancy or regal about Appaloosas. Appaloosas are a stock breed of horse, primarily known for their leopard-like spotted patterns. But Appaloosas are beautiful. Appaloosas are sleek. Appaloosas are muscular. Appaloosas remind me of a Ducati.

"The father opens his eyes.
An impression of where his love once laid remains.
feathers will one day suffocate him."

My father and I ride side by side, across an open plain that stretches beyond the doors of infinity. I feel the warmth of the sun that somehow seems to comfort me from the inside. I look over and realize it is my father smiling at me. My father rarely smiled. At least not around my mother or me. He was not an unhappy man, and in the company of others, those not as close to him as my mother and I, he almost always smiled. But there was something about my mother's and my emotional proximity to my father that seemed to invite a more introspective facade. I'm not sure I understand that about him. I know my mother didn't. My father's lack of a smile in her presence had less to do with his emotional proximity to her and more with an emotional detachment. I can't believe that to be true. Writers do not detach; they rearrange. Now to those that don't understand that process, the order in which writers prioritize their emotional responses may seem to be possessed of the insensitivity of randomness. Like a deck of cards being shuffled by the wind. I knew why my father hardly smiled around us. It was because we reminded him of what he needed to accomplish, and of the consequence if he fell short. There was joy in his heart that we were there, but he prioritized the worry, the concern and the doubt that a provider feels to be expressed before that joy so that he did not become complacent. My father was never unhappy with us, but he was eternally unhappy with himself. That's something some people can never rearrange... depression. No matter what room of your mind you move your depression into, it always ends up being the place where the things you need are. You always have to go back into that room.

> *"If you drink the coffee too fast*
> *Mother*
> *your lips will burn."*

My dad is riding slightly ahead of me now. Have I described my father to you? I don't believe I have...

My father is about six feet tall. He is black haired though gray strands twist their way throughout like an errant child. His hair is not unkempt, but it was never kept. It fell upon his head by virtue of how my father tilted it at any given moment. It's not that he didn't care about his appearance; he just trusted that it was able to take care of itself. My father was right. He was a handsome man, as if the word *handsome* were created for him. I don't believe I've ever seen him in anything but jeans. I don't believe his feet have worn anything but boots. Not even when he was a child.

My father also smokes. I don't smoke, but the fact that he does doesn't bother me. Not like it annoyed my mother. I know why it bothered her, but she can't understand why it doesn't bother me. I'll tell you why… because he's my father. He's the strongest man in the world. Stronger even than cancer.

> *"If you look at the sun too long*
> *daughter*
> *your eyes will melt."*

My father's voice is the most distinctive thing about him. His voice is deep, rich, like a cup of black coffee that contains just a hint of cream when he laughs. He's laughing at me now because as he gallops away he knows I'm a better rider and he knows I will catch up to him. He's laughing because he has not rearranged me.

We stop the horses at the edge of a cliff. Side by side we look out across the serenity of the landscape. I look down into the chasm. What is stronger? A rock that protrudes from the earth or a heart that beats beneath a chest? I look out across the expanse. What is wider? The distance between the edges of land split by God's hand or the gap between the beats of your heart you sometimes fall into when you want to die?

My father turns to me and smiles and the gap that I want to fall into sometimes momentarily closes.

I never told my father about being raped. I didn't want to burden him with the reality of someone doing something like that to his little girl.

I remember a time when I was seven and came in from playing outside. Some neighborhood boys had called me a name as I walked past them. I can't remember what the name was, but I know that it wasn't my name and I wasn't whatever it was. My father was sitting at his desk, writing, when I came in. He watched me after school during the day because that's when my mother worked. My father would have the occasional gig, as he called them, playing piano in a band at nights, but days were ours. I remember that that day my father smiled at me but paused when I didn't smile back.

"What's wrong?" my father asked. When I told him, told him what the boys had callously called me, he brushed past me like an avenging wind. It was so fast that the door slam was the punctuation at the end of my sentence.

I remember looking out from the kitchen window at my father speak to the boys that had dared insult his daughter. My father's back was to me, but I could see his anger reflected in the fright that spilled from each of the three boys' eyes. When my father was done, he turned around. It was then I could see that if my father was able to, he would never let anyone hurt me, and if he were unable to, he would never let anyone forget that they had. When you hold the key to that type of protection, you have to be very careful when you choose to unlock that door.

My father is lighting a cigarette now. American Spirit. Yellow pack. Light flavored. One hundred percent pure tobacco. The smoke from his cigarette is lost in the thickness of the air that surrounds us. I hold on to the moment so that the same does not happen to it.

"Take thy father's hand
there are gestures grand
this day holds the promise of."

Maybe I didn't tell my father about the rape for fear of what he might then think of me. Rape is a crime that in other people's minds must be explained even when there is no explanation, other than fate blew you into a direction with her eyes closed. But that explanation can never suffice. Why? I think because the crime of rape is so horrific, the violation so total, that without someone to lay the blame upon, people would find it impossible to function in a world where they could be blindly misdirected by the blink of fate… And oftentimes, if you are unable to see the monster in the accused, if his looks or his status wraps around his person like a halo, then the accuser becomes the monster.

I never believed that my father would look at me as some type of monster, or that he would look at me with any type of guilt, but he might have looked at the world differently and could he look at the world differently without looking at me differently as well?

I would not be the one to close the openness of the road that lay before my father and me.

"Walk outside into the closing sky
birds fly
one day their feathers will suffocate them
and they will fall
at your feet."

We sit beneath a waterfall that lets out into a racing river that flows because that is what it was born doing. How wonderful not to have to find your purpose. What a fortunate beauty to be born into it. Then I think of a volcano, and it momentarily makes me sad because what if it is your purpose to destroy? What if you are born into this world to wreak havoc? I'm sorry. I must stop. I will not allow such thoughts to intrude upon my Sunday.

It is time for my father and me to have a snack. Mine is a sliced apple I dip into a small container of caramel. I love caramel. I love saying caramel. It tastes just like the word feels in your mouth when you say it out loud. My dad's snack is in the flask I gave him for his last birthday. It is pewter, with a raised ankh on the front made of polished brass. Ankh is the Egyptian hieroglyphic for eternal life. There is bourbon inside. There is always bourbon inside. In that sense, bourbon is eternal, as well. My father takes a drink, then dips his finger in my caramel. He thinks that he is funny. He is. If you were to ask my mother what was my father's one defining trait, I think that's what she would say, even to this day, that my father was funny, even though towards the end, he made her laugh less than anyone. And therein is my mother's one defining trait. Honesty. She would not lie to make my father look bad, even if the lie could be considered the truth depending upon who was telling it.

I do this often when I visit my father on Sundays. I think about the times when we were together as a family. I don't like seeing him alone. I don't like feeling left alone. I don't like my mother being alone. If I can keep us together by remembering the times that we were, then I will excavate my mind until I have stripped it of every memory I have and it echoes with empty recollections.

I look at the beauty of the waterfall. I look at the purpose with which the water rushes over the cliff. I look at the manner in which the water breaks over the rocks as it enters into the river and disappears downstream. That was my parents' marriage. Beauty, purpose, then breaks that fractured and splintered their union, carrying pieces away downstream until they were no longer the two people who fell in love with each other.

"It's all right.
They were only supposed to be in the sky
until you saw them."

My father takes another drink from his flask. I can hear the bourbon soothing his throat in the quiet of the desert. My father loves his flask. And I love that I know it is more for who gave it to him than what is inside it.

I have eaten my last slice of apple, but some caramel remains. I do as my father did before me and stick my finger into the container. As I move it around, the remaining caramel clings to my finger like a cherished memory, like this memory that I will always cherish. I place my finger into my mouth and as the caramel hits my tongue a sunburst temporarily blinds me. I close my eyes and my senses are forced to concentrate only on the taste of the caramel. It is a willing surrender.

"Mmm," I say.

I then open my eyes to see my father is already atop his horse and laughing at me. He is laughing, again, because he knows that I am a better rider, and he knows that I will catch up to him. I smile… because he has not rearranged me.

Nabokov, the Girl on the Wall
and the one in the Bed

Hi. My name is Olivia. Most people call me Liv. My last name is Wiise. Olivia Wiise. That is the name I was born with. That is the name my parents gave me. That is the most personal thing Christian knew about me before he placed his penis inside me.

I remember the rape like the wind remembers to blow when things have remained calm for too long. I remember the rape like the ache of a tooth that remembers that it is slowly decaying. I remember the rape because it is impossible to forget a tear that you can never brush away... even though you momentarily forget it when there are no mirrors to stare into and remind you that it's there.

He feels big inside me, painfully big, but I know it's my fear, my innocence, my virginity, making him seem bigger than he probably is. He is ripping me apart even as I am aware that he is ripping me apart. I try to make a mental note of where the pieces of me are falling so that when the time comes I can gather back as many as possible. The movement of the bed caused by the thrusting of his body scatters some pieces so far away that I know I will never be able to find them. Some parts of me have broken into so many pieces themselves that they can never be put back together again.

My eyes are frozen open. I am too afraid that if I close them, he will think I am enjoying his violation. I want the daggers that come from my eyes to pierce him even though I know they are not sharp enough to penetrate his skin.

He's turning me over… onto my belly. Perhaps I did pierce his skin… or perhaps he wants to destroy my body completely.

My head is turned to the side. I can see his alarm clock on the nightstand. The time tells me in a fluorescent blue glow that whenever I look at a clock and it's 11:31 I will always remember this moment.

He is hurting me.

There is an iPod docked on the top of his alarm clock. I don't know why, maybe my mind desperately needs something to distract it, but I wonder what kind of songs he has on it. Maybe I'm wondering what kind of music a monster would listen to, or maybe I am wondering why a monster would need music at all.

"You like the way that feels?" Christian asks.

Is he talking to me or to himself? Is the evil Christian having a conversation with the Christian that I knew as a child? The little boy that walked me home when I fell from my bike and could not stop crying? Is he asking that part of him if it feels good so that he can then be without internal conflict?

He turns me back over.

"I said, do you like how that feels, bitch?"

OK. He is talking to me. And as I look up at him, I can also see in his eyes that there is no conflict within him. None at all. Maybe that little boy that walked me home never existed. Maybe it was all a dream. Maybe this is a dream.

"Yes," I whisper, because I am afraid. I don't know it now, but I will always regret this answer.

"Good," he says. "Because I'm going to give you some more."

He forces himself inside me… again… No. This is not a dream.

I can no longer watch him as he looks down upon me, as he thrusts and thrusts and thrusts and... I should stop. You will never want to hear that word again.

I turn my head away from him, to the side again, and there I am... standing in the middle of the room watching myself being raped. I look back at myself on the bed. I am so frail, so scared, so naked. Maybe I'm not looking at me at all. It doesn't seem like me. Yet, as I stand there, as I watch this beast convulse on top of the girl on the bed, I can feel his intrusion between my legs, too, so I know that it is indeed me that I watch. Yes, it is I. Even in the dark, even with myself lying on the bed, I can see the tiny scar on the right side of my arm. It's the scar I received when I was five and fell off my bike. Remember? That is when the person that is raping me held my hand and walked me home.

I turn away from myself. I cannot help me. Not in that sense. So I look around the room as if attempting to get to know Christian by the things he has accumulated. I stare at a poster he has on the wall. It is a poster of a woman in a swimsuit. I say woman because I don't know her name. I don't know what she does. And I don't know who she is. I feel like Christian should have that girl in his bed because he probably knows more about her than he does about me. I know that he's known me since I was five, but that was so long ago.

If Christian had bothered to speak to me, if interests and passions did not take us in opposite directions, he would know that I prefer plain M&M's to peanut. That information might seem insignificant to you, but before you put your penis into a girl, I think you should know what her favorite candy is... whether she prefers plain or peanut M&M's. I like biker boots. I specifically like the pair my father bought for me through a birthday gift card to a store he heard me speak of briefly and indirectly. As if he accidentally overheard the sound of a bird's wings flapping and he took note of the direction in which it flew.

I love those boots.

I prefer pancakes to waffles, night to day, showers to baths and eggs just about any way you can cook them with the exception of hard-boiled. I prefer lip gloss to lipstick, spicy brown mustard to yellow and, though I have a gene from my mother that makes me want to sleep late, I am an early riser like my father. If Christian took me out for a drink, that is, when I was old enough to drink, would he know I prefer white wine to red? Would he have gotten to know me enough before that first dinner to know that when I was eight my father gave me a sip from a glass of whiskey and on the occasion that I drink officially for the first time I would love to order a whiskey, but would be too scared? Has he ever heard of the movie *The Cabinet of Dr. Caligari*? If he knew me, he would have because it is one of my favorites. And if he bought me a first edition, would it be Nabokov's *Lolita*?

I'm sorry… I would tell you more, but I want to die and I have to turn around to see what Christian is doing now. What is he doing now?

Christian is having trouble completing the devastation. He makes me stand. Blood trickles down the inside of my leg like a trail of bloody tears left in the wake of desecration. And then… he pushes me down so that I am sitting on the bed before his instrument of destruction. No! I will not let him put his cock into my mouth. I've never ever used that word until now. He has already changed me. Damn him.

"Suck it," he says, oddly attempting to sound seductive.

I remain silent.

"Suck it!" he commands. His poisonous seduction is swallowed by anger like a snake swallowing a rat.

I remain silent.

He takes hold of my hair and leans down. Our faces are but inches apart. For one moment we stare at each other from within the calm of the storm, as the chaos of the situation swirls around us, allowing neither to leave.

Christian whispers to me, "You know you want to... don't you?" He then stands up and pushes me forward from the back of my head.

I know that I will one day be able to numb what he has done below, but I also know that I will never be able to remove the taste of what he would do to my mouth.

"No," I tell him as I push him away. I will always be happy that I did. He takes my hand and forces me to complete my own violation using the blood from inside me, the blood that remains upon it, my blood, as lubrication.

Damn him.

When I am done, I look at the blood that remains on my hand. And that is the reason I am telling you this now. You see, I was in the kitchen cutting a grilled cheese sandwich in half when I accidentally cut my hand. It was a tiny cut, nothing more than piercing the skin. I looked down at my hand and there was a drop of blood. One drop. That's all it takes sometimes to pull me back to that moment, one drop of blood. One drop.

I never ate the sandwich. Oh, and I lied. Peanut M&M's are my favorite, not plain. But when I was looking around at Christian's room, I saw in the dark the bright yellow of a discarded M&M's wrapper on the floor. I will probably never eat peanut M&M's again.

Damn him.

Cicada

I hate Sunday nights. It means the day is over and I am no longer with my father. My father is Sunday to me. And when the night comes it's as if he closes his eyes and can no longer see me. I hate Sunday nights.

I sit on my bed and the light of my laptop illuminates my face. I am looking up a word. I do that often. Look up words. I don't look up specific words, just words that come across my mind in an unspecified way. They are words that have a pretty sound, an unusual cadence. I study their meaning like one would study a lover's face before they ever realize they will be lovers.

I am just beginning to forget about things. Things that I could not forget since I decided to make a sandwich. I have even forgotten about the sandwich.

The door to my room opens. My mother steps in just as I am looking at a word on my screen.

"You know you left a sandwich on the counter?" she says.

I do not respond. I read the word in front of me as if she never entered the room.

Cicada... Then I read the definition: "Cicadas can cause damage to trees, mainly in the form of scarring left on the branches while the females lay their eggs deep within them."

My mother closes the door.

I Will Not Name You for Fear You Will Never Leave

"Sometimes it is only when I look into the darkness
that I am able to see myself.
And I am almost always smiling.
And I am almost never alone.
Though I am the only one I can see.
Warm like a lullaby.
Resigned like a sigh
Will you ever let me go?
Will you ever let me die?"

I am wandering in a field as expansive as an inconsolable cry. There is a tree in the distance whose branches weep upward like a child reaching for his mother's acceptance. The leaves know the futility of clinging to those branches because they bear the color of impending surrender. Auburn is the shade of fire before it burns away all color.

Dragonflies are suspended in the air around me. Their wings flutter at the speed that creates a wind with no direction.

"They're beautiful. Aren't they?"

I turn around. There is no one there. But I feel his presence like the breath that has momentarily fallen in love with my throat.

I will not name him for fear he will never leave.

"Nothing is beautiful here."

"You find no beauty in sadness?"

"No. Why would anyone?"

A dragonfly hovers in front of me as if it is the one speaking. I know it is only there to distract me from being distracted. You can never be distracted from a dream because everything means something, nothing means anything and it all brings you back to the same point before you awaken.

"Then why are you here?"

"This is a dream."

"This lives inside you even when you wake."

"There were things put inside me that I did not want," I say.

"How sad."

"Is that who you are?" I ask.

"This is your dream," I am told. "Who am I?"

I know who he is, but I will not name him for fear he will never leave.

"Dance with me," the voice commands.

"I don't want to dance with you."

"You already are," he says.

I look off into the distance, which is as close as my hand. "I want to go to that tree."

"Why? What is over there?"

"Happiness?" I ask.

"It's your dream—you tell me."

"I don't know," I say.

"Then we should dance until you do."

The dragonfly leaves from in front of me. It was never designed to be still for so long. Neither are dreams and so I am dancing. I hear music that could be humming that swims from the direction of the trees. I know it will eventually wash over me and carry me back to the tree so I am unafraid.

You cannot see him in my arms, but he holds me up. I will not let this dream become the nightmare that is tapping me on the shoulder for my attention.

"No," I say.

"No, what?"

"You're asking for my attention."

"I'm right in front of you."

"No. You're all around me," I tell him as we twirl around the field.

"That's because you won't let me go," he tells me.

"I don't know how."

"Do you want to?"

"Yes," I plead, and now I am literally crying. "I don't want to dance with you anymore."

The humming that once seemed melodic becomes so much louder that my ears bleed from its dissonance. I can feel the tapping on my shoulder again, begging that I turn around. I have had too many dreams not to know that when dreaming, you never turn around.

"Why won't you turn around?"

"This is a dream."

"The tree is behind you."

"I know," I say.

"It's where you wanted to go."

"It's a dream."

"You keep saying that," I am told. And then I am aware that the humming has now gone silent.

"Liv."

I know that voice. It is Brandon's.

"Liv," Brandon repeats. "Turn around."

"He wants you to turn around," the first voice informs me. This I already know. That is what dreams do, tell you what you're already aware of.

"This is a dream," I repeat.

"Liv."

Then the first voice speaks. "Hurry. You need to turn around."

"Why?" I ask.

"As you said, this is a dream. And all dreams end. Don't you want to see Brandon?"

I am more concerned at the moment with a sound I hear. It is a horrific hollow sound that seems to echo without needing to.

"Liv," I hear Brandon beg again. I want to turn around so bad. But you never turn around in a dream.

"I can't, Brandon."

"This is your dream," the voice once again informs me. "You can do whatever you want."

"No. It's not my dream anymore," I say. "It's a nightmare."

"How do you know?"

"Do you hear that sound?" I ask.

"Yes."

"Do you know what it is?"

The voice is silent.

"Cicadas," I say. And then I open my eyes. There are rules to dreams when you lose someone you love. I suggest should you lose someone, you never forget those rules.

And if you are about to sleep... never look up words like *cicada*.

The Briefness of the Beauty of Snow

Gabriel never showed up to classes today. His presence being new, it went unnoticed by most. I noticed. Now classes are over, though for me, they never began. This has nothing to do with Gabriel's absence, however. Classes for me have been over for months. I am unsure if I am learning anything or if the memory that haunts me so vividly still keeps anything else from taking up permanent residency. Are there not three primary functions of your mind? Must not the mind learn, experience and then process both? The flaw then or maybe the mind's failsafe is that while processing certain experiences, the mind must shut down its capacity to learn. Perhaps the process of processing is itself learning, and while the brain seeks to learn from an experience already lived, it cannot also, simultaneously, learn new things. Maybe it deems new information inconsequential in light of what it has already gathered. What if your mind is continually processing a certain experience? Will you ever then be able to learn anything beyond that moment? Maybe the mind doesn't hold the capacity for hope like the heart does.

"What's on your mind?"

Everything, I silently respond before turning around to see that it is Jai who has asked me the question. "What did you say?" I ask, out loud this time.

"I said, what's on your mind? What are you thinking about so intently?"

I have to think a minute before I can answer, and this time, all I can reply is the opposite of what I first wanted to, the truth. "Nothing."

"Nothing," Jai repeats. "How does someone have nothing on their mind?" He wants to play. I'm not sure I am in the mood.

"It's easy," I tell him.

"How?" he asks. I will make him sorry he did, maybe then he will leave me to myself.

"Just try and think of the last time you were happy."

Now Jai is silent. I want to smile, but I can't. I am watching as the light diminishes from his eyes. It is like a stopper has been pulled from a drain that apathetically empties its contents into a reservoir of sadness.

"I remember," Jai says with a grin that reignites the light in his eyes. I grin, as well. Maybe I do want to play. Maybe my heart is not listening to my mind.

"When?" I ask. Suddenly, I hear the rev of an engine. I turn around like a carousel looking for the place it began, but I see nothing.

"Snow," Jai says.

My face turns half away, as if that word, *snow*, were a wind and I was blown into the direction of the past. The past when I last was happy.

Jai begins to tell me the story, but I will be the one to tell you. It's not because Jai cannot tell it well, but because I want to tell it once more, then never remember it again. I think my mind is attempting to wrestle back control from my heart.

It was the three of us, Brandon, Jai and myself. The number three would hold more significance than just the number of people. It was three days before I would be raped. It was three days before the life that was mine would be pushed from a shelf, then put back up after it had been glued back together. It would never be looked at the same again though. It would be like a figurine without beauty or worth, just the ability to occupy the space it once had, hoping no one would notice the cracks.

This night was cold, colder than it had been all year, colder than it had ever been. The three of us had driven together out into the night and into the desert to be warmed by the beauty and space that was always too hot to fully enjoy.

I remember Brandon and Jai howling like wolves at the full moon as if they were drunk from its glow. I remember laughing when Brandon's voice cracked and he sounded more like a frightened baby wolf trying to impress his mother too soon than a wolf ready to give prey pause. I remember Brandon laughing at me because I was laughing at him and Jai laughing at the both of us. Young. Innocent. Happy. We were untouched by the reality of the truth that is real. That you never remain young… you cannot remain innocent… and it is impossible to remain happy. Innocence is a beautiful thing. Like snow. Sometimes it doesn't last as long. Maybe that's why it's so beautiful.

I remember Jai walking back to the car to get our jackets when it became too cold. We foolishly attempted to brave the frost at first, but, as I just pointed out, the truth of what is real sooner or later points out the foolishness of youth. As Jai departed, Brandon put his arms around me and pulled me in.

"How's that?" Brandon asked.

I remember that even though I could see my breath, I felt breathless.

I remember the strangest thing happened.

I still can't to this day explain how or why it happened. I still to this day cannot explain why the bite of a Twizzler makes me smile but they both occurred… Brandon looked down at me, into my eyes, and asked me what was the one thing I'd always wanted to see but hadn't. I asked him why he wanted to know, and he told me it was because he wanted to try and get it for me. My answer was snow. I had always wanted to see snow since I was a little girl but when you're born in the desert a snow's kiss is never meant to touch your lips. I didn't expect Brandon to be able to acquire snow for me. In my mind the best I could hope for was a trip one day to a place where snow was generous with its affection. But again, he wanted to know.

"Snow?" Brandon asked.

"Yes. Snow," I repeated. Then I taunted him. "I'm waiting." The visibility of my breath does not dissipate before a smile draws upon his face.

"Close your eyes and stick out your tongue," he told me.

"Are you going to kiss me?" I asked.

"No," I remember him saying. "The snow is."

How sweet, I thought. How silly and sweet. That may be the best combination in the world to me… silly and sweet. If you find that combination, do your best to never let it go.

I closed my eyes and stuck out my tongue. I remember thinking how cold the air was and I remember wanting the warmth of Brandon's tongue to suppress it. Instead, my tongue became colder… then wetter… I opened my eyes. Brandon smiled as a second snowflake came into my view and landed upon my tongue. I slowly stepped back from Brandon and looked up at the sky… the desert sky… the desert sky raining snow all around us.

"H-How?" I stuttered. "How did you make it snow?"

"I didn't," Brandon said. "You did. You asked for it."

"Brandon…"

Before Brandon could say anything else, and I'm unsure that I would believe anything he said, Jai ran over screaming.

"It's snowing! It's snowing," he yelled.

"We know," I say.

Jai stood beside us, his jaw dropped in awe.

"Liv did it," Brandon joked.

"Did what?" Jai asked.

"Made it snow."

Jai looked over to me. Falling snowflakes invade the space between us.

"I asked for snow," I said.

"You asked for snow," Jai repeated.

"She asked for snow," Brandon said.

"Cool," Jai responded as if we had just told him I ordered a glass of iced tea. And it momentarily made me wish we had glasses of iced tea to drink as it snowed. How silly that would be. How silly and sweet.

Jai offered us our jackets. Brandon took his, but I declined mine. There was no way I was not going to feel the snow upon my skin. After all, I had asked for it. And that is how it came to be that the three of us stood in the desert, bathed in the soft shimmer of the moon, beneath the briefness of the beauty of snow.

Maybe I will hold on to this memory just a little while longer... Yes. I think I will. Its beauty is not in its briefness, but that it happened at all.

The Rev of a Carousel

Rev …

There it is again. The sound of an engine. The sound of a motorcycle engine. I turn my body completely around. Three hundred and sixty degrees. A carousel pushed by the cry of the wind. There is no one there. Maybe it was thunder. Yes. Thunder. The sky is turning dark, though it is not an angry dark; it is more pensive, almost as if expressing regret over its purpose.

My conversation with Jai is done. I don't have the luxury of reminiscing for too long. That is what reminiscing is for me now, a luxury when the present is too distracted to forbid it. I watch Jai walk across the school grounds and past the student parking lot as the rain begins to fall. Regretfully or not, the sky has decided to speak. As I watch Jai disappear farther into the distance, I am reminded of him walking back to the car that snowy night. I look to the sky again, but there is no snow this time. There is no Brandon. Only rain.

Rev…

There it is again. That most certainly was not the sound of thunder. I spin completely around. Again. A carousel propelled by one of the plastic horse's desire to catch a glimpse of a kind face from the last revolution.

There he stands. Christian. He is standing almost exactly where Jai was walking past moments before. It's as if Jai walked right through Christian without ever seeing him or having to stop. How I wish I had that ability.

The rain begins to fall with a greater intensity. Christian is standing with his arms around a girl. She is a young girl. A freshman. I know this because I remember seeing her in the hallways back when avoiding faces was not necessary for my survival.

I think her name is... Danielle. Yes. That is her name. Danielle. Everyone calls her Dani.

Dani is fifteen with brown hair that flirts with becoming red. Freckles indiscriminately dot her alabaster skin, lending a depth to her paleness. She reminds me of a flake of snow. She is so innocent. She is so unique. She is so pure.

Christian kisses her and again I am reminded of the briefness of the beauty of snow. How snow is so innocent, so unique, so pure, until it touches the ground and then waits for its beauty to melt, or worse... be trampled upon.

Rev... There's that sound again. Or is it a warning? I wish it would just tell me. It's so hard to guess in the wind and the rain.

I turn around. Again. But this time I only turn halfway ... as if turning away. A carousel that stops so a frightened child can get off.

Imposing Decay

I begin the walk to my car. The rain allows me no respite. It's OK. I don't want the rain's sympathy. I don't need it. I would rather have its purpose upon me. It feels good, as if I am being washed with my every step. It makes me walk slower even though I know the convertible top to my Mustang is down and rain has soaked the interior. I laugh, thinking how my father would kill me and my mother wouldn't care at knowing this.

This worry, or lack thereof, of the order of things was the only personality trait I felt my parents had reversed. My dad was so easygoing, so relaxed, but if things were out of order, if things he loved or cherished were under the threat of even marginal wear, however expected, he labored over it. As I think about it now, I wonder if that is what allowed him to be so relaxed, the alignment of order; how could anyone ever find true peace in a world where order is always in flux? I think I understand my father more.

My mother, so intense, so stressed in regard to things that had to be done, was not bothered by disorganization or deterioration. My mother never let the decay imposed by rain bother her. I think my mother had it easier than my father. For the first time I understand that she was able to be happier, easier. For it is always raining; things are always deteriorating... Decay does not know the definition of the word *cease*.

As I near the Mustang, I see something has been slipped between the wiper blade and windshield of my car. Even with the wind, the pounding of the rain holds it up against the glass.

My first thought, my first question, is it something from him? Gabriel? Is it an explanation as to why I didn't see him in school today? I wonder these things about his reasons even as I know that he owes me none.

I make my way up to my car and I pick the paper up, cautiously, so as not to rip it. As I begin to read, I wish I had not ever held it in my hands. I want to curse whoever it was that left it on my windshield. It is a flyer announcing a party that will take place tonight at Christian's home. It's the last party before the championship game and it is thrown every year. It usually falls on a Saturday, but there was a wake for Russel that took place that day. I suppose when you're young, to mourn for more than two days is considered self-indulgent.

I stare at the piece of paper as the rain futilely attempts to wash away Christian's name. Like happiness, even decay has its limitations.

Partial Rooms

I hear a voice in the house. The voice is female, but it possesses the authority of a man's. She is asking to be saved, though she is asking with such self-awareness that it's more a command than a request. I find it hard to imagine that if her cry went unanswered, she would not know how to save herself. I know to whom the voice belongs before I enter my mother's back office. That is where the words and music originate, even though the melody softly inhabits almost every room. It's Nina Simone, and she is singing "Save Me." I know what this means... My mother must be beginning a new case.

I gently push a partially open door completely open. My mother looks up from her work and gives me a partial smile. She turns away, back to her words. So used to me not coming in that she seems shocked when she looks back and I have entered.

"Is everything OK?" my mother asks.

I laugh a partial laugh, though I keep it inside. Is anything OK when a parent is surprised a child wants to be in their company?

"Everything is fine," I tell her. "I heard Nina." My mother reaches over and turns the CD player down so we can better hear each other attempt to fight off the silence that usually dominates our conversations.

"New case," my mother says.

"Who?" I ask.

"Lucas Dunagan."

I know that name. Everyone that pays even partial attention to the news knows that name. He raped a fifteen-year-old girl for over four hours. He knew her because her father had purchased a puppy for her from him a month earlier. He bred and sold dogs. That's what he did. I mean, when he wasn't raping young girls. That's why the girl was at his house. She was going to get some items for her puppy that weren't there at the time. Her father was unaware she was going there until she told him what happened days later. Well, she didn't tell her father; the doctor did. She had to be seen by a doctor because she had internal bleeding. She told the doctor what happened and he told her father… after he told the police. That's how horrific the account of the rape was. The reason for the internal bleeding is the reason the trial was moved to our town. No, it didn't happen here, the evil of it was so atrocious that no one in the city in which it happened wanted to be further soiled by having to relive it in court, lest they never feel clean again. I won't repeat the rumors about what was done to the girl, the daughter of the city's prosecutor, but if it's true, she won't ever be able to feel clean again.

"Why would you take that case?"

"I'm the city prosecutor. I don't necessarily have a choice. It was mine the moment the trial was moved here."

"Are you going to go for the death penalty?"

"No, I doubt it will get to that."

"Why? If he did what they say he did, he deserves to die."

"It's more complicated than that," is what my mom tells me. I think people say it's more complicated than that when they are too afraid to admit to themselves that it really isn't that complicated at all, that they have simply decided to make it thus.

"What do you mean?" I ask.

"You know I am not able to discuss details of cases, Liv."

"I'm not asking you to. The case hasn't even begun. I just want to know what you're going to do."

"My job."

"Stop treating me like I'm a child, Mom. Dad never did that. I know about more things than you think I do."

"I know you do," my mother says.

"Then tell me."

"There will more than likely be a plea deal. Simple assault."

"Simple assault?" I echo. "She was raped, Mom. There's nothing simple about that."

"Were you there? Did you see it happen? Do you know why she was there? Did you take her? Did you tell her not to report it for two days? Did you tell her not to go there without her father in the first place?"

Oh my God. I say nothing. Oh my God.

"See. It's complicated. And no one wants to put her on the stand. And to be honest, I don't blame them. If it were you, God forbid, and what they say happened is true…"

"Wouldn't you want to see that person die?"

"Not if it meant you having to die by reliving it."

"She's already dead, Mom. She can only be forgotten or reborn."

"Olivia. Why would you say something like that?"

I hear my mother's question, but it only partially registers. My attention is now focused on the pack of American Spirit cigarettes gathering errant dust on the shelf beside my mother's desk. I know they are not my mother's cigarettes because she doesn't smoke; my mother also doesn't much care for people that do. No. The cigarettes are not my mother's. The pack belongs to my father, as did this office when he still lived here.

I pick up the cigarettes, slowly, carefully, as if the pack had been sleeping and I am afraid to awaken it.

"Those are your father's."

"I know," I say. "Why do you still have them?"

Before she can answer, I have already asked a second question.

"I mean, why haven't you thrown them away?"

My mother puts down the pen that had occupied her hand when I entered and thinks for a moment. She looks up at me… partially. Her stare is almost inward, as if she is looking at herself.

"I don't know," she says.

I look around the office, then I look back at her. "I'm only asking because it's the only thing left on the shelves that's his."

"I know," my mother says this time. And she says it in the same reflective tone that I used when I said it moments earlier. "Everything else was inanimate," she continues. "Furniture. Tools. Things. I guess I thought the cigarettes were the closest thing he had to plant life, the tobacco being organic and all, so I had trouble throwing them away."

"But you hated when he smoked."

"I don't like it when anyone smokes."

"Yeah," I agree. "But you hated when Dad did. I remember you arguing with him about it all the time."

"It wasn't all the time," she counters.

"It was enough times that he felt he had to hide it from you."

"Is that what you think he did? Hid it from me?"

I nod. Yes.

"He wasn't hiding it from me, Olivia. He chose not to do it in front of me. And I chose not to be in front of him when he did it."

"So you pretended it didn't happen?" I ask.

"I suppose," my mother responds. I pull a cigarette from the pack and look at it as it is held between my fingers.

"Do you think that works for everything?" I ask my mother.

"Are you going to start smoking now?" she responds, avoiding my actual question.

"Do you?" I ask again.

"Do I what?"

I place the cigarette lengthwise beneath my nose and pull the aroma of the tobacco from the thin paper that wraps around it like a lover's arms. "Do you think pretending something didn't happen works for everything?"

"Maybe temporarily." My mother surrenders. "But things don't just go away if you ignore them."

I lower the cigarette and look at my mother.

"Daddy did."

My mother looks at me as if my words slapped a cup of coffee from her hands, leaving her more awake than she wanted to be.

"I didn't ignore your father," she begins to explain. "I ignored some of the things he did."

"What's the difference?" I ask.

"I don't know," my mother admits somewhat honestly. "I only know the longer we were together, the harder it was to distinguish the two."

I hold the cigarette up to my mother. She looks at it, past it and to me. "Would you let him smoke if he came back?" I ask her.

"He's not coming back," she says.

I place the cigarette back into the pack and then I extend them to my mother.

"Then why don't you throw away the pack?" I hold a partial breath. My mother leans from her chair and reaches for the pack. I am unsure if I move it partially closer or farther away. I know that I move.

My mother takes the pack of American Spirits from my hand and tosses them into the small trash can hidden partially beneath her desk. I immediately want to go and retrieve them, rescue them… That's what I would love to do. That is what I feel that I should do. But unfortunately it's more complicated than that.

"I'm going for a walk," I tell my mom.

"You just got home," she says. "And it's so dark out."
I smile... partially.
"It's dark in here, too."

The Breaches of Faith

It still rains. It is still as it rains. It is especially still inside the mourning walls of the abandoned church. I don't know if I came looking for God or Gabriel. I do know that neither of them is here. There is only me. There is only rain.

Where is he? Where is He?

Drops of rain enter the house of the holy through the breaches in the roof. Is that His acknowledgment of me? Is He giving me in the rain something that was closer to his presence than I have been since what feels like forever? Is he telling me I am not alone? That would be so easy to believe if I thought it was only raining upon me. Then I would feel special. Then I would feel not so alone. Then I would feel like acknowledging Him with prayer. The only thing I feel is wet.

I wonder when it rains upon Lucas Dunagan again if he will feel as if God is speaking to him. I wonder if Lucas Dunagan prays. If he does, I wonder if God answers Lucas's prayers or if like the trial, because of his actions, Lucas finds God has moved to a different venue.

I wonder about the girl... I wonder about... I wonder about... I stop. Suddenly I feel like praying. I feel like praying as I am baptized by rain that is only able to do so because at some point someone got mad at God. I extend my hand out to capture the drops of rain. I will give him one verse for every drop that lands on my palm.

One drop…

"Hear me, Father. I am one of your sheep. Though I am no longer as soft to the touch. Though I am no longer as easily led. I am no longer looking for you to shepherd me."

Rain falls around my hands, in between my fingers, but not another drop hits my palm. Have I angered him so soon? I have only just begun.

There it is… Two drops.

"Are you listening still? Were you ever listening? Did you listen when I cried for him to stop? If you did, why didn't you make him?"

Three drops…

"If you are not there when someone needs you, then why do you require constant need? There are so many things I want to say to you, so many things I want to ask you because by not answering my other questions, you only leave me with more. Is that part of your mysterious ways? Or is that just indifference? Are you listening to me, Father? Father?"

Four drops…

"Why did you allow your son to bleed? Father? Why did you allow him to die? I'm just a girl. Why should I think you would care more about me?"

I lower my hand. I don't want to pray anymore. But I haven't finished. I… I raise my hand once more.

It takes a moment but, five, five drops…

"Did you think I was gone? Are you as tired of hearing my voice as I am? Then take it away."

Six…

"Why is it so easy to hate you?"

Seven… Seven drops.

"And when will you let me know it's OK to stop?"

A gust of wind rushes past me, also having entered through the splinters of faith. It lays an errant piece of paper at my feet. Where did it come from? How far has it traveled to get here? Perhaps God has decided to answer me in a letter.

I look down at the piece of paper. It is dark, but I need not pick it up to know what it says. I have seen this paper before. I saw it earlier today. Yes, it has traveled far to find me. It is a flyer, a flyer for Christian's party. Christian's party being held tonight.

I wonder about that girl he was with in the parking lot.

I turn and I begin towards the exit of the church. Just before I am about to leave, I remember something. I turn back and look inside. I stare at the damage of the roof and the punctures of the walls and I wonder how it still stands.

I step outside the church. The rain has finally stopped. My conversation with God must be over.

"Amen."

Only Every Third Word Counts

Brandon and I had this game between us. I think about it as I drive from my home to Christian's. We called the game Only Every Third Word Counts.

The game was simple. Sort of. One of us would say a sentence, any sentence. If you re-spoke the sentence using only every third word, it would form a second sentence. The sentence you really meant.

"Just because I don't say love doesn't mean you are not Brandon."

Silhouettes Are Not the Ghosts You Run from They Are the Ghosts You Become

I step outside my car and I close the door behind me. It is 90 degrees at night. Desert towns have no logic to their temperature– sometimes it is so cold and sometimes it is so hot. Hot. I remember what Christian said that night. Hot. He used the word *hot*. There's that cold feeling again. It's not a cold like when you walk inside from a hot day and open the freezer and immediately feel frost upon your face. That cold feels good. It is more like the cold you feel when someone pushes you into a pool as you stand on the edge, already having decided you did not want to go in.

I am in front of Christian's house; his grasp feels imminent. Remember only every third word counts and reread that last sentence.

The house, with its indulgent brick and secretive wrought iron, appears to me more as a mausoleum than home. I walk a hundred yards towards the structure before I look down and realize I am still standing beside my car. Somehow, if I am to do this, my body must reunite with my mind, my heart must stop beating and I must realize ghosts only haunt you when you run away from them.

I look at the house again. Every curtain over every numerous window of the home is sheer, as if the occupants want you to glimpse their decadence without being able to touch or judge it. I stare at the intoxicated silhouettes, stumbling, anonymous images at a party I want not to attend and wish for them to remain just that, silhouettes. I have to be strong though. And I have to realize that I too will remain a silhouette if I don't get nearer to them.

I notice one silhouette in particular. No, it's two. Now it's one again. I know it. Like the flyer, I have seen it before. It's the silhouette I had glimpsed in the rain in the parking lot of the school earlier today. And now I understand my visual confusion. Sometimes a snake wraps itself so tightly around its prey, it's impossible to know where one begins and the other ends.

The one are now two again and my eyes track them as Christian slithers towards the back and then up the stairs with his intended, Danielle, so closely behind him it's as if she is gliding on the scales of his back.

I know what is at the top of those stairs. I have made the ascent though the circumstances of my steps were under more threatening temptation. I am unsure I can climb them again without equal motivation. I am unsure I can open the door to the room she will soon be in. Christian's room. That is where the three of them will be alone… Just her, Christian and the girl in the poster on the wall. I have to go in. I have to go upstairs. I have to say something because I have been in that room, and I know that the girl on the wall… she will remain silent.

Do You Want to Fuck

I don't remember opening the door to Christian's house. I don't remember having to open it. I don't know if I ever closed it after I left. After...

"Do you want to fuck?"

That is the assault upon my ears before my eyes are even able to focus on the assailant that uttered the words. I turn and I am looking at a boy becoming a man who will always be a boy. I suppose that I could have faith that he will eventually mature, but there is a tattoo of a naked girl on his biceps that saves me the disappointment in hoping that he will.

"What did you say?" I ask. Sometimes it is not enough to see the flames; you must be burned before you realize you're in hell.

"Do you want to fuck?"

I stare deep into the vacuum where his eyes take up residence and wonder would he say that very thing if he were around his mother. I wonder, would he let someone say that to his mother? I am so empty of compassion that I wonder if he would say that to his mother. And would she do it because he had the decency to ask first?

I look away. I have to because sometimes the abyss enters you through your gaze.

The horror of what I then see I cannot look away from. How can *he* be here? Why would *he* be here? I demand to be told. I have walked across the entire room towards him before I look down and realize I have yet to move. Again, as it would turn out, I don't have to. He turns around and sees me and now walks over to greet me. I grit my teeth as if I were biting down my nerves in order to remain calm. He stands before me.

"Hi, Jai," I say.

Jai doesn't respond.

"Come with me," I tell him. He follows without saying a word.

The Long Ascent up the
Spiral Downward

I cannot help but think as I ascend the staircase leading up to Christian's room that it spirals like the coil of a snake. Is that coincidence in design or is it architectural assimilation? Was it once straight, only to bend and curve with the weight of every bad deed Christian burdened its purpose with?

Jai is closely behind me. He knows that we are going to confront Christian. He knows that it is because of Danielle. But he does not know exactly why. I never told Jai I was raped by Christian. Jai is as unaware as the rest of the town. He only knows that something happened, something that may have escalated into the something more that resulted in Brandon being killed. Did I have a specific reason for not telling Jai about what really happened? Was there a reason I didn't let one of my closest friends know that I had been raped? No. There wasn't. I didn't tell him because he never asked. At times I found that odd. There were things I was sure he knew. There were things that I was sure he had heard. And there were things I was sure he thought. But he never asked me about anything. Not even at Brandon's funeral. I assumed he had his reasons and I didn't want to force anything on him. Not like things were forced upon me. I know that in his heart he wants to explain to me why he is here. Why he is feeding from the belly of the beast like every other parasite that crawls around downstairs, but he doesn't try. Maybe he knows there are no words that can reach me. The beast consumed me, and the first thing I allowed him to devour were my ears so I wouldn't have to hear his breathing, so I didn't have to hear my tears, so I didn't have to hear him say he was sorry afterward. Though, I needn't have worried about that last thing.

No. There is nothing Jai can say to me right now that would make me despise him less as we climb the stairs together. I focus on navigating the spiral. I look at my feet and I want to remember what Brandon would call them but I can't because I feel them become heavy as if they realize we are nearing the top.

I stop... We have reached the top... I know because I can see his door. I know because I can hear my heart. I know... because I can feel my face burn, waiting for the tear I will not allow to run down my cheek.

"Come on," Jai says, attempting to pull me closer to the door. I am a stone and his hand is a feather.

"No. Wait," I say.

"For what?" he asks.

I am paralyzed by the memory of one of the worst times of my young life. I need to think of one of the best if I am ever going to be able to move.

I close my eyes... This will only take a moment.

Magenta

Everything surrounding me is oversaturated with color. It's as if the walls of my mind are bleeding the memory and everything is rich with the blood of its own color. Memories somehow never let you forget that that's what they are.

I am on the beach. The sand beneath my tiny bare toes is so white I feel as if I'm standing on snow. My feet sink as I race across its unevenness as fast as my eight-year-old legs will run. I am the fastest person in the world. Nothing will be able to catch up to me and make me leave this time or place. The sound the ocean makes, an ocean vaster than my eyes can take in, is loud, like a lion's roar. It competes with the melody of children's voices as they converse with the birds that talk back from above the little kids' heads. I think the birds are thanking us for coming.

Waves build and playfully roll towards me, knowing full well I am safe on the sand, but it is cute how they tease me before they break. I stop and look out into the ocean. I smile at the waves as they taunt me only to then tickle my feet.

I remember now, not then, about a poem my father wrote my mother. I read the poem one day when no one was around and I had done what children do when parents leave them alone, which was go through their things. I remember there were many poems in the purple folder I found hidden between my mother's legal books, but I remember one in particular. I remember the poem for the specific lines where my father implied he could lose an eternity of his soul within the blue of my mother's eyes. That's why I remember the poem... because my eyes were green. I was so jealous. I started to crumple the poem, but my fingers wouldn't allow me to destroy something my father had created. I straightened the paper back out against my chest, then placed it back between the other poems. But I never forgot that line. Why am I telling you this now? Because as I remember back, I remember that that's how blue the ocean was that day, as blue as my mother's eyes.

I remember the sun that day. The sun above both sand and sea was a child's crayon yellow. I stare up and into it. I am so close to the edge of the ocean that my face is caressed with a mist of water the heat from the sun quickly evaporates. Thank you, sun.

I hear bicycle bells.

I turn away from the ocean and look over to the pier as a family of four rides past on their bikes. There is a father, mother and two small children. One is a boy that looks to be about my age with hair almost as long, and the other child is a girl, three, maybe four, with training wheels on her bike. I see that tied to the seat of her bike, held by a long twirling ribbon, is a balloon. The balloon is an odd color. One I've never seen. I stare at it as the little girl rides past. The color of the balloon is so pretty. It's how I feel as I play on the beach with my father and mother.

That would be the only vacation we took as a family. The only time I was ever out of the state in which I lived. I remember that everything about that day felt magical, as if I were inside that little girl's balloon. I don't know why, but even then, at the age of eight, I tried to feel and touch and taste and see everything that was around me because somehow, almost instinctively, I was aware that I might never feel this exact same feeling again. More importantly, I was somehow aware that there will come a time when I want to remember how I am feeling at that moment; not because I want to, but because I will need to.

I even remember the poem my father wrote my mother.

> *"Your eyes compel like the trumpet of angels.*
> *Is that why I feel as if I've died?*
> *As if my soul were being emptied of everything I was and everything I could be because now it has changed.*
> *Did you steal my eternity before you blinked?*
> *And when I look into your eyes again, is that why I see me inside?*
> *How cruel your gaze*
> *how gentle your smile*
> *how is it possible*
> *they both beguile?"*

My mom is walking towards me as I stand on the beach. She is smiling at me. My father was right—she does have beautiful eyes.

The Reverse of a Carousel

I am standing before a naked girl sitting up on a bed. Her feet dangle from the edge as if reaching for the floor but unsure it is there. She has the struggled stare of a mannequin longing for sight. She should pray her sight doesn't return. Not just yet. She does not want to see the monster that stands before her, though I can look at the damage upon her bruised skin and tell that she has already felt him. I look over to Christian's dresser. There is a bottle of pills that contain Danielle's stare.

I turn and glare at Christian.

"You didn't even give her a chance to fight back. Did you?" I say.

"She didn't want it." Christian says and then smiles as if I had just complimented his hair.

I am sick.

"What happened?" Jai naively asks. I don't have the desire or time to inform him.

"Jai," I command him. "Put her clothes on and take her downstairs."

Jai turns to me. "What about you?"

"I want to be alone with Christian."

"Why?"

"Don't worry about it, Jai. Just get Danielle dressed and get her out of here."

Jai looks at me. I can see in his eyes that he is wondering if I am myself at all. He has never seen me yell and that is because I have never yelled. I'm wondering if this is me as well.

"You sure?" Jai asks, so that he can be sure.

"Yeah, she's sure," Christian answers for me. I don't correct him.

Jai carefully though hastily dresses Danielle. She is only able to give him the assistance a one-year-old child might be able to give a parent attempting to clothe her. I watch as her shirt covers the bruises on her breasts as it is slipped over her head and pulled down her body. It's so easy to conceal hurt when it manifests itself on the outside. Jai cannot get her pants on quick enough as I no longer wish to stare at the bruises on her legs.

Jai takes Danielle as gently as he is able to by the arm and then walks her past both Christian and me. Christian says nothing as we both watch Jai take her down the stairs.

It is now only Christian and myself in a room only one of us ever left the first time I was there.

"Did you come back for more?" Christian asks. I try to keep my eyes from breaking as I respond.

"What's wrong with you?"

"I don't know what you're talking about," he says glibly though I doubt he even knows that he is being glib.

"Do you think what you're doing is right? Did you see what you did to her?"

"No. I didn't," he says. "Maybe next time I'll tape it so I can see what you're talking about."

"I bet your mother would be so proud of you."

"Fuck you!" he spits out.

"You're about to graduate, Christian," I say. "Are those still the only two words you can put together?"

Christian slowly steps toward me. It feels as if he has brought the entire room closer.

"How about this?" he begins. "Fuck you, you fucking whore!"

Give me a moment and I will continue the story. I just need a moment please... OK. Let's start again from the last thing Christian said to me. "Fuck you, you fucking whore!"

A tear escapes my eye. It is not a tear for me. It is a tear for my father. No father should have a daughter to which something like that is said. I feel as if my father is standing beside me as it is uttered and he is unable to do anything.

"Why are you crying now?" Christian starts, but my knee won't let him finish. He should have gotten dressed before he stepped so close to me. He is writhing on the floor as I turn and leave his room.

I am down the spiral staircase so fast it's as if the structure regurgitated me from its insides.

Jai is waiting for me beside the door with Danielle wilting in his arms like a dying flower.

"Are you OK?" Jai asks.

"No," I respond. "Not until we're out of here."

Most of the partiers remain oblivious to the wreckage slowly expanding around their celebration. I go to grab Danielle's arm, but someone grabs mine and turns me around.

"You didn't give me a chance to finish what I was saying."

I am staring at Christian, who spits that out through teeth that in the time it took him to put pants on have become more like fangs.

"Get your God damned hands off me!" The crowd is slowly becoming a part of the crash site now.

"This is my house," Christian barks. "I'll do whatever I want!"

Jai wants to intervene, but there is already a girl in his arms.

Christian places his hand around my throat and starts to back me up towards the nearest wall. No one around me tries to stop him. Instead, they accommodate him by parting to clear his path.

"Let her go!" Jai yells.

"Just leave, Jai," I manage to say before Christian tightens his grip around my neck. "Just leave—"

Boom! Christian hits my head up against the wall with such force that I am unsure whether it is my skull that has fractured or the wall, that is, until I feel the warm warning of blood trickle down my neck.

"Aren't you going to cry again?" he says with gleeful anticipation of it occurring.

"No," I tell him. "I refuse to give you any more of my tears."

"You don't have to give me anything," he threatens. "If I want something from you, I'll take it."

I swear I hear the people around me cheering.

Again I wonder what happened to the boy who was nine, the boy who stole a rock for me. I find the answer within my question. Who "stole" a rock for me. Even the nicest of his gestures were gift wrapped with misdeed or bad intent. Christian is now the young man who the young boy was always going to become. I was just a puzzle piece that made up a portion of the landscape of his destiny.

"You've already taken everything, Christian. There's nothing left to take."

I don't know why, but he loosens his grip around my neck. I don't think it's because of compassion. I think it's because he is getting off on my confession. Whatever his reason, it allows me to continue.

"But you know what?" I tell him. "Every bit of me you consumed is rotting out your insides and no matter what you do, no matter how hard you try, you will never be able to spit me out the way that I am able to spit out you."

And that is what I do. I spit more of him, remnants of hate, back into his face.

Christian is confused where I thought he would be angry. Hurt where I expected rage. For a moment he reminds me of the little boy I once knew.

Moments never last...

Christian takes his free hand, the one that is neither restraining nor choking me simultaneously, and makes a fist. The fist is slowly raised to my quivering face. I close my eyes...

I am now back on the beach. I am remembering the playful battle between a little boy's tongue and the heat of the sun. Both attempt to diminish a tower of ice cream that spirals up from a cone in their own separate ways. I look on as tears of vanilla run down the side of the cone, weeping joy. I can feel the coldness as the ice cream seeps between the gentle grasp of his tiny fingers. I can taste the ice cream as it tickles the boy's tongue and makes him giggle. I smile, knowing that the sun, monolithic mass that it is, will not defeat the insatiable hunger of a child.

"Open your eyes!" Christian demands. I comply. But it's OK, because unbeknownst to him, even with my eyes open, I remain on the beach watching a little boy defeat the sun. Hit me. It will not shake loose this memory.

"Does anybody care if I teach this whore some manners?" Christian asks those who surround us with an appetite for the dish he has just offered up.

"Leave her alone," Jai shouts as he continues to lend stability and protection to Danielle. The words have no sooner left his mouth than Murdoc is at Jai's side to silence them.

"No. No one cares what happens to her! Especially Jai," Murdoc states. Murdoc then turns and looks Jai directly in the eyes. "Right, Jai?"

Jai does not respond. He doesn't have to. His presence at the party answered that question for me before it was ever asked.

"See," Christian says to me. "No one cares what I do. They certainly don't care about you!"

The rev of a motorcycle and everything stops.

There is a second rev… A louder rev… And the momentum of events changes, as if they are being pulled against their will in another direction, like a carousel that suddenly reverses itself. A third rev… It is too late for anyone to get off.

The sound of glass shattering is seldom good. Rarely welcomed. Sometimes, though, that breaking noise, the act of glass splintering and the dance of fractured particles landing at your feet can sound like a symphony.

Gabriel's motorcycle, his Monster Dark, appears more to me as an angel of light as it crashes through the privileged pane of Christian's front window.

The Monster Dark lands completely intact, though Gabriel does not sit upon it.

All eyes turn to the front door as it is opened and Gabriel steps in.

Christian follows my eyes as they look over to Gabriel. He loosens his grasp around my neck, finally realizing his party is over.

Gabriel slowly steps over towards Christian and me. The crowd parts in the wake of Gabriel's determined steps, though this time they part not out of anticipation but fear. Christian releases his hand from around my throat and I pull in air like a child's first gasp and release it like a dying man's last.

"I don't remember inviting you," Christian says with an arrogant lack of fear.

Gabriel equally but more gracefully shows he is unafraid with a smile that is his only reply.

Christian takes the hand that had moments earlier threatened me and attempts to redirect it and its momentum toward Gabriel. Arrogance is so often preceded by stupidity. When you're a quarterback, your arm is probably as equally important as your heart. Why would you allow your heart to beat beyond the rib cage that protects it? Especially out of something that so invites consequence that is nothing more than a vulgar display of power? Do you understand what I'm saying? I doubt Christian would have before he gave Gabriel the offer of his unprotected arm. Gabriel immediately grabbed hold of that arm and halted the threat of Christian's punch. Christian is paused by the quickness of Gabriel's reaction and the strength of his grip. Christian looks at his own arm and the manner in which Gabriel holds it. What an interesting but sad look, the look of awareness within the sudden onset of consequence. There now is the fear Christian had so foolishly lacked. One act on Gabriel's part and it could change every act that awaits Christian's life. Gabriel takes his other hand and extends it toward me. Once I have taken hold of his hand, Gabriel releases hold of Christian's arm with the other. Neither Christian nor anyone else in the room moves as Gabriel walks me over to his bike. He lifts his bike upright and rolls it toward the door. I hand the keys to my car to Jai, and Jai quickly takes Danielle out of the house. I turn to Christian. I cannot describe the look on his face other than to say it is concrete with anger. After all, this is his house.

"No one else knows what you did," I say to him. "But I do. And if you ever touch or talk to her again… If you occupy the same space for more time than it takes you to walk away … I will not remain silent this time. I will scream so hard I'll wake up the devil and he realizes you are gone. And then you'll have to run from someone other than me."

Gabriel swings onto his bike, then extends his hand to me once again. I take hold of it and he helps me onto the back of his motorcycle. I wrap my arms tightly around him. I cannot even hear the rev of the engine as the motorcycle starts because my heart beats louder. I lay my head gently upon Gabriel's back and close my eyes, and I wait for him to take me to the beach.

The Night Is a Sandless Shore

We ride into the night. The increasing wind folds itself around my body like his protection. "Faster," I whisper. And the rev of the motorcycle's engine makes my heart quake like a lover's sigh.

Deschanel

Do you know the actress Zooey Deschanel?

Aside from acting, Zooey also paints. And, oh yeah, she sings quite beautifully, as well. Everything about Zooey Deschanel is beautiful. Her face. Her hair. Her voice. Everything except her name. Her name is not beautiful, more than it is otherworldly. It is an impossible combination of something so whimsical sounding… "Zooey"—go ahead and say it and try not to think of an elephant eating peanuts while sitting in a lawn chair, and another last name, "Deschanel," that drips with privilege and purpose. Placed beside one another it is an essence that does not naturally exist. And if you have ever seen Zooey Deschanel, you understand that neither can she. She has to be an illusion. And if not, why are there not more of her in the world? Why would God make so few of her? Why would he give us one more reason to hate him?

Danielle now lays safe in her bed, though her eyes remain open and her gaze still reflects a chemical unawareness.

I sit on the edge of her bed, both of us half-bathed in moonlight that intrudes through her windows. Maybe even the moon knows not to give her too much light too soon. As I sit on the bed I wonder if a hospital bed, with police asking her questions instead of me stroking her hair, is the right place to be. Is ignorant bliss sometimes better than harsh reality? Is it right for me to decide whether it is for someone else? I remember back to the conversation I had with my mother earlier. I did not see anything. She cannot remember anything. If I had to testify, would I have to say that I saw her kiss Christian willingly at school? Would I have to say that it looked as if she enjoyed it? Did that imply consent for anything that happened after? Will boys ever be able to understand the equation of how much consent is implied within a kiss?

I scan the items in Danielle's room. Though she is only two years younger than me, as I look around I am initially struck by how many things I had long since discarded that she decided to keep. It is her room and so I will respect her privacy and not list them, but I will say they are things, cute things, playful things we love as girls but understand, mournfully so, that we must let go as we become women. I am somewhat envious she chose to hold on to them longer than I did. I wonder what she knew that I didn't.

As I look over to a chair in one of the corners of the room, I realize that I am being looked at, as well. Stuffed white fur, big black eyes and a familiar pink bow tied in her hair... "Hello Kitty," I whisper underneath my breath as I smile the tiniest of smiles. If the Hello Kitty could read my thoughts, she would hear me tell her how she used to belong to me, as well. Across the dark I stare into her impossibly expressive eyes and tell her that she was always my favorite. I must admit to Hello Kitty that I also had a Tigger stuffed doll from *Winnie-the-Pooh* that was also very close to me, but he was never as special as you, I say. I hope that she believes me. I'm sorry, I say. I don't know what I did with you. But if I were to find you, would you still be my friend? Or would you be mad at me because I abandoned you? I'm sorry, I say again. It didn't seem like you were allowed to go where I was going. The more I think about it, maybe I was wrong.

"Where am I?" Danielle asks, interrupting my conversation with Hello Kitty as she begins to emerge from her chemical state.

"Home," I tell her.

"What happened?" she asks.

"What do you mean?" I respond, somewhat hoping she doesn't emerge too quickly from her haze, hoping she doesn't ask too many questions.

"How did I get home?"

"I brought you. Your parents let me in."

"My parents..." She worries.

"It's OK," I comfort her. "I told them you weren't feeling well. They were just happy you made it home safe."

"They didn't know I was going. They told me not to."

"Don't worry about it. You're fine now."

"I don't know you," she finally realizes.

"My name is Olivia. Liv. Everyone calls me Liv."

"You're the girl whose boyfriend died."

It turns out she does know me. Or who I have become. I am the girl at school who is defined by tragedy.

"Yes," I say. "That's me." And then the question I had hoped to avoid even as I knew it was destined to be asked.

"What happened at the party?"

Someone help me. What happened at the party? The longer I remain silent, the quicker she will realize that something did happen. Silence betrays more than words sometimes.

I look back over to the stuffed Hello Kitty cat. I swear I hear her go, "Shhh." As if it wants its innocence to remain relevant, even if just for the night.

Kitty... I think. Her eyes are unrelenting in their plea.

"Nothing," I lie to Danielle. "Nothing happened. You were drunk. You fell down. You have a few bruises, but they will go away." Instantly I feel bad.

"Did I say goodbye to Christian?" she asks.

"No. I did it for you."

"Why did you do it for me?"

"He doesn't want to see you again," I tell her. I don't feel bad telling her that at all.

"Why? Did I do something wrong?"

"No," I quickly say. "That's just how he is. Don't worry about him. He's not worth it."

"He's nice," she replies.

"No. No, he's not, Danielle."

"My head hurts," she says softly.

"Close your eyes," I beg.

I think *(500) Days of Summer* is my favorite Zooey Deschanel movie. I believe it best captures every disparate aspect she possesses that renders her special, so not of this world. I wonder how long it took Zooey to grow into her name. No child is born displaying qualities that would make such a name seem appropriate, though it is now as uniquely hers as her DNA. So, I wonder when she became Zooey Deschanel? At what point did she inhabit her name? And as I look at Danielle slowly close her eyes, I wonder if she'll ever be able to inhabit who she once was.

I rise from the bed and walk over to the window. It is not yet raining, but like every night inside me I can tell that it soon will. I turn and look back at Danielle. Am I looking at myself the night Christian raped me? Was I curled in my bed in that same manner? Was there someone before me? Was there someone that could have said something and prevented me from becoming them? With everything that Christian has given me unwanted, now he gives me this guilt. I cannot be the one who forces Danielle to remember, and as wrong as this may be to say, I hope Christian drugged her so much that she never does, but I can't remain silent, either. Not anymore. I look over to the Hello Kitty stuffed cat. It will be OK, I tell Hello Kitty. I will speak for Danielle. I will make sure she holds on to you for a little while longer. I smile the tiniest of smiles. I bet Zooey Deschanel likes Hello Kitty.

Horses Pulling Promises Underwater

I see Gabriel off in the distance, leaning upon his motorcycle just outside the abandoned church. He is softly lit by the light of the moon, though much of what I know of him remains concealed, like a promise made in a desperate moment. When I left Danielle's house, he was gone. I had been left alone and I didn't know why. This is the only place I knew to go. I leave my car along the road and walk towards him. The nearer I get, the farther away he seems, as if my every step closer pulls him slowly in the opposite direction.

"Gabriel," I cry as I get nearer. My eyes never leave his for fear he might disappear in the uncertainty of my peripheral. "Gabriel!" I am breathless by the time I am nearer him.

"Why did you come here?" he asks me, and it wounds me like a promise forgotten.

"Why did you leave me?" I ask back.

"You don't need me, Liv. You're going to be fine," he says to me.

"I know I'll be fine. As long as you're here."

"No," he disagrees. "You don't need me."

The expression shifts upon my face quicker than a promise given for gain.

"I do."

"No, Liv."

"How can you say that? You saved me tonight."

"Is that what I did? Are you sure?"

I know that I am sure. I was there. I saw what he did. I am swimming in more confusion than I can keep my head above.

"Christian was going to hit me. You stopped him."

"He was never going to hit you," Gabriel says. "He only wanted to make you think he was. He only wanted you to be afraid, and you weren't. He knew he couldn't hit that out of you."

"I still don't understand why you have to go."

"I don't know that you can understand."

"Try," I beg. And then follows the silence I have come to fear so much.

"I have to go," Gabriel begins, "because it's impossible for me to stay."

"Anything is possible. Isn't it?"

"No, Liv. I wish I could tell you yes. But not this. To stay isn't possible."

"Why?"

"I don't belong here."

I step closer in case I have to wrap my arms around him and disappear along with him should he try.

"You belong with me," I tell him, almost begging for him to agree.

"Not anymore."

I feel my head submerging deeper beneath the water. No promise will be able to reach me.

"I don't understand what you're saying, Gabriel," I say. "I don't know what you mean. Why can't you be with me? Why do you have to leave?"

Gabriel places his hand against the side of my face. I want to melt within the spaces of his fingerprints. I want to be everything he touches.

"You're strong on your own now."

"I don't care," I tell him. "I don't want to be on my own."

He removes his hand from my face, and I am no longer a girl anymore, for everything that left with his hand can never be reclaimed.

"You're not alone."

"What if I say I love you?"

"You can't love me," he says.

"Why?" I demand to know.

"Because," he begins, "I can't let you."

"Tell me why?" I scream. "Why?"

"I can't," he says with the coldness of a promise never to be kept before it was ever made.

"I hate you!" I say. It feels as if the words go past Gabriel and are swallowed by the church.

Gabriel leans down closer to me. His eyes never leave the wanting of him in my own that betrays my last words.

"That is what will keep you strong."

He goes to lean back up and I throw my arms around his neck and pull him into me.

"No. I take it back! I don't hate you! I take it back! Now you can't leave! You have to stay! You have to or I'll die!"

"Liv," Gabriel says to me. I remain silent, afraid any word I say may be the wrong word, the last word before he has to go.

Gabriel places his lips next to my ear. My entire body quakes. Is this the promise that will let me breathe again? Is this the promise that will not fail to reach me? I listen as Gabriel whispers into my ear words that form a sentence I do not immediately understand.

"What do you mean?" I ask Gabriel as he gently breaks my embrace.

Gabriel smiles, turns and gets atop his motorcycle. He starts the motorcycle engine amidst the sound of tears scarring my skin as they run down my face.

"I don't know what it means," I repeat.

"You will," Gabriel says.

I step back from him, not because I want to, but because I know I cannot keep him any longer, just as I knew I couldn't keep Brandon in the desert the night I told him what happened to me. Like that night, I know I will never see Gabriel again, either. He turns away, puts his motorcycle into gear and disappears into the darkness, leaving me standing in front of the church, a mourner at my own funeral.

Untitled

I pull the blankets of my bed over my head as if I'm closing the lid of a casket. My thoughts cannot decompose fast enough. Time cannot eat away my flesh with sufficient hunger. I need a feast of clocks and I need to be laid bare as their banquet. I hear the angry yell of thunder outside my window, and I hope that somehow the rain finds its way in and washes away my ashes so nothing remains of my existence but the guilt of those who failed me.

I am carrion lying beside a deserted road, long forgotten by anything that might recall I was once the owner of a portion of the sky. I am emptied of purpose. Not even the birds of prey that pick at the remnants that remain of me shall wake me. Rip it away. Tear it if you must. There is nothing left that I feel, not even the memory of how I once felt.

The rain begins to fall.

Why is my mind still thinking? Why is it so lucid that I can count the raindrops that fall outside my window? Why won't my mind be as still as the rest of me? I cannot fight not thinking anymore. It is too tiring and I am too tired. I allow my thoughts to focus back upon things that concern the living and that's when I remember…

Brandon's letter!

I rip the covers away from my body. This corpse no longer has the luxury of sleep. Purpose has tapped me on the shoulder and I have awakened. I almost fall from the bed faster than the drops of rain hitting the window as I grab Brandon's letter from my nightstand and pull it close to my chest. I try and catch the new breath given me only moments before because I know that in moments Brandon will speak to me. I don't care that it will be for the last time; I'll hold on to his words with the same suffocation that sadness folds around me.

The rain falls harder.

I sit on my bed, in the center, my legs folded. I look at the envelope as if I were looking into Brandon's eyes. Because of that I know when I open the envelope that it will be as if he blinks, so I keep the envelope closed for a minute more. OK. I am ready. I tear the envelope open with the gentleness of brushing away a hair from Brandon's face. I unfold the letter with the care one might use unfolding the wrapper of a favorite piece of candy saved until the end of the day. I do not immediately begin to read the contents of the letter. No, I first recognize Brandon's handwriting and take a moment to dwell inside that familiarity. A deep breath. A sigh. I read. It is a short letter, only five words. But tears from my eyes moisten the paper before I have read the last one.

I read the letter again. Then I read the letter again. Each time I feel my soul spill from my body, then reenter before it can be mourned. You should be able to trust your eyes. Isn't it impossible for them to deceive? Yet I read the letter again. And then I read it again because my eyes are either dreaming or deceptive. Maybe they are both.

The letter cannot be true. The letter cannot mean what it doesn't say. I want to die, because if it is not true, then it will be worse than death.

The rain...

Kiss the Resurrected, Curse the Dead and Be Careful Not to Confuse the Two

I step through the entrance to the abandoned church with greater anticipation than even the devil might. I clutch Brandon's letter in my hand tighter than a crucifix. I can feel the words embedding themselves upon my palm.

I step inside farther, the splintered wood beneath my feet betraying every cautious step. Who is it warning?

"Brandon…" I say, though I am well aware it is spoken too softly to wake the dead.

"Brandon." I am louder. But I am still afraid of being too loud.

"I read your letter," I tell him. "I read it over and over again."

I listen for his acknowledgment between the sounds of the drops of rain.

"I know what it means. I understand now."

I wait again.

"You don't have to say anything," I assure him. "Just let me know what you said in your letter was true. Just let me know it means what I think it means."

"Brandon…" I say even louder. "I believe you. You're right. I know you are. I believe."

I listen again. Why is the rain so loud? "Brandon!" I say. This time I scream it.

A fluttering sound pulls my head upward in time to see a winged creature leaving through an opening in the roof for the rain and sky. Was that Brandon? Was it his soul? Did I scare him away by calling too loudly? I race outside into the pouring rain to try and see him again.

"Brandon!" I yell into the darkness. "Brandon!"

I look up to the sky and there is nothing, only rain to mingle with my tears. A gust of wind snatches Brandon's letter from my grasp and carries it upward. I reach up to the sky, but the heavens will not help me by coming nearer. I curse God again. If heaven will not bend for a weeping girl's hand, then why does it exist?

I yell into the wind one last time.

"Brandon!"

The wind never carries anything back to you. I curse it, too, along with God.

Awkward Hippos

Every new day seems to bring another first. Today it is the first time I have been inside Brandon's home since he died. I'm finding it difficult to breathe. I don't know if it's because I'm staring at a picture of him or because the house seems so airless. Brandon's presence was the home's pulse and without it, with him gone, the house is being kept alive artificially.

I pick up the photo I am staring at. It is a photo I remember very well. His mother framed the picture less than a week after I took it. Me. It's a special picture. Special because it is probably the only picture of Brandon in existence in which he is not smiling. It was near impossible to get a picture of him not smiling. Brandon was always smiling. That's one of the things I loved about him. And when he tried not to smile, Brandon had the awkward smile of a child attempting to contain his excitement over a shiny new toy. That's one of the things I loved about him more.

I stare at the picture as I remember the day and the moments before it had been taken. Brandon was mad at me. Well, he was as mad as he could ever get at me, which is to say he was slightly annoyed in the way you might be when someone takes the last French fry from your plate. We had been at the zoo almost three hours and Brandon kept asking me which animal was my favorite. How do you answer that? They are all so different. Some are certainly more unique than others, but to pick a favorite seemed so unfair. I did feel more sympathy for the ones that seemed to know they were in a cage or confined by bars. Brandon would tell me they were better off that way because they were more protected. They didn't have to worry about the dangers of the wild. I don't know that I ever fully believed that. I don't know that Brandon did, either. I just knew he was trying to make me feel better. Brandon was always trying to make me feel better. Something more I loved about him.

Just before I took the picture, as Brandon was posing, I said, "Hippopotamus." When he asked me what I was saying, I told him that the hippopotamus was my favorite animal because it had ears like him. He knew I was only teasing him, but he wouldn't give me the satisfaction of a smile. Snap… The picture was taken.

Brandon didn't have ears like a hippopotamus. I loved Brandon's ears. They were big, big on the inside because he listened to me. Brandon was always listening to me.

"Hippopotamus," I say softly. And suddenly I feel awkward. As if I should not have spoken the word. As if I no longer have any right to. You see, I said it that day not because it was my favorite animal, not because it reminded me of Brandon, but because it's a fun word to say. Like being with Brandon that day was fun. Being with Brandon was always fun. Suddenly I am tired of telling you things that made me love him.

I put the picture down. I know why this house feels abandoned.

There Is No Door I Will Not Walk through to Get back to You, Not Even Death

I have come to a place at Brandon's house where I can breathe. I am outside, out back of his home. The heat of the shining sun feels good on my face. It burns away the artificiality I felt when inside. I also cling to its warmth. I must. I find myself unprotected sometimes from these intermittent feelings of coldness. They overwhelm me like an avalanche of snow burying a butterfly in the springtime.

"There you are," Brandon's mother says. I turn around to greet her.

"Hello, Mrs. Green."

"I looked for you inside the house."

"I just needed some air," I explain. The look on her face tells me I needn't have. We take a seat on a swinging chair that is supported by the left arm of a towering oak. Even though it's winter, there is still an abundance of life all around. It seems as though it only gets cold enough inside me to kill anything.

"What can I do for you, sweetheart?" Mrs. Green asks. It takes me more than a moment to answer.

"Brandon…" I push out and then stop.

"What about Brandon?" she inquires, interrupting my odd silence.

"Brandon once told me that Mr. Green was not his real father."

I stop this time because the look in Mrs. Green's eyes politely asks me to.

"How did he know? How could he?"

"He found the papers given when Mr. Green adopted him."

"I should have burned those the day I got them," Mrs. Green says.

"Why? Brandon loved his father," I tell her. "That's not why he told me."

"Then why did he?"

"He wanted me to know everything about him," I confide. "That's why I told him everything about me. That's why I made the mistake of…" I stop myself again.

"The mistake of what?"

"Nothing," I say. Awkward pause. "Can you tell me who his real father is?"

"Why do you want to know?" she asks.

"I'm not completely sure. I want to know more about Brandon, I suppose. Everything I can."

"There's nothing Brandon's real father can tell you about him."

"Why not?" I ask.

"Because," she begins before an awkward pause intrudes again.

"Because, what?"

"Because he died before Brandon was born."

"How?" I have to ask.

This time the pause is neither awkward nor unexpected. I watch as Mrs. Green searches my eyes out to either make sure I am ready to hear what she is about to say or that I can be trusted with the information. She may possibly be looking for both.

"Do you know the burned-out church on Redemption Road?" she asks, and I nod, yes.

"The church where the preacher hanged himself."

"Yes."

"Did Brandon's father go there?" I ask.

Mrs. Green doesn't answer my question as asked. She instead tells me something with her expression that I should find difficult to believe, but in a way, something I have no trouble believing. Something I want to believe.

"The preacher..." I begin.

"Yes," she confirms. "That was Brandon's father," she says.

The swing stops. I don't know if it was her or me or if it simply stopped.

"But I thought the mother and child died," I state.

"No one ever knew who the mother was. It was just easier for people to believe both were dead. It gave closure where there otherwise could be none."

I rise from the swing and look away from Mrs. Green and off into the distance behind their home.

"It is him," I whisper under my breath, though not low enough not to be heard.

"Who?" Mrs. Green asks. "It is who?"

I turn back to her. "Brandon." I am careful to say it in a manner that will mute the shock of what I am actually saying.

"Brandon?" Mrs. Green repeats.

"Brandon," I too repeat. "He's come back."

Now Mrs. Green rises from the swing. She takes two steps closer to me, though they are pensive steps.

"What are you talking about, Liv?"

There is a rush of panic in my eyes. A rush of panic for her to believe me, and a rush of panic for what I am about to say to be true.

"The letter you gave me from Brandon."

"Yes. I remember. What did it say?" she asks.

"It said, 'Only every third word counts.'"

"What?" she begs.

"Every third word," I say again. "That was our game."

"I don't understand, Liv."

"Gabriel!" I shout. "Gabriel is Brandon. I don't know how, but he has to be. Only he would know."

"Only he would know what?"

"That only every third word counts." I am trying to explain something that cannot be explained and trying to get someone to believe something I am unsure I believe. "Brandon and I were the only ones that knew about the game. We made it up. The letter. That's what it said. Only every third word counts. And then what Gabriel—"

Mrs. Green takes me by the arms, interrupting my last sentence. She cannot steady the excitement in my eyes, so she stills my body.

"I don't know why you're saying this, but Brandon is dead, Liv. Dead. And no matter how much you or I want him back, he's not coming back. Ever."

"Mrs. Green—" I begin, but she will not let me finish.

"I don't care what the letter said, Liv. Brandon is dead. And no stupid game is going to make me believe anything other than that."

"It wasn't a stupid game," I persist. "It wasn't. Don't you believe he could come back? Don't you want it to be true?"

Mrs. Green turns and steps away from me as if disgusted by the very question I have just asked. She then turns back before she answers.

"Do you know why his father hung himself?"

"No," I say. "I don't."

"I'll tell you why then. Because he couldn't find redemption for what he'd done. And what had he done? Fallen in love with someone? Is that such a sin that he should pay the way he did? Is it so wrong that he should be judged by the people he refused to judge?"

"No. It's not," I softly offer up.

"I didn't want redemption," Mrs. Green continues. "I even turned away from God for making my beloved think that he couldn't live without his forgiveness. I stopped going to the church at all. So how did God punish me? He took away my son … the only piece of his father I had left. And now you want me to believe someone that cruel would allow my son to return?"

"Don't you even want to know how I know?" I ask. "Don't you want to know what Gabriel whispered to me in front of that very church?"

"No," Mrs. Green says with a coldness that even the sun that beats down upon me will not warm. "Brandon is dead. And the dead don't come back. They just wait for you to come to them."

Algebra and Ecclesiastes

I do not like math and I do not understand religion. One relies on equations difficult to understand and the other theories impossible to prove by equations. One uses abstracts and the other needs abstracts. One allows you no room to be wrong about its interpretation, and the other... allows you no room to be wrong about its interpretation. Can any of these things be said about words? No. I do not like religion and I do not understand math.

It was wrong of me to go to Brandon's mother and tell her what I did. What was I thinking? How could I be so insensitive? How could I expect her to believe?

"For the living are conscious they will die," Mr. Mortenson recites to me as I sit across from him in his empty classroom. "But as for the dead, they are conscious of nothing at all."

I had come here after leaving Mrs. Green's home, though I waited until his class was over, a class I should have been in.

"But what if he came back for me, Professor?" I implore. "Don't you believe love is stronger than death? I know he loved me."

"Also," Mr. Mortenson continues, citing more verse. "Their love and their hate have already perished, and they have no portion anymore to time indefinite in anything that has been done under the sun."

"Then you're telling me, according to what's written in the Bible, Brandon's mom was right?"

"What did she say?" Mr. Mortenson asks.

"Why believe in a God without mercy? If death is so finite, why believe at all?"

"God is a merciful god. Is that not what Scripture says?"

"What you just cited is saying there's no way Brandon could come back to me!" I exclaim. "What's so merciful about that?"

"Liv," Mr. Mortenson begins. "What I gave you was a verse from Ecclesiastes that explains the state of the dead. Nothing more. Not things that might occur after. And that is also a Christian belief. The one I chose to give you first. The world is full of many beliefs that are there for all to take in."

"I want to believe in what Brandon told me."

"What did he tell you?"

I pause. Am I about to make the same mistake again? Can I trust that Mr. Mortenson is a man of ideas and not just one that teaches them?

"It wasn't what Brandon said, Professor. Gabriel said it."

"Then tell me," he asks. "What did Gabriel say?"

"He whispered to me, 'There is no door I will not walk through to get back to you, not even death.' What he said was longer, but that was what was hidden in every third word. Every third word. That was something only Brandon and I did."

"Olivia…" Mr. Mortenson starts. And he reminds me of my father whenever he would have to tell me something bad, like when my dog passed. That's the only time he would ever call me Olivia. "As a teacher I might introduce you to information. I may explain it, even elaborate upon it. But it is not my job to tell you what it means. You have to decide that on your own. Literature is not math. Philosophy is not algebra. There are no absolutes beyond the word *absolute*. As with many people, the older I get, the more some beliefs change and the more others remain the same. I think the only thing that alters a person's beliefs more than age is loss. Maybe that's the merciless irony of this life, that with more age there is more loss. But you can't let anger over loss cloud your heart and your mind. Acceptance is sometimes the only healer."

"Are you asking me to accept Brandon is gone forever?"

"I'm asking you to make it to class, Olivia. Anything outside of that, you need to come to on your own."

"Maybe it's because acceptance comes easier with age," I tell the professor. "Or maybe it's because I can only read Ecclesiastes. But I have held Brandon. He came back to me. I have to believe that. I have to."

"Why?" he asks.

"Because if it's true, and I don't believe it, Brandon may go away forever."

Every Kiss before Judas

"Why were you there, Jai?"

There is no immediate answer to my question as I now stand before Jai, outside the school, in a courtyard of students. I can read the expression on Jai's face and know that he wishes he were one of them.

"Jai," I repeat. "Why were you there?"

"There" is the party and "why" may not need to be understood by you, but it must be by me or the next anonymous blur that sweeps by me will hold more importance than this person I once knew as my friend.

"No reason," he tells me. I want to slap him, but I am not violent. I have just somehow become the vessel that absorbs it.

"I know you had no reason to be there," I spit back. "You had at least twenty reasons not to be. So why were you there?"

"I don't know."

"Jai," I plead, "I'm trying to understand so I don't get upset."

"You're already upset. So what difference does it make?"

"I'm upset, Jai, because I don't understand why you were at a party thrown by someone that you know did something horrible to your friend! What were you thinking?"

"Maybe I wasn't thinking. Maybe I had no reason. Maybe I was just there."

"I know you, Jai. You don't do anything without a reason."

The courtyard has emptied. Class must have begun. It is now only Jai and me.

"Do reasons matter, Liv?"

"What?"

"Do they?"

"Of course reasons matters," I tell him. "I don't want to hate you."

Jai laughs. I stare at him wondering at whom I am staring. Am I different or is he?

"I'm all alone, Liv."

"What are you talking about, Jai?"

"I don't have anyone to tell me when I'm doing something wrong or be happy for me when I've done something right. I'm alone. It's up to me to decide what the difference between the two are and if it matters if I even care."

"You had Brandon. You have me. You don't think I care? You know I do."

"How? How do I know? You just told me you don't want to hate me, which means that right now you do. How can you hate someone you care about?"

"I hate that you were at the party, Jai."

Jai smiles. "You're so good with words. It's the same thing, Liv."

"Just give me a reason…"

"What if I gave you the reason? What if you still hated me? What if the reason made you hate me more?"

I am silent as I try and understand what he is not trying to tell me.

"See," he says. "You're finally starting to understand."

"Understand what?" I ask.

"That it doesn't matter what my reason is?"

"What did you do, Jai?"

Jai does not answer. I step closer. It doesn't seem to concern him.

"What did you do?"

"Do you think Judas committed suicide," Jai begins, "because he felt guilty about betraying Jesus, or because he used something so beautiful as a kiss to do it?"

"Jai... What did you do?"

"Do you think his reason matters?"

Flickers

I am reaching into the trash. I am reaching into the trash. I am reaching into the trash. I say that three times because that is what it feels like I have been doing forever now. But this time, I am literally reaching into the trash. My hand is in the tiny trash can in my mother's office rescuing my father's pack of American Spirit cigarettes.

I glance around the office as I retrieve the pack and pull it from imminent destruction. I am still alone.

I sit down in what was once my father's chair, the only other item in the office that belonged to him. Again, I look around the office to see if I am still alone. I am. I take my left hand and I gently slide it across the length of the wooden armrest until I feel the hidden clasp. It is a clasp only the maker of the chair, my father, and I know exists. I unhinge the clasp and then lift the top of the armrest open. Inside, in its own compartment, is a sterling silver Zippo lighter. It is more slender in width and smaller in size than a standard Zippo, but it is a Zippo nonetheless. And it is adorned with a pattern of filigree whose design seems as random as a flame's flicker.

I slide a single cigarette from the remaining ten or so within the pack and roll it gently between the fingers of my right hand. I saw my father do this and when I asked him why, he told me it was because the tobacco in American Spirit cigarettes was packed differently than that in other brands. Slamming the top of the cigarette box against the palm of your hand, as was most smokers' ritual to tighten the tobacco, was a useless gesture. With American Spirits, the desired aim was to loosen the tobacco to enrich the flavor, thus you rolled the portion of the cigarette below the filter between your fingers slowly. I learned a lot of things from my father, some as random as a flame's flicker.

I have rolled the cigarette enough, but I do it for a few more moments. Anything that makes me think about my father I always want to do for a few more moments than I have to.

I place the cigarette in my mouth. I can already taste the tobacco. As I have never once smoked, I assume that that is what the taste is. It's a deep, rich taste. I don't know that I like it, but I know that I am going to continue. I flip open the top of the Zippo lighter. Click. What a unique sound that is, the click of a Zippo lighter opening. Unlike any other click you will hear. A click ironic in the sound of its beauty because once you hear it, you know something is about to burn.

I light the cigarette. The tip ignites into a brilliant orange that slowly relaxes into a deceptively cool amber. No wonder fire burns so many. It is impossibly seductive.

This seduction of smoke will be a trial by fire for my virgin lungs. My lips softly embrace the filter and I inhale, pulling from the filter a tighter embrace. Death immediately struggles to exit my body. No, Death. Not now. I will not allow you to. Your essence will not be forcibly evacuated or expelled. No. I will not cough out your destruction. Instead, I will release your toxic transparency slowly, pulling from it the things I want before letting what remains escape, discarded within the shifting smoke. And the direction I blow your dissipating death in will be as random as a flame's flicker.

I twirl in my father's chair as I exhale. The rapidness of my spinning swirls the smoke around me like a ribbon so that I am never without the thought of my father as I become dizzy. I inhale again and then spin again…

I am no longer spinning in the chair. I am seven and I am sitting in the kitchen on a Thursday morning watching my father as he attempts to make me breakfast before school. A bowl of cereal would have been fine. Fruity Pebbles' brand is staring at me from the top of the refrigerator and I swear I see the prehistoric cutie laughing at my father like I want to as he burns the eggs. But he's my father, and he's making the eggs for me, so I leave the laughing to her.

"How do you like your eggs, Dandelion?"

"Burnt," I say, trying to help my father out.

He smiles as I watch the smoke rise from the pan. Then I realize, maybe that's what made me remember this, the smoke…. I stop spinning and I am back in the chair. I put out the cigarette and sit back in my father's chair, lingering with the smoke that will soon be gone faster than a flicker.

I miss you, Daddy.

If You Have Come Back from the Dead, Do Not Leave Again without Taking Me

There is no death in me but love
the love of things
holding hands
your eyes
sodomizing dragonflies
with you.
There is no death in me but love
no desert promises
no beauty of ruins
but there is always your smile when Kinski is on-screen.
There is no death in me but love
and this is how I know the wind is a mistaken name
and that all monsters dark are necessary
and that you wouldn't want to make the same mistake twice
for every gesture frail
for every somewhere a bell is ringing
lies the threat of the dissipating dusk
and me becoming the carrion of his absence
the abandoned and the reborn.
There is no death in me but love
this is how I know the beach is no place for lovers
this is how I know there is a fountain that burns
and that if I ask do animals have souls they sell

the response will bounce off the echo of rocks.
There is no death in me but love
so onto whom does the blood from your fingers fall
and if the percussionist pauses for a piece of candy
will he gain riches
or will the rabbit the lion and the wind
carry his beat and whisper whores
to those that dive into pools of you?
There is no death in me but love
this is how I know there are no accidental gestures
no happy fracture
no resurrection
but my heart will still beat
with the momentum of sons
greater than a feigning corpse
whose death becomes revenge by mourning
graced with strawberry intentions.
There is no death in me but love
and if his eye was the pen of his greatest work
that work wreaks more havoc than the desecration of thunder
and if it is a choice between bourbon and caramel
if it is the distinction between Nabokov the girl on the wall and the
one in the bed
I will whisper cicada
but I will not name you for fear you will never leave
nor will I admire the briefness of the beauty of snow
but I will look into your eyes
I will feel the rev of a carousel
I will fight the imposing decay
I will close every door to partial rooms
to get you to stay
and close these breaches of faith
reminding me with your silly way

that only every third word counts.
There is no death in me but love
this is how I know silhouettes are not the ghosts you run from but the
ghosts you become
and if one asks, do you want to fuck
you have begun the long ascent up the downward
and something so pretty as the color magenta
will not stop the reverse of a carousel
that is taking away your dreams
of things like Deschanel
and horses pulling promises underwater.
There is no death in me but love
thus none of my tears are untitled
and I know if I am to hold on to you I must kiss the resurrected
curse the dead and be careful not to confuse the two
speaking of two
we are sometimes two awkward hippos
but I love you so much there is no door I will not walk through to get
back to you not even death
and I would read algebra and Ecclesiastes
and I would protect every kiss before Judas
to keep our souls intertwined
and dancing like flickers.

It took me four days to write that poem. I did not leave my room until I was finished. I'm not sure that it is finished. Poems are funny that way, but I do know that there is no death in me but love.

Dandelions

Do you think a brick trembles when held by an architect's hand? It is not Sunday, but I need to see my father. In my head I am still spinning in his chair and now I am compelled to touch his hand, to hear his voice and to see his smile. I want to fall into the arms of my creator and feel born again within his embrace. I want to tremble like a brick does when held in an architect's hand.

"How's my little dandelion?" my father says. Dandelion...

How I miss being called that every day. The English name Dandelion is a corruption of the French *dent de lion*, meaning "lion's tooth." A dandelion is a large genus of flowering plants in the family Asteraceae, and like other members of this family, they have very small flowers called florets that collected together form a composite flower head. Dandelion was the nickname my father gave me. He said I possessed many beautiful attributes that collected together made me who I am. Did you know that many Taraxacum species, of which the dandelion is one, produce seeds asexually by apomixis, which means the seeds are produced without pollination? This results in offspring that are genetically identical to the parent plant. I will say that again. This results in offspring that are genetically identical to the parent plant. My father didn't know this when he nicknamed me. Knowing that fact, knowing my father, always makes me smile.

"How is your book?"

I always ask my father this. And he always does the same thing. He takes his index finger on his right hand and taps the side of his head just above his eye. And that is why I always ask, because I have faith in my father that one day his book will go from thought to page. I want my father always to know that, that I have faith in him.

"I want to talk to you, Dad."

"Would you like some lemonade?" my father asks.

"Fresh?"

"Of course," he says.

"That would be great," I say.

My father smiles.

My father's smile makes me remember a line from a Kate Bush song. My father loves Kate Bush. "Uniquely exquisite" is how he most often referred to her. "Transcendental" was a close second. I remember the first time he watched me as I listened to "Running Up That Hill." He smiled as if he'd introduced me to the sky. Transcendental... Kate Bush asks this question in one of her songs: "Have you ever seen a picture of Jesus laughing?" Then she asks, "Wouldn't you think, he had a beautiful smile? A smile that heals." That is my father's smile. Beautiful... Healing... Transcendental...

I watch as my father makes us two glasses of lemonade. He never begins the process until everything is in front of him. Two glasses. Ice. A knife. Sugar. And, of course, the most important thing to have when making fresh lemonade. Lemons. My father has eight lemons on the counter, four for each of us. Well there were eight lemons on the counter, now there are six and two on the floor. My father bends to pick the two lemons up and as he rises three more roll off to join the other fallen. This add and subtract game goes on for about a minute. I half suspect my father is doing it for my amusement, and I dismiss the other half of what I believe, that he is just clumsy, because the first thought is better.

I watch as my father slices the lemons with the care and precision of a surgeon and then I continue to watch as he squeezes them with the goofy recklessness of a clown. I wonder what a philosopher such as Aristotle would think of the metaphysical implications of a man whose existence could be related to the manner in which he makes a glass of lemonade. I wonder if Aristotle's dad ever made him a glass of lemonade as good as my father's.

My father leads me to his balcony, five stories above, overlooking a desert backdrop that seems to belong entirely to him. The sun is so bright that my father asks me if I would like the sunglasses that he has placed on his own face. I smile but say no. I want to see everything around us as it is. Every color is so vibrant and alive it's as if it were freshly painted for this moment and I will not insult the artist. I admire the backdrop that is the sky. It is a pinkish hue, stabbed by a setting sun, bleeding the pink and laying its head upon scattered clouds of blue.

"What did you want to talk about?" my father asks me.

I stare at his face. Even behind his sunglasses I can see the kindness in his eyes. My father could never hide that, even on the rare occasions when he was not too kind.

"Do you remember when I was nine?" I ask him. "You had a pair of sunglasses that you always wore?"

My father thinks, about the sunglasses, and where my question is going.

"I'm not sure," he says. "I had a lot of pairs of sunglasses."

This was true.

"These were your favorite. I remember Mom asking you why you always had them on and you said it was because you thought they made you look like Mickey Rourke in—"

My father finishes my sentence.

"*Rumble Fish*." He smiles. "Then she told me she hated *Rumble Fish*."

"Yeah. So you wore them to dinner that night."

"I remember," my father says.

"She was so mad," I add. "She didn't notice me feeding my peas to the dog."

"I saw you," my father says.

I'm surprised.

"You never said anything."

"Why would I?" he says. "I hated peas. If they had peas in *Rumble Fish*, I bet Mickey Rourke would have hated them, too."

I smile, but it quickly fades. Perhaps too quickly. It betrays what I am thinking.

"What's wrong, Dandelion?"

"Do you remember what happened to them?" I ask. "The glasses?"

"I lost them, I think."

"No," I tell my father. "I put them on one day when you were gone. I wanted to see if I looked like you. When I took them off to put them back on your dresser, they fell and I broke them. I kept them under my pillow for four days and tried to fix them, but I just made them worse. I buried them in the sand out in the back yard."

"Liv…"

I wish he had called me Dandelion. "Yes, Dad?"

"Is that what you wanted to tell me?"

I don't know what to say. No, it's not what I wanted to tell him, but I don't know that I can tell him anything else.

"You loved those sunglasses," I say.

"I liked the sunglasses, Liv. I love you. There's a big difference."

"I'm sorry."

"For breaking my glasses?" my father asks.

"No."

"Then for what?" he wants to know.

"Because," I begin. "I was raped."

My father removes his sunglasses and places them onto the table beside his glass of lemonade. Perspiration from the ice slides down the glass and onto one of the lenses of the sunglasses as if my father had shed a tear before removing them. I feel like I have just exploded in front of my father's very eyes in just the way in which the wind disrupts a dandelion. My father stares as if he has watched someone pull me from the ground, displacing my roots, and "whoosh," watched as they blow and pieces of me scatter. I am nothing more than florets in the air that his eyes search desperately to put back together as the flower I was before the revelation. And what does my father do? My father puts his arms around me and pulls me back together before parts of me drift away forever.

"My dandelion," he calls me. "Are you OK?" The softness in his voice betrays the fact that he knows I am not. I stay in his arms before I say anything and I think that says everything.

For the next half hour I tell him as much as I can without telling him more than I think he needs to know. I make him promise not to tell my mother. When he asks me why I chose to tell him, I say, "Because." He accepts that. And he knows that me needing that "because" to be accepted and not further questioned is the reason I asked him not to tell my mother.

"I'm going to tell you something I've never told anyone," my father says. And it's the first time he's ever told me that. He sighs and tells me how when he was thirteen, he got into the kind of trouble that was a rite of passage at that age but criminal intent a few years beyond it. He alludes to shoplifting, but I don't ask because as with my story, the details were not as important to me as the sharing was. His overzealous father sent him away to a juvenile camp for a month to make sure it never happened again.

There, my father tells me, are boys much older, much stronger and much more inclined to such activities as the one he simply did on a dare. My father pauses and I try to recall if I'd ever saw him pause. I don't think I have. He continues by telling me of one night when some of the boys, three or four he says, though in his frightened eyes they were one, pulled him from his bed and forced him into another room. They first forced him to disrobe, then, after making fun of him, one of the other boys, the biggest, started to remove his own clothes while the others held my father down. He remembered hoping his father was going to open the door and tell him this was all just meant to scare him. When the boys began to turn him over, he knew this was not going to happen; his only thought was when it was over and he was allowed to go home, how he would curse his father to his face. Fortunately, before anything physically invasive was able to occur, a counselor intervened. Every night after that, for the rest of his time at the camp, my father locked himself in the room where the assault was to take place while the other boys would try and get in. They taunted him by whispering the vile and disgusting things they would do to him if they did manage to get in. My father would just cower in the dark. To this day, when alone at night, my father tells me, he still sleeps with a light on. I ask him if he ever cursed his father when he got back home. While he was away, his father left both him and his mother. He never saw him again.

"When it was happening, this horrible thing," my father says. "I hope you never cursed me for not being there to stop it. And if you did, I'm sorry."

"No, Daddy," I tell him. "I only cursed myself." Now I pause. I think about the experience my father had. I ask him. "If I locked myself in a room—" My father doesn't let me finish.

"I would break down any door to protect you."

"Any door?"

"Any door, Dandelion. Even death."

There is no fear of mortality in me anymore. It is gone. There is just a sadness for Death as he must now realize both my father and Brandon are stronger than he. How insignificant Death must feel in my presence. It makes me smile.

My father rises. "I'll be right back," he assures me then he steps inside his home.

I look out at the vastness of the desert before us. Like death, it's no longer as imposing as it was moments before my father told his story. If he could traverse worlds to reach me in death, surely he could cross the desert's expanse in mere seconds to reach me. It is just now, in this moment, that I think I understand what love does... It strips away the physical, the tangible, for it has no need of the boundaries or limitations of flesh. Love resides in a space where there is nothing but an absence of space. This is why nothing can get in its way.

My father steps back out onto the balcony. There is a chain with a crucifix dancing at the end. Both shimmer in the sunlight.

"What is that?" I ask.

"It's the only thing I ever kept from my father," my own father tells me.

"Why did you keep it?" I ask.

"I think I kept it because I knew it was valuable," my father begins, "and because of that I guess I always thought my father would come back for it. And if he did, that meant he would have to see me." My father looks at me and smiles. "I don't believe that anymore."

"What would you have said to him?" I ask. "Do you know?"

"Goodbye." My father says as he clasps the chain around my neck.

"Would you ever come back home, Dad?"

"No," my father says as if he knew one day I might ask the question.

"Is it because of Mom?"

"Yes." He nods as he lays the crucifix gently upon my chest. "When I could have gone back I loved her too much to ever hurt her again."

"How do you know you would have?"

"I just know," he says. "Now it's not where I belong."

"I wish—" Again, my father doesn't let me finish. He knows the sentence would be too painful. Not for him, but for me.

"Don't blame your mother for us not being together," he tells me. "She was never less than anyone I couldn't love. I can't say the same about myself."

"Daddy," I say.

"Yes, Dandelion?"

"Could you make us some more lemonade?"

As my father rises he takes his sunglasses and gently places them over my eyes, which are red from crying.

"You look just like me," he says.

"Oh, no," I say. And it makes my father laugh. "Have you ever seen a picture of Jesus laughing? Wouldn't you think he had a beautiful smile?"

My father has the most beautiful smile in the world. The world has no space for anyone else's smile.

Does the Bow Make the Violin Cry on Purpose or Is It Just the Inconsistency of Its Touch?

My mother sits in front of the television. It is a rare moment when she actually appears to be relaxing. I sit beside her on the couch. She looks at me, and I am sure she is thinking that this is a rare moment, as well.

"What are you watching?" I ask.

"Some old movie. I'm not sure what it's called, but it's certainly weird."

"Who's in it?"

"No one you've ever heard of, I'm sure."

"Try me."

"Peter Weller?"

The name does not sound familiar. I look at the television screen. His face is not familiar, either, but I love his voice. It is deep, gravelly and authoritative.

"Do you remember Mickey Rourke?" I ask my mother.

"Every woman my age remembers Mickey Rourke," my mother tells me. "He was gorgeous when he was younger. Not that he isn't still today. Though it's an odd type of handsome now."

"I thought you didn't like him."

"Why would you say that? And where were you all day today? I tried calling you..."

"I went to see Dad."

"On a Thursday?" Then it hits my mother. "Is that why you asked me about Mickey Rourke?"

"Yeah," I say. "It made me think back to when you and Dad talked about him. I didn't think you liked him."

"No. I loved Mickey Rourke. It was almost impossible not to. I wasn't too crazy about your father trying to be him."

"Why not?"

"Mickey Rourke played horrible characters. No one you would ever want to be in love with, sweetheart. Besides, I loved your father for who he was. Most of the time, that is."

"What about other times?"

"I don't want to say bad things about your father, Liv. We had our problems like any other married couple."

"Do you wish you had tried to stay together?"

"I did, Liv. I tried a lot of times."

"I want to go stay with Aunt Gale. Transfer to the high school in her district and finish the year out there."

My mother mutes the sound on the television and turns to me. "Why would you want to do that?"

"I have my reasons."

"Well, you need to tell me."

"No, Mom. I don't. I'm almost eighteen."

"Almost."

"Mom…"

"Did something happen at school? Is someone bothering you? I'm your mother, Liv. You need to tell me."

"Why? So you can plead it down?"

I rise from the couch.

"What does that mean, Liv?"

"I just don't think we look at things the same way, Mom. Like you and Dad didn't."

"You're not your father, Liv."

"Neither are you," I say, and I immediately regret saying it. "I'm sorry, Mom."

"You don't have to apologize. But if something's wrong, if someone is bothering you, then you do need to tell me. No. I'm not your father. I'm your mother. And that still means I love you."

"Mom. I'm fine. I just don't want to go to Lago anymore. There are too many memories with Brandon there. I thought I could handle it, but I was wrong. I can't. Can you just accept that I'm making the right decision? The right choice for me?"

"Have I ever not let you make your own decisions?"

"Not without explaining."

"I have to have more of a reason."

"What if reasons didn't matter?" I say, echoing what Jai said to me days before.

"They always matter," my mom says, and I wouldn't have expected a prosecutor to answer any other way.

"I know, Mom," I say. "It's just this time, I'm not so sure I can explain."

"You promise me no one is hurting you?"

"Yes, Mom. I promise. No one is hurting me." It's not an easy thing to lie to a prosecutor and have them believe you. My mom never asked me if someone *had* hurt me.

"OK, sweetheart," she says. "Why don't you sit back down and finish watching the movie with me."

"OK," I say. I sit down beside my mother but before she restores the volume to the television I stop her. "What's your favorite Mickey Rourke movie?"

She takes a minute to think, and I can see in her eyes when she has the answer. "*The Pope of Greenwich Village*," she tells me.

"Why that one?" I ask.

"Because," my mother begins, "that's the one that he reminds me of your father most in."

I turn toward the television and my mother and I continue watching the movie. *The Adventures of Buckaroo Banzai.* My mom was right. It is a weird movie. But we laugh together several times. And as much as it makes me sad, laughing with my mom without my father there, it also makes me happy. Sad and happy. It's like the two sounds that come from a violin.

If I Could Kiss You before the
Smoke Expires

I never returned the pack of American Spirit cigarettes that belonged to my father back to the trash bin. They should have never been placed there. Nothing owned by my father should be discarded. Instead, I have them in my room, on the nightstand beside my bed. Every now and again I flip the top open and smell the tobacco aroma to remind me of him. It's not that I need that particular sensorial trigger; it's just that it evokes a specific image of my father to me. It's an image of uncharacteristic restraint. My father rarely smoked around me, but when he did I knew it was with an awareness that I was watching. And I could tell my father tempered his enjoyment of the vice for fear I might be influenced by it. There were rare occasions when my father didn't realize I was watching him smoke. There was the time he worked on his car. Then there was a time where I saw him simply pulling upon a cigarette as if it were the fuse that was going to ignite some creativity buried deep within him and bring it to the surface. In those instances, as he smoked, there was a swagger to his mannerisms, a relaxation in his eyes that was sweet but slightly dangerous. In his casual flick of the ash was a disregard for everything that had nothing to do with that moment where he was smoking a cigarette. I imagine watching him so coolly unconcerned must be like watching Mickey Rourke in a movie.

As I sit up in bed, watching the moon outside my window warm the night sky, I cannot resist the urge to remove one of my father's cigarettes and light it. There is a half-empty can of soda on my nightstand perfect for me to use as an ashtray. The soda is warm now anyway. I take my father's Zippo lighter, also removed from its original place, and flip open the metal top. Click. There is that sound again, though echoed in the darkness it sounds even more ominous. I use my thumb to pull down on the wheel that provides the necessary spark. Fire. I place the flame from the lighter up to the cigarette and light it. I flip the top back down on the Zippo as the now bright orange tip of the cigarette burns away portions of the dark. I inhale. Slow. I exhale. Slower.

"You don't smoke."

I look over to the window. Brandon is sitting in the chair that is backed up into the corner.

"I know," I say to him. "But you're not really here, either."

Brandon smiles. I smile because I always did when he did. I know this is a dream, but sometimes knowing you are dreaming doesn't make the dream any less real. Sometimes knowing it's a dream and knowing you will eventually awaken makes you appreciate the things that happen within the dream even more. I have become very familiar with the laws that govern dreams.

"Are you sure?" he teases.

"You'll be gone as soon as this cigarette ends," I tell him.

"So what are you going to do?" he asks.

"Smoke slower."

Brandon smiles. I smile again.

"I told my father about the rape."

Brandon's smile disappears.

"I thought you didn't want to."

"I didn't."

"Then why did you?" he asks me.

I slowly exhale smoke into the air. I look at it aware that I am looking at an hourglass whose sand vanishes instead of falls.

"I didn't want you to be the only one who knew. I didn't want to feel like it was a burden that kept you from—"

"From what?" Brandon interrupts.

I take another drag of the cigarette. I don't want to smoke so fast, but I am nervous at knowing he will leave when I am done.

"From going to where you belong." I exhale.

"I belong with you, Liv."

"I know, Brandon. And I belonged with you. But not anymore. I don't want to keep you here, in this place, this world, because you worried about me. I thought if someone else knew…"

Brandon rises from the chair and steps over to my bed. He sits beside me.

"You're not keeping me here, Liv."

"It doesn't matter now. My father knows. There's no need for you to stay even though I want you to."

"Liv," he says. "I'll always be here with you. It doesn't matter what you do."

I flick the ashes from the end of my cigarette into the soda can and go to take another puff. Brandon softly takes hold of my arm.

"What's wrong?" I say.

Brandon smiles softly as he releases hold of my arm. "You're smoking too fast."

Brandon's right. I don't want the dream to be over. I don't want him to be gone just yet. I don't want him to be gone at all, but…

"I'm sorry," I say.

"It's OK."

"What if I never wanted to wake up, Brandon?"

"Awake from what?" he asks.

"This dream."

"You have to," Brandon tells me.

"Why? Why do I have to? Why can't I just dream this forever?"

"Liv…"

"Tell me. Why can't I just sleep forever?"

"Because," he says, "you're going to run out of cigarettes."

Do you ever think of how little you laugh in dreams? I wonder why that is. Is it because laughter is something too real to exist in the dream world? Or is it because we rarely laugh when we are awake, so we don't want to waste those moments when we sleep? I don't care. I am laughing now.

"I miss your laugh," Brandon says to me.

"I miss everything about you," I reply. Then I notice the heart pendant I gave him in the desert is no longer around his neck. "You're not wearing the pendant I gave you."

Brandon's mood shifts like smoke after the wave of a hand.

"You didn't take it off, did you?" I ask.

"No. I didn't."

"What happened to it? Where is it?"

Brandon rises from the edge of the bed. He backs away towards the wall like smoke being pulled from a room.

"Brandon…" I say, hoping my words will pull him back, closer to me.

"Not everything can go where I am," he tells me without coming closer.

"But that was my heart," I say, rising from the bed.

"Your heart is still with me. You have to trust me," Brandon says.

Even in the dark, I can see within Brandon's eyes that I can trust him.

"Liv," he says to me. I don't like his tone.

"What?" I ask.

"Your cigarette…"

I look down at the cigarette that has been burning of its own volition in my hand. It has reached its end. I watch as the burning color fades, leaving only smoke to remain.

I look up to Brandon.

"Can I kiss you before the smoke is gone?"

"Liv…"

"Yes, Brandon?"

"It's gone."

And so is Brandon.

The Burning Color Fades, Leaving
Only Smoke to Remain

When you awaken from a dream you never wanted to leave, the realization that you are awake comes within fractions of a second. The feeling of what you have lost by waking, however, defines the word *eternal*.

I am awake. My father's cigarettes remain on my nightstand. They are untouched. Another reminder that it was all a dream. There is not even the smell of tobacco in the air, only the emptiness of night.

"Liv."

A voice… I turn my head and look across the room. Brandon is standing there.

"Brandon!" I cry.

"Shhh…" he whispers. "You're still dreaming."

I leap from the bed into Brandon's waiting arms.

"I thought you were gone," I tell him.

"Never before a kiss goodbye," he says.

"No. A kiss is not enough," I exclaim.

"Liv."

"No, Brandon! It's my dream. I control it. And I want you to make love to me."

"This is all in your head, Liv. It won't be real."

"Nothing has felt real since you died," I say. "This is the most alive I've felt in forever. I can touch you. I can feel you. I can smell you. I want the memory of this, of you inside me."

"Even if it's just a dream?"

"I don't care. I'll stay asleep until it's over. I'll sleep forever if that's how long it lasts."

"And what will you do after?" he asks. "When you have to wake up?"

"I will wear this dream like a second skin. And always remember it as our first time together. As my first time."

"It will be your first time," Brandon says. Then he kisses me and lays me gently upon the bed.

The room darkens, as even the moon seems to shut its eyes.

"I love you, Brandon," I say.

"I love you, too, Liv."

We make love, somewhere between night and day, somewhere between the real world and the dreaming, somewhere between what is and what can never be, somewhere within the eternal.

Silent Alarms

It is Friday, and a whole town holds its collective breath like a man in a mask waiting for the trembling hands of a bank manager to open the vault. This vault won't be opened until 7:00 p.m. and it is only 9:00 a.m.

I am holding my breath as well but only because I am standing in the high school hallway and I see Christian walking towards me. I have not seen Christian since the party on Monday. It alarms me that I have not thought about him since then. Am I healed or too hurt? What's he going to say? And if I am healed, will his words hurt me? If I am too hurt, will his words make it so I can never be healed?

I count the steps he is taking towards me. One. Two. Three. Has he somehow read my mind? Does he know that I plan to leave? Did he somehow figure out that before I leave I am going to the police? Does he have some sort of internal alarm?

Five. Six. Seven. He's just about up to me... I listen for the bells telling me to run. I listen for the ringing telling me to clench my fist. I listen for the alarms telling me I should be alarmed...

Christian walks right past me without saying a word. What is even more telling is that I don't turn around to see if he has done the same.

I know I am not healed, but I know I am not too hurt, because as I exhale I know Christian no longer alarms me.

Catastrophic Tears on a
Butterfly's Wings

"Thank you."

I know who it is before I turn around and confirm that I am correct. I recognize the fragile space between her words.

"Hi, Danielle."

"Everyone calls me Dani."

"I know."

"You can call me Dani."

"OK," I say.

"I wanted to thank you for making sure I got home from the party the other night."

"You don't have to," I begin.

"I want to," she says. "I looked for you the last few days but…"

"I wasn't feeling well," I say, and I'm not sure that I am actually lying.

"I wanted to let you know you were right about Christian, too."

"What do you mean?" I ask.

"He won't talk to me anymore. Every time I try, he tells me to get away from him."

I look into Danielle's… Dani's eyes. They are wounded, though not fatally. It is as if they possess the tiny tear that might be found on a butterfly's wing, which while unnoticeable to the naked eye, will never allow the butterfly to fly perfectly again.

I don't say anything. I'm afraid to. I'm afraid of where my words may lead. I'm afraid that any words I say might rip that subtle tear and make it more noticeable, which might make it more damaging.

"I don't remember much from that night," she continues. Then she looks at me, waiting, waiting for me to fill in the blanks and I can see her confusion pulling at the tear.

"You fell, Dani. That's all."

"That's all?"

"Yeah," I say, and this time I am positive I am lying. "It's OK. Every girl falls at a party at some point, in some way or another. You made it home safe. That's what's important."

"People look at me like they know something I don't. Or like they're trying to figure something out."

"Don't give those people anything," I implore her. "Don't look any of them in the eyes. Never look anyone in the eye who is not worth your stare."

"How do I tell who is and who isn't?" she wants to know.

"By the way they stare at you," I say.

"I don't want to hurt anyone's feelings. Christian—"

I stop her. "Christian can't be hurt. Not by people like you or I."

"What kind of people are we?"

"Girls that fall at a party and are able to get up and smile."

Danielle finally smiles, and, for a moment, the tear in her eye all but disappears.

Root Beer Floats

The wind blows past me, circles around and ultimately blows through me as I walk across the school courtyard towards Jai. I look up at the sky, and it fills my eyes with blue. I am not fooled. There will be rain tonight. I have been told by my belly even God will be watching the game tonight and, for one reason or another, he shall weep over its outcome.

"Jai," I say as I approach. "Jai." Jai cannot hear me over the music that fills his ears via the earbuds inserted in them. I eventually am close enough that he turns around and quickly deactivates his iPod and removes the earbuds.

"Hey, Liv."

"I need to talk to you, Jai."

"OK," he says.

It takes me a minute to tell him. "I'm leaving."

"What do you mean?"

"Leaving. Going."

"Going where?"

"Away, Jai."

"Away from what?"

The wind stirs around us.

"Have you noticed," I ask, "that it doesn't seem like the wind has ever stopped blowing since Brandon died?"

Jai doesn't answer.

"I'm going away from everything," I say. "I'm moving to my aunt's. I'm going to finish the school year there."

"Why?"

"I can't be here anymore."

"Why, Liv?" Jai asks. "Nothing bad is going to happen anymore."

I have to laugh. I do it softly.

"Bad things haven't stopped happening, Jai. And after Monday, I expect things will only get worse."

"What's Monday?"

"It doesn't matter," I say. "Graduation is an important memory, and I don't want that memory attached to this place."

"Will it make a difference, Liv? Things that happen to us follow us everywhere. Believe me," Jai says. "I know."

"There has to be a place that doesn't feel like here."

"Well, if I'm wrong," Jai says, "and you do find a place to hide, let me know. Hopefully it will have root beer floats. And hopefully it won't ask what you've done. But I don't think such a place exists."

"What do you want to hide from?"

"Everything," Jai says.

The wind stops.

"Well," I continue, "I just thought you'd want to know because I'm leaving tomorrow."

"You're not staying for the game?"

"Goodbye, Jai," I say, then turn and walk away.

"You think Brandon came back," Jai yells. I stop. "Don't you?" he adds. I turn around. I want to see his face. "You think Gabriel is Brandon."

I walk back towards Jai. There is fear in his eyes. "What did you say?"

"I think so, too." He exhales.

"You do?" I ask.

"Yeah," he says, as if an incredible weight has been shrugged from his shoulders. "I do."

"Come with me," I say.

"Where?" he wants to know.

"Somewhere where they have root beer floats."

The Laws That Govern Ghosts

We sit in the back of a diner. It is the local diner, and as local sometimes means, it is the only diner the town has. If you want more, you have to go to the next city over, but they probably don't have root beer floats. There are two in front of us, though Jai's is just about half-gone.

"I love root beer floats."

"I know," I tell Jai as he nearly finishes the remainder of the contents of his glass before setting it down.

"You think I'm crazy, don't you?" Jai asks.

"I don't think you're crazy, Jai," I say, and I don't, because if I do, then I'm crazy, as well.

"That's why I didn't say anything before. But what happened at the party. How Gabriel just appeared. How he was there for you. I knew you had to think the same."

"What happened at the party?" I ask. " Is that the reason you think Gabriel might be Brandon?"

"There are other reasons. And I'm sure you have some of your own."

"Really? I haven't told you whether I believe it or not."

"I know you do," Jai says as he leans in from across the table. "Otherwise you would already be gone. You wouldn't wait around for the game tonight. You want to see if he's going to come. Gabriel… Brandon…"

"I don't know if that's the reason I'm staying. Maybe I'm staying because I want to see Christian lose. Even though that's stupid of me."

"Why would that be stupid?"

"Because even if he does lose the game, I won't get back anything he took from me. Especially Brandon."

"But what if I'm right? What if Brandon is already back?" Jai asks.

"I don't know."

"What do you mean?"

"I want to believe it, Jai. I want to believe more than anything that Brandon came back. That maybe somehow he did find a way to be with me, maybe to make Christian pay for the things he did. But…"

"But what? That would be great."

"Would it?"

"Of course it would. Why wouldn't it?"

"Because I love him," I say. I can see from the look in Jai's eyes that he does not understand. I try and help him to. "What if it's me that's keeping his soul from resting? What if I'm responsible for Brandon being in some limbo that he can never leave because of his feelings for me or mine for him? Do you know what that would feel like for him? Can you even imagine being trapped between what you felt and what you can no longer feel? If it's true, he must be incredibly lonely. He must be dying inside over and over again because his spirit can't rest. What's so great about that? And—" I stop.

"And what?"

"Have you ever read a ghost story?"

"Yeah."

Jai looks confused at what seems an abrupt change of subject.

"They never stay. They always have to go back. So I would lose Brandon all over again. I cannot handle that. I can't."

"So you think it's true. You do think Gabriel is Brandon."

"You're not listening to me, Jai," I tell him. "When I first thought it might be true, I was so happy. I couldn't wait for Gabriel to tell me it was real, that he was Brandon, but that was selfish of me. I just want Brandon to be at peace, even if it means I never will be. Maybe that's why I'm staying for the game, to make sure that if he did come back, nothing happens to him."

"I don't believe you. What if there's a way for Brandon to stay? To remain as Gabriel?"

"Life doesn't work like that, Jai. You don't get to keep the things you love."

"How do you know?" he asks. So I tell him.

"Look down," I say.

"What?"

"Your root beer float is gone."

Open Casket

I don't expect to find Brandon at the abandoned church. But I want to talk to him and I believe if I do it there, at the church, I have the best chance of him hearing me.

I step within the disintegrating walls. I clutch the crucifix given to me by my father. A crucifix I never remove from my neck even if the weight of it and the betrayal I feel from it will sometimes burn.

I am overcome with the overwhelming sense of abandon that Brandon's father must have felt. Knowing what I now know, this house seems as empty as Brandon's home did without him. I now think that with the father gone, burning the church was an act of mercy. I feel no salvation here as I did once before, only shame.

"Brandon," I whisper. Then I speak louder so he hears me over the decay. "If you can hear me, I want to tell you something and I want you to listen. I want you to listen to what I tell you. You're free. Are you listening to me? You're free. Find your way to where you are supposed to be. Find your father if you can…"

I clutch the crucifix tighter, maybe looking for strength, or the strength to believe.

"Don't come to the game tonight. Please. I'll be OK. I don't want you to do anything that might compromise the person that you were. Not for me. I'm fine, Brandon. I will be fine. As long as I know you love me. And I do."

The more I speak, the more I believe and therefore the angrier my tone becomes.

"Are you listening to me, Brandon? Do not come to the game tonight. Go home. Go where you belong. I don't need your protection anymore. I need to protect you. And I need for you to let me."

I feel moisture on my face, and at first I think it is rain. It is not until I wipe it away and feel the temperature of a tear that I realize I am crying.

"I love you, Brandon. Eternal."

All Fathers Come from Hell

Somewhere a father is talking to his son. A father is always talking to his son. Whether that son chooses to listen to that father defines who he will become or avoid becoming.

Christian's father has never said more than seven words to me. These are the 261 words he has just said to Christian.

"Who are you? You're my son. What are you? You're a football player. Not just a football player. You're a quarterback. Which do you think is more important to me? I'll tell you. What you do. Because that's what defines who you are and if my son is not a quarterback, then I don't know who you are. Your name is my name. And you have had everything that name gives. Do you think it was free? Without any cost? I don't give out charity and anybody that takes charity is a worthless piece of shit. Did I raise a worthless piece of shit? Are you going to shit on my name? No. I won't let you! So how are you going to pay me back for everything I have given you for the past eighteen years? You're going to start by winning this game tonight. That's your down payment. That is the first sign of respect you will give me. You will look me in the eye holding the championship trophy, you will hand me that trophy, shake my hand and say, look, Dad, I am not a worthless piece of shit. I pay my debts. I want to keep your name. That is how you are going to pay me back. If you don't win the game, if you don't bring me that trophy, then I want you to look me in the eye and I want you to apologize for wasting eighteen years of my life when I could have been on a golf course every fucking weekend."

Not all fathers come from hell. But they all have the ability to make sure that's where their sons end up.

Helicopters

Strange thing about helicopters... the thing that gives them their power, their strength, is also the most dangerous thing about them. The rotor of a helicopter, from which it derives its purpose, its ability, its strength, is also a helicopter's most fragile element.

Christian and Murdoc are standing in a corner of the locker room, hidden away from other players, as they dress for battle. What they do not need to put on, what they wear beneath their skin, is their purpose, their ability, their strength. And it gives both an intensity that revolves around them like the blade of a helicopter.

"You make sure you protect me out there tonight," Christian barks at Murdoc.

"You think you have to tell me that? I've got you protected on field and off," Murdoc barks back at Christian. "There are friends of mine... friends of ours at every entrance in case Motorcycle Boy decides to show up. And believe me—they're not worried about being expelled. They don't have to be. They don't go here."

Planes are forced to go from one point to another. It is the limitation of their design. Planes are not allowed to be inert. Change is inherent in their purpose. It is the destiny of their function. Helicopters, however, have the ability to hover. They can become airborne while never having to depart from the point from which they have arisen. This might seem advantageous, but it can also be dangerous. Staying in one place is not always the wisest plan.

"Fuck Motorcycle Boy!" Christian shouts. "If I ever see him again, I'm gonna wrap that motorcycle around his neck and send them both to the same place I sent Brandon!"

Murdoc pulls Christian farther back into the corner, if that is even possible. "What you better do is shut the hell up! You don't know who's listening! Besides, we didn't do anything to Brandon."

"Are you afraid?" Christian asks.

"Afraid of what?"

"Afraid of Brandon."

"Why the hell would I be afraid of Brandon?"

"Maybe you think he's come back or something?"

"What are you talking about? Is that what you think? That Brandon's some ghost? You think that was the reason Russel quit the team?"

Christian now pushes Murdoc back up against the wall, reversing Murdoc's equally aggressive pull.

"Did I say that? Is that what I said? No! It wasn't! So keep your goddamn hands off me!"

"Good," Murdoc says. "Because I don't believe in ghosts! And you don't need to, either. They don't exist! And if Russel's father hadn't shot that quitter in the head, I would have."

"You would have had to beat me to it," Christian offers. Both stand there for a moment, hovering above their own vileness.

Planes can fly side by side. They can fly so close together that their wings just about touch. If the pilots are capable enough, their wings can touch. Helicopters are incapable of that maneuver. The intensity of the rotor dictates that anything it comes too close to will either be destroyed by it or destroy it.

"We don't need him, anyway," Murdoc says. "All we need is your arm and the win."

Christian steps up to Murdoc so that they are but inches apart from each other.

"My arm is the win. Don't forget that. On the field, or off."

"I won't. Don't worry."

"Good," Christian continues. "And when we're holding that trophy after the game. When I am holding it, make sure you come up and say, thanks, Christian. Thank you for making me look great. Thank you for doing what no one else in my family could. Thank you for giving me a way to get out of this shit-hole town!"

Christian and Murdoc stand there, hovering in a sandstorm of their own self-importance.

On August 24, 2001, Air Transat Flight 236, an Airbus A330 carrying 293 passengers and 13 crew, ran out of fuel over the Atlantic Ocean. All four engines on the Airbus A330, the plane's primary source of power, either flamed out or stopped cold at 33,000 feet. The pilots of the Airbus A330 with 293 passengers, managed to glide the plane for over an hour to a successful landing in the Azores with no loss of life. All 293 passengers survived. Such an amazing accomplishment is beyond the singular mindedness of a helicopter's design. If its main source of power should fail, if the purpose of the helicopter's rotor, which is to revolve so intensely that nothing or no one can get near it, should be interrupted, there would be nothing or no one that could save it. It should be said that the Airbus A330, with 293 passengers aboard, was assisted in a safe landing by the deployment of the plane's ram air turbine, a small propeller, with nonlethal blades, that provided power for critical sensors and instruments to fly the aircraft.

Do you wonder if those small, yet significant, blades ever aspired to be the rotor on a helicopter?

I Can See the Coliseum from inside
the Lion's Mouth
(Pre-Show)

The lights to the football stadium where the game shall be played shine so brightly, I think it is day, momentarily forgetting that as I approach the coliseum-like structure, we are all actually underneath a blanket of darkness. I am still conflicted about my presence, but I think it is that sense of conflict that has brought me here. If I did not believe this night would affect me regardless of my presence, then the night would not have me.

It is taking longer than it normally would for the journey from the entrance of the team-neutral school to the parking lot. Students who wisely chose to walk are not only passing my vehicle, but also the vehicles that are virtually stopped in front of me. I watch as students once known to me as friends walk by without ever acknowledging the fact that we have either grown up together or around each other. It is as if I have been swallowed up by the beast that is adolescence, and I am watching from the inside as I am being slowly digested. Sad is the creature that is too apathetic to purge itself of something that doesn't agree with it. I hope it chokes on my disregard.

I can see from the rearview mirror that Sara Welsh and two friends are approaching. Sara's twin sister, Eva, committed suicide freshman year, when, for reasons no one is quite sure of, the male upperclassmen suddenly decided one sister was better than the other, even though they were identical in almost every way. Sara stayed at my house for more than three months until her parents moved into a house that didn't contain the ghost of her sister. We became like sisters ourselves. If I remember correctly, I walked her up to the coffin so she could say goodbye to her sister during the wake, as she was unable to take the few steps on her own. If I also remember correctly, I did not see her at Brandon's funeral, but I don't hold that against her. Her boyfriend, Kyle Cross, the football team's leading rusher, was not there, either. I would rather believe that she was consoling him because he was too distraught to attend, rather than she simply didn't go because she was not allowed. Apparently, no one on the football team was allowed to go to Brandon's funeral. Either that or no one on the football team could handle death. Yes. That is why she chose not to attend. Her boyfriend couldn't handle the sadness. If that makes me naïve, I apologize. I cannot think badly of a friend that lost a sibling. I... wait... here she comes... I watch in the rearview mirror as she sees me see her pretend not to see me. I watch as she walks right past me, and the car Brandon allowed me to use to pick her up from the hospital, when she and her family were done identifying her sister's body. Give me a minute... Anyway, I don't have it in me to think that someone could be so cruel as to not be there for me as I was for them. I hope I never do.

Love's Grievous Intent
(First Quarter)

I've sat in my car now for thirty minutes. I find myself frozen by a roar the stadium itself cannot contain. I have been to enough games at Lago High that I can speak the language of the collective spectators without witnessing what they are seeing. The game is in its first quarter, no more than thirteen minutes in, and we have already scored once. The opposing team has yet to respond in kind. I turn up my CD player. Martin Grech plays on repeat. "Open Heart Zoo." I hear another roar, which overpowers Martin's fragile soprano. We have scored again. Then there is a knock on my window. I turn and see Jai standing outside my car, so I turn off the radio, open the door and step out.

"Why aren't you inside?" I ask. "The game's already started."

"I know," Jai replies, though it doesn't seem necessarily that he wants to. "I don't really care about the game."

"Then why are you here?" I ask.

"I came to see you."

"Why?"

Before he can answer, we are interrupted by the roar of a lion that is amplified by the nature of its hunger.

"What happened?" Jai asks.

"We just got the extra point," I tell him.

"We." He smiles. "You sound like you're rooting for our team."

"Force of habit," I say. "Why did you want to see me?"

"You're leaving still?"

"Yes," I say.

"Then there are some things I need to tell you. Things that I did to you I'm not proud of."

"Like what, Jai?"

"We've known each other for so long..." He hesitates.

"I know. We lived on the same street for almost twelve years. I think I've known you longer than anyone else in Lago. You were the one that introduced me to Brandon."

"Yeah," he says, though it is with an awkward intonation.

"Is this about Brandon?" I ask.

"Yes. I mean no," he says, quickly changing his mind. "It's about me. The things I did."

"What did you do?"

"I took a cookie from your lunch bag when we were in kindergarten. You thought your mom forgot to pack one, but she didn't. I ate it. It was oatmeal raisin, I think."

"That's OK, Jai. I hated oatmeal raisin. That was my mom's way of getting me to eat oatmeal, which I hated, too."

"I cheated off you in algebra," Jai tells me. "It was our ninth grade exam."

"I think I got a D."

"Yeah." Jai smiles. "So did I. I forgot how bad you were at math."

"Is... that it?" I ask, knowing, somehow worried, that he can't possibly be done.

"No."

"What else?" Jai pauses and I hate it. I hate pauses in anything other than a poem. "Jai?"

"When I told you Brandon wanted you to meet him at Christian's that night..." Another pause. I am hating Jai at this moment.

"You what, Jai?"

"I tried to tell you before. A few days ago, but I couldn't."

"You tried to tell me what?"

"I lied."

"What do you mean you lied?"

"That's not what happened," Jai says.

"Then tell me, Jai. Tell me what happened."

The sound of the crowd has died down. First quarter is over.

Those That Know Iago
(Second Quarter)

You should be able to sit outside and listen to music if that is what you choose to do. But this is high school. There are a lot of things in high school you should be able to do but can't. And the things one chooses to do often seem to be the wrong choice.

"Where's your friend?" Murdoc asks, having stepped over to where Jai once sat alone.

"What?" Jai asks as he raises his head.

Russel repeats the question for Murdoc after removing the earbuds from Jai's ears. "He said, where's your friend?"

"What friend?" Jai asks.

Before responding, Russel grabs the MP3 player from Jai's hands and examines it.

"Look at this, Murdoc." Murdoc looks at the somewhat primitive device as Russel turns to Jai. "How many songs can you hold on it? Five?"

Jai rises from the courtyard bench and attempts to take back what is his. Russel tosses the MP3 player to Murdoc. "Can I have my player back, please?" Jai requests.

"Well he did say please," Murdoc says to Russel.

"Then I guess you have to give it back," Russel responds.

"Here you go, Noodle." Murdoc extends the MP3 player to Jai's waiting hand, then feigns taking it back. "I'm just playin' with you, Noodle," Murdoc says as he finally hands the player to Jai.

"My name is not, Noodle. It's Jai."

"Shut the hell up, Noodle!" Russel spits.

"That's not nice," Christian says as he walks up, smiling like the devil moments before he was to tempt Christ.

"Noodle knows we're just teasin'," Russel halfheartedly defends himself. "It's all good."

"Where's your friend?" Christian asks.

"We've already asked him that," Russel states.

"Twice," Murdoc adds.

"What friend?" Jai repeats.

"How many friends do you have, Jai?" Christian responds. Jai looks back at Christian.

"Brandon?"

"Yeah," Christian says. "That's the one."

"I don't know. I think he's having lunch with Liv."

"Perfect." Christian smiles. "That's exactly who I wanted to talk to you about."

"Liv?"

"Yeah. Liv. I want you to invite her over to my house tonight."

"Why?" Jai rightfully inquires.

"None of your business why," Murdoc interrupts.

"It's a good question. He has a right to know," Christian informs Murdoc. "Because, Jai, I want to talk to her."

"About what?"

"This fool asks a lot of questions. Don't you, Noodle? Don't you?" Russel yells.

"His name is Jai," Christian defends him disingenuously. "And I don't care if he knows," Christian says to Russel before he turns back to Jai. "I want to talk to her about some things. Personal things. Things people in school don't need to know about."

"Why don't you ask her to come over yourself?"

"Ah, there's the rub," Christian intones with a complete unawareness that he is quoting Hamlet's "To be or not to be" soliloquy. His mind is but regurgitating echoes of sentiments too deep for him to understand, too meaningful for him to retain. "I don't know that she'd come if I asked her to."

"Then why would she come if I asked her?"

"Because," Christian begins. "You can tell her I want to plan a surprise party for Brandon. Tell her you'll be there, too. She trusts you."

"So why would I break that trust?"

"What are you afraid of? That I'm going to hurt her? I just want to talk. What I want to talk about is, like Murdoc said, really none of your business."

"How do you know I can get her to come? How do you know she trusts me?"

"She likes you. I can tell."

"She's my friend."

"We're all friends..." Christian pauses. Did I tell you how much I hate pauses? "So you'll do it, right?"

Love's Grievous Intent Part 2
(Third Quarter)

So begins the rain. The darkening skies did not lie. Let it pour. I am too angry to cry. Let the sky weep for me. And do not stop until you no longer hear my voice.

"Why did you do it, Jai? Why?" I scream as clouds mirror my darkening heart.

"You don't understand," Jai responds.

"Then make me understand. And don't tell me your reasons don't matter! Reasons have never mattered more. So tell me, why?"

"I don't know that I can," he says.

"Then I hate you!"

"No," Jai begs. "I don't want you to hate me."

"Do you know what Christian did to me?" I ask. "Do you?"

"No," he tells me. And I can see in his eyes that he is not lying, though it does not soften my heart to him. "Brandon wouldn't tell me. All he said was that Christian hurt you."

"Hurt me?" I push Jai up against my car with force I was unaware my body had access to. "Do you think Christian would have killed Brandon if all Christian did was hurt me? He was hiding something else!"

"I'm sorry, Liv."

"He raped me!" I beat those words into Jai's body with fists that pound harder than the rain pounding into the ground as it falls around us. "He raped me!"

"Liv! I didn't know that would happen! How could I? I would have never done what I did."

I stop hitting Jai and step back from him so that I don't hit him again. And I want him to see my face, look into my eyes when I tell him what I do. "It doesn't matter, Jai. It's your fault. Your fault Christian raped me and it's your fault Brandon is dead."

"Liv..."

"What, Jai? What could you possibly say to me that would matter?"

"I did it because I loved you."

The crowd in the stadium cheers. We have scored again.

"You what?" I ask with the indignation given fools who remain untouched by their lack of wisdom while those around them suffer the fate of folly. "Brandon was your friend, Jai. Your best friend."

"I know he was. But I knew you first. I loved you first. I just didn't know how to tell you."

"So instead you decided to lie to me so I would be raped?"

"No. I just thought he wanted to talk to you. I was just hoping to make Brandon jealous. I thought he would break up with you and it would just be you and me the last year of high school. It was stupid. I never meant for anything that happened to happen."

"That's another lie. If Brandon had left me like you wanted him to, I would have been devastated. And I am. And you wanted Brandon gone. And he is. You got everything you wanted, Jai. Everything." Another cheer envelopes us. The extra point is scored.

"I just wanted you to love me like I loved you."

"You'll never have that now. Will you?"

"Liv…"

I move up to Jai, within inches of his trembling body, and I am now as close to him as I will ever get again.

"Don't you ever say my name again. Not even to tell me goodbye."

If You Are Reading This,
Then I Am Already Dead
(The Clock Is Stopped)

I should have run when he opened the door. If you're a girl, don't ever forget that sentence. Don't ever ignore a feeling you have never had while in the presence of someone you trust. I should have run when he opened the door. Now I can never run far enough.

"I didn't think you'd come," Christian says to me. Christian has never done anything to hurt me, so when he says that to me, why does my heart skip a beat in fear?

"Why wouldn't I?" I ask him.

"Well, I'm glad you did." He smiles. "Come in."

I step in, and my eyes immediately recognize reason for concern, though my mind is slower to process it. Both Murdoc and Russel are sitting on the couch in the expanse of the living room, both holding bottles of beer.

"Where's Jai?" I ask.

"He's on his way," I am told, without realizing that everything that is being said that might keep me from harm is a lie, and the things that will prove to be true, I will wish were not.

Christian motions to the couch. There is a seat available in between Murdoc and Russel. I choose a brown leather chair with an ottoman in front of it to sit upon. I do, however, push the ottoman away, not feeling comfortable enough to take advantage of its purpose. I will come to regret that decision.

"Want a drink?" Murdoc offers.

"I don't drink," I tell him.

"We won't tell anyone," Russel tries to comfort me.

"No, thank you. I'm fine," I say.

"Too late," I hear as Christian brings over two glasses of wine. "I already poured you something."

"I don't want a drink."

"It's just wine," Christian argues.

"I know. That would be a drink," I respond.

"She's good." Russel laughs aloud. "I can see why—"

Whatever Russel was going to say is quickly interrupted by Christian's yell. "Shut up!" Russel stays quiet.

"He can see why what?" I ask.

"Nothing," Christian reassures me. "He's drunk."

"Are you?"

Christian puts the wineglass intended for me on the table beside the leather chair. He sits down on the ottoman so that he is directly facing me. I told you I would regret not using the ottoman. "Not yet," he says.

"So why do you want to throw Brandon a surprise party?" I ask, thinking this is the reason I have been invited.

"His birthday is coming up soon, isn't it?" Christian responds.

"I know," I tell him. "But I didn't know you even liked Brandon."

"Why wouldn't I? We go... I mean, we went to the same school. He was captain of the swim team. I'm captain of the football team. We both like you..."

There are moments when you will experience epiphanies in your life, and if you are lucky, if you are leading a charmed life or if you simply have a guardian angel who never sleeps, that epiphany will come at a time when the insight matters and its worth has yet to expire like milk you can no longer consume. It was at that moment, Christian telling me that he liked me, that I wished I had never walked through that door. Unfortunately for me, the milk was already wreaking havoc on my insides.

"When is Jai coming?" I ask.

"He'll be here soon," he lies. "Have a drink of your wine."

"I told you I don't drink," I say again.

"Take a drink!" Christian yells. And that is when I know that when the front door of his house opens so that I can leave, I will not be the girl I am at this very moment. Just as quickly as that revelation chills me, Christian calms down. "I'm sorry," he says. "I shouldn't have yelled. You don't have to drink if you don't want to."

"I don't want to," I say for what feels like the hundredth time.

"That's cool," Christian says as he rises, turns away and takes a drink of wine from his glass. I want to jump up from the chair and race for the door, but my legs know what my heart does not, that I would never make it. "You know what I don't understand," Christian continues.

"What?" I ask.

"Why did you and I never get together?" He turns back to me.

"What do you mean, get together?"

"He means fuck! How come you two haven't fucked?" Russel offers, and Christian's rage is immediately back.

"Shut up, I said! I'll tell you when I want you to speak!"

I had heard from one person or another that Christian, if not a racist, at the very least entertained racism. I didn't want to believe that about him. I don't want to believe that about anyone, though I know it is true. And while Christian's words bore no evidence that would convict him of such, his tone was more than circumstantial.

I rise from the chair, but I have taken no more than the intent of a step away when Christian is standing in front of me. "Where are you going?"

"I want to go home," I say.

"But we haven't finished talking about the party."

"There is no party."

"There will be," Christian says. And for some reason, I think about the first time my father must have held me.

"Sit down," he commands. And so I sit. "What did you think you were coming over here for?"

"I thought," I say, "to talk about Brandon."

Christian retakes his seat on the ottoman directly across from me. "You don't have to lie to me. Brandon isn't here. Neither is Jai. And he's not coming. It's just you, me and opportunity."

Christian consumes the remainder of his wine, as if the words he has just spoken scorched his throat as much as they burned my ears.

"I want to go," I begin to plead. "Will you please let me go, Christian?"

Christian takes his hand and places it upon my trembling leg, just above my knee. "I can't."

"You can do anything you want to do," I tell him.

"I know I can," he says to me with great foreboding. "That's why I can't let you leave."

There is a pause… Then Christian seems to have a moment of clarity that I'm not sure if I can believe is real. Maybe it is the tears falling from my eyes or maybe my guardian angel has awakened. "OK," he says. "I'll let you go, but you have to do one shot with me."

"I don't want to do a shot," I say even as I wish alcohol were drenching those very words as they left my mouth so I could leave.

"You want to go home, right?"

"Yes," I say.

"Then, one shot," Christian says.

"One?" I repeat so that it is said again, hoping that will be some kind of contract between us.

"Yes. One."

"Then you will let me go?" Again, I want the terms of the contract to be clearly stated.

"Yes."

It's easy to have faith in things you want to believe. I think that's why so many people have faith in someone they have never seen.

"OK," I say. "I'll have one."

"One?" Christian asks as if he now needs to be sure of a contract he has written, before signing.

"Yes," I repeat. "One."

Christian waits while Murdoc retrieves a bottle of tequila and two shot glasses. I did not see where they were, but they had to be closer than they should have been, considering the room we are in and the size of the home. I can't let the realization of that fact and its implication overshadow my hope that I will get to leave soon. Murdoc pours the shots and Christian hands me one glass, then takes the other. He raises his glass. "To us," he toasts.

"I can't do that, Christian," I tell him.

"Do what?" he asks.

"Toast to us. I'm Brandon's girlfriend."

"OK. How about to our last football season?"

"OK."

Christian reraises his glass. I look at him. I look deep into his eyes, searching for a glimmer of nobility. "One. Right?" I ask when I can find none.

"Yes," Christian assures me with a smile. "One."

I close my eyes and tip the shot glass back. The contents pour into my mouth, past my tongue, barely wetting it before scarring my throat on its way down to pollute my insides with its intent. I open my eyes. Christian's glass remains full.

"I think I'll do mine later," he says on his way to betraying our contract. My heart sinks, drowning beneath the liquid that promised to save it. I watch as Christian then puts the shot glass on the table beside the chair. I stare at the glass. It is still full, like a promise God has yet to answer. I think that's why so many people don't believe in him.

I jump up and race for the door. I will later regret this. I am about one hundred feet away from the exit, but it may as well be one thousand. And though I can see my destination, it is as if I am running through a labyrinth, and at every turn I am running towards the future that was mine before I stepped through that door. I see my dad telling his little girl to go faster. Run, he says. Run, Dandelion. Then I see my mom smiling because she knows I'm about to make it out of the house. Her arms are open, and I know that when I make it into them she will hold me. I know as she comforts me she will tell me things about boys and men so I never find myself in this situation again. She's going to tell me how when she was growing up she had boys try the same thing. And she's going to tell me how she got away, just like I did…

I am at the front door of Christian's house. My hand is on the knob. I will open it and Brandon will be standing there to take me home. Somehow he knew I was here. Somehow he knew what Christian was planning. And somehow, he made it, in enough time to rescue me…

I fling open the door. There is nothing outside but darkness. Slam! The door is closed. Christian turns me around and backs me up against the door so that it cannot be opened again. I look into his eyes. There is nothing there but darkness.

"The party's not over yet." He smiles to me.

"You said I could go," I cry.

"I said you could go after we did one shot. I haven't done mine yet."

My cell phone rings. Though it is in my pocket, I can tell from the specific ring, from the melody, that it is Brandon.

"Do you want me to get that?" Christian asks with no purpose other than to taunt me.

"No," I tell him.

"You sure?" he asks.

"Yes," I respond, wishing that Brandon could hear Christian's voice, even though I haven't answered his call. The phone stops ringing.

"Christian..." I say.

"What?" he asks.

"Please..."

"Quiet," he whispers, putting his finger up to my lips. "You'll have plenty of time to beg."

"Christian, don't."

"Don't what?" he wonders.

"Don't do this," I plead. "Your parents..."

"They're not home. They're never home. Just like your dad."

I want to kill him. Not for what he is doing. For what he has just said.

"Don't move," Christian tells me. Then he uses his left hand and holds me against the door by my neck in case I try to defy him. He then takes his other hand, his right hand, and slides it in between my clothing. "Haven't you heard?" he asks me. "I have the best hands in school." This is where I stop thinking. This is where I stop feeling. This is where his hand wrongfully beckons a girl to become a woman. "Touchdown," he exclaims. Tears stream down my face, past my neck and in between the fingers of the hand that restrains it, as if a river, searching for compassion from the rocks as it rushes over them. It is the only moisture he will force from my body...

After a minute, that will affect me for a lifetime, he stops. And with the gentleness of a man asking a woman if she would escort him to a dance, he asks me if I want to go upstairs to his bedroom.

"No, I don't," I manage to push out with lifeless breath.

"Are you sure?" he asks me without purpose.

"Yes," I reassure him without purpose. "I'm sure."

"You're already mine," he then tells me. "There's no going back. There's only going upstairs, where there's just you and me. Or"—when the devil says "or," you know it's already too late—"there's staying down here, where there's you, me, Murdoc and Russel. It's up to you what kind of party you want to have."

The horrified look in my eyes answers for me, as my voice cannot be summoned from its hiding place in my throat.

"Good," Christian says softly. "It will be more fun with just the two of us." He finally releases my throat, then takes my hand with the instrument of his violation and leads me back into the living room where Murdoc and Russel sit.

"Liv wants to go upstairs," he tells them, then turns back to me. "Don't you?"

This I trust you know, but allow me to say it. Every answer you read from me, every word, is given in the same slow and hushed manner that death must employ when whispering in the ear of a child.

"Yes," I say.

"Yes, what?" Christian asks.

"Yes," I repeat. "I want to go upstairs."

"You want to go upstairs with who?"

I don't want to go upstairs. I want to die. But I know if I stay down here, the death will be something I will never live through.

"Yes," I say again. "I want to go upstairs with Christian."

Murdoc raises his cell phone and touches the touch screen. My words are played back to me from his voice recorder.

"Your voice sounds so sweet." Russel laughs.

"I bet everything is sweet about her," Murdoc adds.

Christian raises his right hand and brings his fingers to his lips. "Real sweet."

I look over to the shot glass once again. I want to jump inside of it and drown. After I do, I hope someone will then light the contents on fire and force Christian to consume my desecration.

"Let's go upstairs," he says, more politely than anything else that has been vomited from his lack of conscience.

I look at the full glass of wine earlier offered to me. I will try and submerge my feelings in its apathy. "Can I have the glass of wine?"

"I thought you would want it." Christian smiles, a smile that quickly disintegrates into a smirk directed towards Murdoc and Russel.

I pull my body over to the table and remove the glass of wine. It is red wine, deep red, like the blood of a sinner. I try to keep my hand from trembling so the waves of merlot do not betray my desire to not give Christian the added excitement of my fear, lest he lust for me even more. I raise the glass to my lips. I know the contents will not be enough to numb me, but I hope it will be enough to erase the taste of Christian's rotting breath, should he press his mouth against mine.

"Go ahead, drink," Christian says to me.

I tip the glass up and tilt my head back. The wine races over my tongue and down my throat as if aware of its purpose and the urgency with which I need it performed. There are cheers from the crowd as the present bleeds into my recollection of the past. I know that our football team has scored again. The score is 20 to 0.

"Damn, girl!" Russel exclaims. "You a pro!"

I turn and hurl the empty glass at Russel. It misses him, smashing instead against the wall behind him. "Don't talk to me!" I yell. Both Christian and Murdoc laugh.

"C'mon," Christian says with a joviality in his tone as if this has all been funny games. "Let's leave these two to clean up." He leads the way. I follow slowly behind. I am at the foot of the spiral staircase. This is the very first time I will ever ascend them, though it will not be the last. My feet feel as if they are encased in cement and I cannot tell you how it is that I am lifting them to climb. I also cannot tell you why Christian starts the following conversation as we ascend…

"Have you seen the *Twilight* movies?"

I am so taken aback by the randomness of this question that it almost pushes me down the few steps I have managed to climb. I have to make sure I heard correctly.

"What did you say?"

"The *Twilight* movies. You know, the ones with the vampires and werewolves."

"Yeah. I know them," I say.

"Did you like them?"

I stop. "Why are you asking me this? Why do you care?"

Christian stops and turns to me. "I want to know what your opinion is. You like a lot of cool things. What do you think about the movies?"

"I haven't seen them." I surrender.

"You don't like vampires?"

"No. Vampires don't scare me."

"Why not?"

"You have to invite them in."

Christian laughs, turns and walks back up the stairs. "Yeah. Who's going to be afraid of teenage monsters anyway?"

How tragic is irony sometimes?

We are at the top of the stairs. I am looking at his closed door.

Christian steps over to the door and turns to me.

"You sure you want to come inside?"

I turn and look at the bottom of the spiral staircase. Murdoc and Russel are at the bottom. I look back to Christian.

"Yes."

"Yes, what?"

"Yes. I want to come inside."

"After you," he says.

I look downstairs again. Demons never leave their posts. Evil never sleeps. They will be there until I go into Christian's room or come back down to them. I turn and walk past Christian into his room. Christian follows me inside and shuts the door.

No… I am not afraid of monsters that have to be invited in. I only fear those who invite themselves.

Twenty Seconds from the Moment You Tap God on the Shoulder (Fourth Quarter)

The rain stops midair. The drops are frozen, as if someone has tapped God on the shoulder while he wept, and he stopped momentarily to turn around. Something is wrong. I roll down the window to the Mustang and I begin to asphyxiate. There is no air. The world is holding its breath and everything has stopped around me. I quickly roll up the car window so that the air inside does not escape. I sit in my car, watching, waiting, wondering whether the world outside is being strangled around me. How long will it be until the grip tightens enough that I, too, will no longer be able to breathe? I hold my breath in anticipation of it being held for me. Then, slowly, like the wail of a child that must penetrate the deepness of sleep to reach its mother's ears, I hear the roar of discontent. It builds in intensity as the rain begins again. The world gasps, then exhales and then begins to breathe again. I know the pattern of that breathing. I told you—I know the language of the crowd. The opposing team has scored after an interception thrown by Christian. The score is now 20 to 6.

I jump from my car and run toward the field. I run so fast it feels as if I am running in between the raindrops. Are my feet even touching the ground or am I being carried by the aural waves of anger that pour from the stadium? The opposing team has scored the extra point. The score is now 20 to 7.

I am allowed entrance into the crowded stadium. I do not have to push past anyone in the crowd because everyone is in their seats. I find myself standing against a rail, watching a battle take place beneath a deluge that is incapable of slowing or stopping it.

I look up at the scoreboard and it confirms what I had been able to ascertain just by listening. The score is 20 to 7. It is the fourth quarter and there are less than three minutes remaining on the clock.

I watch the kickoff and I watch us return the ball to our own forty-yard line. No one minds that I am standing in front of him or her because the entire stadium is now on its feet. Christian steps out onto the field. I want to look away, but I can't. He lines up and takes the snap. There are two receivers he can throw the ball to, but I, along with the rest of the stunned crowd, look on as he ignores both; instead he focuses downfield, where no man visibly stands. He brings his arm back and readies the ball, then throws it into the direction he was looking, as if the football were a bullet and he were trying to shoot someone. The projectile is snatched from the air by the first person able to reach it, and that is not someone in a Lago High football uniform. Don't anyone breathe. Don't anyone move. Close your eyes and if you do not watch it happen then it couldn't have occurred. Or shouldn't have. Touchdown. The score is now 20 to 13. Christian should be walking off the field as teams prepare for the extra point, but he stands, transfixed, looking in the same direction he flung the costly pass. I watch as Murdoc walks over and whispers something in Christian's ear. It is only then that Christian removes himself from the football field.

The other team does not attempt an extra point. Instead, they go for the two-point conversion. The score is now 20 to 15.

I look around the entire stadium, unsure what I am searching for. What was Christian looking at? Who was Christian looking at? Is it or he still here? Lago High takes the field for what could be the last time. The rain stops. Even those above want an unobscured view. How special Christian must feel to have God's undivided attention. Did he not realize that once you've made friends with the devil, God's attention is not necessarily something you want?

We are returning the ball after the kick. The stadium gets louder with every yard we gain. By the time we are stopped at our own ten-yard line, I am almost deaf.

First down, and though Christian seems completely focused, there's no man open. He must throw the ball away purposely this time. It is now second and goal. The time on the clock is fifty-four seconds. A touchdown will be the win even without the extra point.

The ball is snapped and Christian steps back. I don't know why, but my eyes race around the stadium. Christian's body stalks the field, stopping upon a receiver that is wide-open. Victory and a life he will never deserve are but a ten-yard pass away, so why does Christian drop back, as if he is being charged, and throw the ball to no one? Where there should have been cheers and a celebration, there is only the sound of rage, and it resonates with venom that is most deadly when coming from the mouths of the young.

We call the last time-out and the coach marches out onto the field to speak with Christian. I do not celebrate, for twenty seconds remain on the clock, and even I know that all Christian needs to do is take the snap, drop to his knee and allow the clock to run out. The crowd knows this, as well, and this may be the only reason Christian is still alive. The coach storms off the field and the teams get into position for the last play of the game.

The final snap... Christian now has his hands on the football. I have told you, Christian is always holding a football. Christian goes to take the kneel, and there are some that will tell you that he hops up instead; there are some that will tell you that it looks as if he is lifted up, prevented from kneeling. I will tell you that for a fraction of a second, I saw both of his feet off the ground.

"Take the knee!" the crowd yells. Christian stands there, frozen.

Boom! Christian is on the ground, hit by a defensive end who should never have had the opportunity to reach him. A collective gasp as the ball rolls free of Christian's grasp and is picked up by a lineman, who then completes a run that makes sure the championship trophy remains free of Christian's grasp, as well.

The score is 21 to 20. Final.

I smile, not because we lost the game. I don't want to be someone who rejoices in another's sadness. I smile because I knew Brandon had not listened to me.

Boo

As you sit and stare like you've seen a ghost
what continues to haunt you?
Is it the friends that pass you by as if they were at your funeral?
Do you wonder why they can't hear you breathing?
Maybe it's because you're still holding your breath.
Do you want to reach out from the casket you lay in, lined with
regret, and scream that you're alive?
Or are you better off perceived as dead?
You are, aren't you?
Dead?
Are you not now in your father's eyes?
How does it feel to be orphaned at such an age?
How will it feel the first time you sit down at the table and eat with
two people that don't know you're there?
Or care?
Can you hear your father screaming from here?
The whole town can.
Why don't you ask them what he's saying?
Or do you already know?
Are you still holding your breath?
It doesn't matter.
Your father still knows where you are.
What did that ghost whisper in your ear?

Was it something bad?
Did it scare you?
Will you make a girl scream to drown out your own screams?
Will you make her say things
repeat things
like you repeatedly lost the game?
Will it still feel the same?
Is your hand as heavy as your guilt?
Is that why you couldn't throw the ball?
Did you not see the guy waiting to catch it?
He saw you.
So who did you see?
What was he wearing?
A uniform?
Or was he unadorned?
Do ghosts wear jewelry?
What do they whisper in your ear to distract you when you should be
paying attention to something else… like that guy waiting to catch
the ball you should have thrown by now?
That receiver won't ever wait on you again.
Maybe you will wait on him
while he's standing in a fast-food restaurant line.
Would you like fries with that?
I said would you like fries with that?
Would you?
Do you wish that you had paid better attention in class so that you
wouldn't have to ask that question?
You do realize you will have to get a job.
No one is going to pay you to play anymore.
And even if they do, you will find that you can't perform.
You can't perform.
You can't perform.
What did I say?

I said you can't perform.
Is that why you force it?
Will you ever be able to walk the length of a football field and not
think about how you failed?
Will you ever be able to step back onto a football field? If you do,
don't you think that ghosts will be there?
Are you scared?
Not like the movie Twilight,
instead
don't you have real fright?
Don't you?
I said don't you?
You should.
Because nothing you ever do will be good.
Nothing will.
I said nothing...
And as you sit there looking like you've seen a ghost,
when the devil sees you first
I wonder if he will think he is looking at his own reflection?

The Apologizing Sky

The sky at night is so pretty after it rains and the clouds choose to remain as pillows for the moon. Is that the cloud's apology for tearing up the sky? A soft place for the moon to rest its head? Do you wonder if the moon ever accepts the apology? If the moon ever lays its head down to rest? If it does, is that when just a sliver of the moon lights the sky so the world doesn't go completely dark? Or when the moon gives only that amount, is it trying to plunge the world into darkness because the apology is not enough? Is that sliver that remains to light the sky at night then the only part of the moon unable to hold on to anger? Is that tiniest bit of forgiveness salvation, or is it pity? Which one is more saved, the one who receives forgiveness or the one who gives it?

The distance from the field where the game was held to the abandoned church is approximately nine miles. It is nine miles that Jai chose to walk in the rain instead of remain at the game. For all that Jai has done, those things admitted and the ones still secret, is nine miles enough of a distance to compose a proper apology? But he is going to try, and that is why he finds himself standing beneath a sleeping sky in front of a building that has been unable to close its eyes.

Jai recites a passage under his breath as he walks up to the door.

"Even though I walk through the valley of the shadow of death I will fear no evil..." Jai crosses the door into the church, then completes his thought. "Because I have made friends with it."

"There's no one here to confess to, Jai," Gabriel says as he appears from the back of the church. "There hasn't been for a long time."

"Is it my turn now?" Jai asks.

"Your turn for what?"

"Vengeance."

Gabriel walks toward Jai. Jai has to wonder if that is the answer to his question.

"Avenge not yourselves, beloved, but give place unto the wrath of God, for it is written, vengeance belongeth unto me, I will recompense, saith the Lord."

Gabriel stands directly in front of Jai.

"I'm not the Lord, Jai. I'm just a teenager."

"I'm sorry," Jai responds.

"Sorry for what?"

"Don't you know?"

"No. I don't, Jai. Is there something you want to tell me?"

Jai reaches into his pocket and removes the iPod, the same iPod that he is never without.

"I want you to have this. I mean, I want Brandon to have it."

"Brandon can't use it where he is."

"It's an iPod," Jai says.

"I know what it is, Jai."

"It cost me three hundred dollars," Jai continues. "I paid for it with money that Christian gave to me."

"Why would Christian give you money, Jai?"

Jai pauses. Gabriel waits for his answer.

"I don't want it anymore."

"Why would Christian give you money?" Gabriel repeats. Jai still has the iPod extended to Gabriel, but Gabriel will not take it into his hand.

"Christian told me he just wanted to talk to Liv," Jai says. "I didn't know he was going to do anything else."

Gabriel does not give Jai the respite of a reply. Jai waits for it until he knows it isn't coming.

"I thought he just wanted to talk."

Gabriel's silence begins to echo throughout walls that should not be able to contain an echo.

"Brandon, please… take it."

"Brandon is dead," Gabriel says.

"But—"

"He's dead, Jai."

"He's not coming back?" Jai asks.

"He can't."

Jai slowly lowers the iPod to his side. He stands silent for a moment, like a secret that no one wants to hear. Slowly he turns and walks toward the exit. Jai speaks while continuing to walk away from Gabriel. "Is this my vengeance?" There is no response.

Jai stops and turns back around. Gabriel is gone.

Color and Conclusions

"You look like you've seen a ghost," Murdoc says as he leans down to a statue-still Christian. Murdoc is the only person to remain in the locker room with Christian, who has remained seated in his own refuge since the end of the game. Murdoc's comment begs Christian to look up.

"You saw him, too?" Christian asks.

"Saw who?" Murdoc responds.

"Gabriel," Christian says, his eyes pleading for Murdoc to answer yes.

"Gabriel? Where?"

"On the field! You saw him on the field?"

"Are you high?" Murdoc spits out. "What are you talking about?"

Christian leaps up and is now eye to eye with Murdoc.

"Gabriel! Did you see Gabriel on the field?" Christian screams.

"No!" Murdoc yells back. "All I saw was you blowing the game!"

"I didn't blow anything," Christian argues. "Gabriel was on the field. I saw him. He kept getting in my way. I was trying to hit him, but it's like the ball went right through him."

The confusion in Murdoc's eyes quickly transforms to pity. "There was no one on the field but players. Mainly our players! And that's who you should have been trying to hit. You blew it,

271

dude. The perfect season, the championship, and if you think any of the colleges are still interested in you, then you're crazy. Crazier than you sound right now."

Murdoc turns to walk away, but Christian grabs him by the arm and spins him around.

"I know what I saw! He was on the field. I saw him."

Murdoc looks into Christian's eyes.

"Do you see him now?" Murdoc asks.

"No," Christian answers.

"You sure?"

Christian looks around even though he knows he doesn't have to.

"Yeah. I'm sure. Why?"

"Because even if you don't see them, ghosts always see you. So you're more fucked than you think you are. See ya around, buddy."

Christian looks on as Murdoc turns once again and begins to walk away. Murdoc gets farther this time, almost out of the locker room before Christian calls out to him.

"So that's it? You're out?"

"Yeah. This is the part of the movie where we go our separate ways. Only the way I'm going is up."

"Really?" Christian asks.

"Yeah," Murdoc says. "Really. *I* didn't fall apart out there on the field tonight. You did. My stats are intact, brotha. So unless you know something I don't…"

"Yeah. Actually I do know something which apparently you've forgotten," Christian says as he walks up to Murdoc. "I know you've done everything I have. With almost everyone I have. Yeah," Christian continues. "I know your heart is as black as your skin and I know that don't wash off."

"So. What if it don't?"

Christian steps even closer to Murdoc, as close as he possibly can without touching him.

"So? So if there are ghosts watching me, that means they're watching you, too," Christian says. "Which means you're more fucked than me, because in the movies, the black guy never makes it to the end. Brotha."

The Memory of Glass

Murdoc walks from the stadium towards the parking lot where his Cadillac Escalade is parked. All other vehicles and their occupants have abandoned the area. Murdoc's bag of gear is slung over his shoulder and his keys are in his hand, but one thing is missing. He should have been leaving to cheers, instead the noise of self-satisfaction has to substitute in his head.

"Vodka…"

Murdoc stops. Vodka? Was that the word he just heard from a disembodied voice as if spoken by someone months ago and just reaching his ears now? Murdoc half looks around as he hovers for a moment. One… Two… Three. Murdoc begins toward his vehicle again.

"Would you like some vodka?"

Murdoc freezes. This time he is sure of what he has just heard if not exactly certain from whom and, more importantly, why.

Murdoc drops his bag of gear and looks around him, turning the circumference of a circle with the halting movement of someone afraid of ending up back where they began.

"Christian," Murdoc yells.

"I said you look like you want some vodka."

This time Murdoc spins around faster and yells louder. "Christian!" Again, there is no answer, but there are more words…

274

"This one's on me."

Murdoc is now less concerned with finding out the source of the voice than with escaping it. He races for his car, faster than he has ever run on a field, leaving his bag on the ground behind him.

Murdoc makes it to his car, but someone or something has been there before him. All four of his aftermarket Goodyear MTR tires are flat. Murdoc purchased those special tires himself with money he took from other students. He walks around the entire car to confirm what he already knows. He then clutches his keys and looks out into the darkness at what he doesn't know.

"I didn't do anything," Murdoc screams. How is it possible a person can lie like that when they are essentially talking to themselves? You never have to tell a mirror what you've done; it already knows. Even if you break the glass, the memory remains within every shard, waiting to cut you once you think you have sufficiently swept it all away. Murdoc is shattering into thousands of pieces at this moment and every one of them knows what he's done.

Murdoc leans his head against the passenger door of his car and closes his eyes. Again he hears a voice, a voice this time calling out his name.

"Murdoc…"

Murdoc opens his eyes and sees the reflection of Gabriel in the driver's side window, standing behind him.

"Catch, Murdoc!"

Murdoc turns around and brings his hands up to his face as if expecting something to be coming towards it, something that can do as much damage as the truth often can. "I didn't do anything," he cries.

Glass never forgets…

Death Is the Errand and the Fate

"So," begins Christian. "You finally make it over to see my house?" He is talking to Brandon, who stands across the length of the pool in Christian's pool house. Both Murdoc and Russel are standing on either side of Christian. As for Christian, he chooses to remain seated in the deck chair, reclined in the manner an emperor might, drunk on his own delusion. There is a football in his hand that he tosses in the air as he speaks to Brandon. Brandon is there breaking the last promise he made to me. Never make promises in the desert. There's not enough of anything to keep them alive.

"You didn't bring Liv," Christian continues. "I guess it doesn't matter. She's already seen it. Right, Murdoc?"

"I know she's seen your bedroom," Murdoc offers. All three laugh.

"Yeah. She saw it from more than one angle," Christian stabs.

The heart pendant I gave Brandon only hours earlier hangs from his neck. He looks down upon it, then back up to Christian. "His vanity swelled him so vile and rank that he could hear no other voice but his own," Brandon begins to quote.

"What?" Russel asks for all three.

Brandon enunciates each next word so there will be no such confusion. "He deserved to suffer and die."

"What the hell are you mumbling about?" Murdoc asks. "I think you been out in the desert sun too long."

"It's from *Beowulf*."

"*Beowulf*?" Russel asks. "What's that, like, some monster movie?" Again, all three smile.

"Yeah." Brandon smiles, too. "Something like that."

"What do you want?" Christian asks. Brandon takes one step closer and Christian immediately rises from his chair.

Brandon stops. He is now about sixty feet away from Christian.

"I want to show you what happens to people like you. People who do the things that you do."

"Why don't you just tell me?"

Brandon takes a few steps closer. He is now about fifty-five feet away from Christian.

"They have seen my strength for themselves..." Brandon begins anew.

All three listen as Brandon takes a few more steps closer. He is now about fifty feet away.

"Have watched me rise from the darkness of war, dripping with my enemies' blood..."

Brandon steps closer. He is now forty-five feet away from Christian.

"I swam in the blackness of night, hunting monsters. Killing them one by one..."

Brandon steps closer for the last time. He is now forty feet away from Christian.

"Death was my errand and the fate, they had earned," he ends.

"I don't know why you're so mad," Christian now begins. "I did you a favor..." How can someone's words be viler than even the actions they imply? "I showed her everything." Why would you spit into someone's blood after you have impaled them? "And you know what?" Christian asks.

"What?"

"She showed me things, too. Great things," Christian continues. "Wild things."

"We wanted to show her some things, too," Murdoc taunts. "But she got all shy."

"I don't think your friends in prison will be shy," Brandon says.

"No one's going to prison because no one did anything." Christian smiles. "I know you'll find this hard to believe, but Liv went upstairs with me because she wanted to. She practically begged me to take her upstairs. Right, boys?"

"That's how I remember it," Russel says.

"She was begging for it," Murdoc adds. "Begging."

"Repeating a lie," Brandon says, "doesn't make it truth any more than doing something where no one can see you makes it right. You know what you did. And so will the police."

"You think so?" Christian asks. "The instant replay shows something different." Christian turns to Murdoc. "Murdoc, let's go to the tape."

Murdoc pulls his iPhone from his pocket and activates the voice-recording feature. A familiar voice pierces Brandon's ears. "I want to go upstairs with you, Christian."

"You bastard!" Brandon hurls toward Christian.

"Bastard?" Christian mocks. "That ain't very literary. Where's your fancy quotes now?"

"You forced her to say that," Brandon rightly states. "She's scared. I can hear it in her voice."

"You can?" Christian asks rhetorically. "That's not what I hear. Murdoc, let's go back to the tape."

Murdoc replays the voice memo.

"Doesn't sound like fear," Christian states. "Sounds like she can't wait. Play it again," Christian commands, and Murdoc obliges him.

Brandon turns to Murdoc. "Give me the phone."

Christian smiles as he continues tossing the football up into the air.

"Play it again," he yells to Murdoc. Murdoc plays it again.

"I wouldn't play it again if I were you," Brandon threatens.

"You're not me," Murdoc responds.

"You're right, Murdoc. He's not. So play it again."

Murdoc plays the voice recording again.

Brandon, only forty feet away from Christian and the others, moves to take the phone from Murdoc's hand. Before Brandon can take his first step, Christian calls out to him. "Brandon."

Brandon turns to Christian.

"Catch!" Christian screams, then hurls the football with all the strength in his arms and lack of compassion in his heart at Brandon. The football smashes into the side of Brandon's head, knocking him from his feet into the pool beside him. Brandon's body hits the surface of the water like a slap in the face, and then his body sinks beneath the water.

Why is it vultures never circle themselves? Are they too close to others' decay to smell their own rot? Christian, Murdoc and Russel all step to the side of the pool and look down upon Brandon's unconscious body.

"I thought he was supposed to be a good swimmer," Russel jokes.

"Well, he sure as hell can't catch a football," Christian says. "Russel," he commands. "Get College Boy out." Russel jumps into the pool to retrieve Brandon; then Christian turns to Murdoc. "Go get him something to drink. I'm sure he's going to be thirsty when he wakes up."

Murdoc does his master's bidding and leaves for the bar across the deck. Russel brings Brandon's body to the surface and Christian helps pull him from the grave he himself put Brandon in.

"I don't think he's breathing," Russel states, as Brandon lies motionless.

"Why don't you give him mouth-to-mouth?" Christian asks with no real concern.

"Do I look like I make out with guys?"

Christian kneels down and looks at Brandon's closed eyes. "Why don't you say something smart now, College Boy?"

Russel still stands, but he leans over Brandon's body, enjoying Christian's assault. "What was that book he was quoting from?" Christian asks no one in particular.

"I think it was *The Wolfman*," Russel states.

"No. No," Christian says. "It was something else."

"*Beowulf*," Murdoc corrects as he walks over with a full bottle of vodka in his hands.

"Yeah," Christian says, momentarily looking up. "That's it. *Beowulf.*" Christian looks back down at Brandon. "What would Beowulf say now?"

Christian takes his fist and pounds it down upon Brandon's chest. Brandon spits out water while simultaneously trying to breathe in air.

"He looks thirsty," Christian says, turning to look up at Murdoc. "Don't you think?"

"He definitely looks like he could use a drink." Murdoc laughs. Murdoc unscrews the top on the bottle of vodka. He tosses the top to the floor and looks down at Brandon. "Would you like some vodka?" Brandon continues to spit up water and gasp for air. "You look like you want some vodka."

Brandon attempts to rise but is restrained by both Christian and Russel. Murdoc holds the bottle over Brandon's mouth. "This one's on me."

Murdoc pours the vodka straight into Brandon's mouth, choking Brandon even though he is no longer underwater. Brandon turns his head to the side in an attempt to spit out the substance, but Russel uses one hand to grab hold of his head and prevents him from expelling the poison. There are three of them, and they are strong.

"The strength in my beloved's heart is not physical.
It rarely is with those that dream.
And that is why those that create are the easiest to destroy.
Cursed be the architecture of life."

"Give him one on me," Christian urges. "I don't want him to think I'm a bad host."

"It's your party." And with those words Murdoc pours more vodka down Brandon's throat. "What does he care anyway? He's not driving."

"That's a good idea," Christian says.

"What?" Russel asks.

"Let's take our friend for a little drive."

That is how the four of them end up in a car. Murdoc driving his Hummer, Russel in the passenger seat and Christian in back, holding up Brandon, who watches the passing exterior while his interior slowly dims.

"Have another," Christian says, taking the bottle of vodka and pouring more down Brandon's throat, which has long ago surrendered its reflex and no longer struggles. Then Christian begins speaking to Brandon as if they are two long-lost friends on their way to a party or some mutual function where they will sit and reminisce.

"You know, Brandon," Christian begins. "I did know Liv first. Years before she ever met you. I don't know if she ever told you, but I was the one that stole a rock for her from a museum we went to when we were younger. I know what you're thinking, it's just a rock, but she wanted it and I was the one that got it for her. Who knows why girls like the things they do. I thought it was cool that she liked rocks. I liked rocks. So tell me... what gives you the right to come around years later with your stupid books and poems and take her away from me? You know what I don't like? Poems. I hate poems. They're stupid. Just because they rhyme I'm supposed to be impressed? A rock can smash your face in. Can words do that? I tried writing Liv a poem once and it turned out like shit. I can't even remember the stupid name. You know what I did with it? I buried it under a rock and then, and this is the really good part, I pissed on it."

Murdoc and Russel laugh from the front seats of the car.

"Do me a favor though," Christian continues. "Don't tell Liv—she'll think I'm insensitive. Hey, that kinda rhymed, didn't it? Maybe I could be a poet."

The car pulls around the back of Lago High to the indoor swimming pool. The locks on the door will prove no match for brute intent. In moments they are inside.

"I think this may be the first time I've been in here," Murdoc says as he and Russel enter the pool area.

"I know it's the first time I've been in here," Russel adds.

"One of you want to help me with our friend here? He seems to have had too much to drink," Christian says.

Murdoc and Russel take hold of Brandon from both sides and hold him up with Brandon's back to the edge of the pool.

Christian steps up to Brandon and lifts Brandon's head up so that he can look Brandon in eyes.

"How long can you hold your breath?" Christian asks.

"Come closer," Brandon says.

"Why?"

"I want to tell you something."

"More quotes?" Christian hazards. He then takes a step closer to Brandon, and, though Brandon speaks directly to Christian, Murdoc and Russel hear, as well. "I'm listening," Christian tells Brandon.

"When you reach for the sky," Brandon begins, "the stars will laugh at my behest... and angels will look away from the dispensing of my wrath."

There is a stab of silence before Christian has the nerve to ask, "Who said that?"

"I did," Brandon responds.

"Push him in," Christian commands.

Russel looks at Brandon, and Brandon stares back into Russel's eyes.

"How long can you hold your breath?" Russel asks before he releases hold of Brandon. Before Brandon can steady himself, Murdoc pushes him backward into the pool. Splash. Brandon's body immediately sinks to the bottom. His eyes remain open as his spirit escapes in tiny bubbles that rise to the surface of the water and release Brandon's last breaths.

"His eyes are still open," Murdoc says.

"So what?" Christian asks. "He's dead."

Christian walks away with Russel as Murdoc stands and stares at Brandon's eyes through the water and the darkness.

You Were Like One of the Little Boys
Playing around Us

I don't know that a night has comforted my body with sleep without also tormenting my head with what Brandon's last thoughts were as he drowned. I do know the dream that sometimes overtakes the nightmare. It is Brandon, telling me what his last thoughts were as we sit across from each other in the exact setting it took place. So here I am again, looking across at Brandon, at a table in a children's game room, with the disembodied voices of children running around us.

"I remembered our first kiss," Brandon says.

I smile.

"Do you remember where our first kiss was?"

"Of course I do, Brandon," I tell him. "Every girl remembers her first kiss. Especially if it was from their first love."

"Where was it?"

"Don't you believe me?"

"Of course I do." He smiles. "I just like hearing you say it."

"Chuck E. Cheese."

Brandon laughs. I want to laugh, too, but my eyes tell him to stop it.

"I'm sorry."

"It's OK," I say. "You were the one that worked there."

"I know," he tells me. "At least I didn't have to wear the rat costume."

"If you had worn the rat costume, I think I would have kissed you earlier."

"You're not funny."

"A little?"

"Yes, Liv. A little," he says. "Do you remember what we were talking about?"

"I remember that it wasn't actually a date. You were working and you sat down with me during your break."

"I bought you pizza."

"No. You took half a pizza from the table behind us while the kid was playing Skee-Ball."

"Oh yeah... I didn't like that kid."

"Neither did I," I add.

"I did buy us the sodas."

"I think you got those free."

"Yeah. You may be right. I did. Wow. I was a horrible date."

"No. Not at all. You held a woman's baby while she played a game with her four-year-old. That was sweet. You also almost tripped when you rushed to save your coworker in the rat costume from some child who was punching her. Very sweet. And if I remember correctly, you did get the kid from the table behind us another pizza when he came back. And free tokens."

"I just wanted to get rid of him so we could talk."

"I know. That was the sweetest thing of all."

"We talked about our favorite movies. Yours was *Breathless*, by Godard, which I thought was odd for someone so young."

"I thought you liked the film."

"I did. But a black-and-white film from the French New Wave about ill-fated lovers? I mean, Liv."

"Never watch movies with your dad. Your taste will eventually become his. I remember your favorite. The way you smiled when you mentioned the title. You were like one of the little boys playing around us. But I think you were more excited than any of them."

"That's because it's such a cool movie."

"Yeah. That was the word you used, over and over and over again. Cool."

"Incredibly cool. So ahead of its time. And the themes it explores. Who are we? Why are we here? How long do we have? And the soundtrack! And the photography!"

"You're sounding like one of the little boys playing around us."

"Is that bad?"

"No. I love it. And I love *Blade Runner*. And you are right. It is a stunningly gorgeous film and there is no other like it."

"The villain! Roy Batty!"

"Yes. Rutger Hauer."

"The coolest villain ever!"

"There's that word again. I remember you being this excited. It's like I'm sitting with you in the booth. I can't hear any of the noise from the children or the games because your voice won't allow the intrusion. Your enthusiasm begs my complete attention and I surrender it. You were saying about Roy Batty?"

"To feel so sympathetic to someone that must do horrible things because he was made into a monster."

"He just wanted to live, to be with the girl he loved."

"His soliloquy before he dies, the beauty in the last line. 'All those moments will be lost in time... like...'"

"Tears in rain," I say.

"That's right. You knew it. You finished it for me, Liv."

"That's when you kissed me."

"Yes. That's what I remembered as I lost my breath, Liv. I remembered our first kiss."

The dream always ends the same. By returning to a nightmare.

"I'm sorry," Brandon says.

"Why?" I ask.

"Someone is telling me to close my eyes."

"Why?"

"Because I'm dying. Remember?"

That is when the laughter of the children around us stops.

"Oh. Yeah," I say.

"Do you think ghosts are monsters?" he asks as he rises from the table.

"No, Brandon," I tell him. "I think monsters create the need for ghosts."

Brandon turns and begins to walk away...

Watermelon Feet

And then, as if Brandon is aware that I could never wake from a nightmare so cruel, he stops and turns, then walks back to me. He kneels at my feet and takes my hand with his.

"I want to tell you," he begins, "my favorite things I will learn about you before I'm gone."

"OK," I say. My hand trembles for more reasons than my skin can comprehend.

"You wear contact lenses, but when your eyes get sore, like when you forget to take them out at night, you wear your glasses the next day. You hate your glasses. Your mom picked them out for you when you were younger and you think they look stupid. You could not be more wrong. You still have your pink Barbie Big Wheel you got for your fourth birthday. You kept it because you want to give it to the daughter you want to have. You want to name your daughter Ridley. If you have a boy, you will still name him Ridley. You're a vegetarian, though not vegan. Eggs and cheese are your favorite breakfast. You have not always been a vegetarian. You stopped eating meat at age seven. Chicken tenders were the last meat you ate and the hardest for you to give up. You enjoyed eating them with your father when you two would go to fast-food places on the weekends. You love animals. All animals. Horses are your favorite. You saw a dead horse alongside the road when you were nine as your dad was driving back from a carnival. You have never gone to another carnival. When you were ten, you cut off your very long hair and donated it to Locks of Love. You own six pairs of shoes, though I have only seen you wear two pair. Your favorite pair are your red Chuck Taylors. Your second favorite is a pair of green ones. Every now and again when the mood hits you, you will create a third pair from the two by wearing one red and one green at the same time. The left foot always has to have the red shoe on, never the green. You would never tell me why. You would also never explain your love for the band Duran Duran. I'm not certain which of the five members is your favorite, but I do know your favorite song by them, 'The Chauffer.' You are afraid of spiders but once owned a pet snake. You also owned a pet rat after you decided you could not feed it to the snake."

Brandon rises while never letting go of my hand."You named the snake Tristan, and you named the rat Isolde."

Brandon releases hold of my hand and leans down so that we stare into each other's eyes.

"I can't tell you anything else that says more about why I love you," Brandon continues, "than the selfless poetry of that act."

"Brandon…" I say.

"I really have to go now. He's telling me to close my eyes again."

Brandon has never said this in my dream. And as he turns and disappears, I wonder where he is going and wish that I could follow.

The Road That Begs Collision

"Close your eyes!" Murdoc repeats as he opens his own and finds himself in the present, leaning against his Escalade and screaming to no one. He calms as he hears the sound of a car coming toward him from the distance. He moves away from his own car and steps out toward the road to identify the oncoming vehicle. It is not until the car is nearer, then stopped beside him, that he recognizes the driver.

"Noodle." Murdoc sighs.

"It looks like you need a ride home," Jai says as he looks over at the four deflated tires that anchor Murdoc's Escalade to its parking space.

"No shit," is Murdoc's reply. Then, without further invite, Murdoc opens the car door and steps inside Jai's rusted but running '78 Firebird.

"Don't you want your bag?" Jai asks.

"Just get me the hell out of here," Murdoc barks.

Jai puts the car in Drive, swings it back around toward the road and takes off into the darkness.

"I don't think you've ever been in my car," Jai says.

"Look at it," Murdoc states. "Why would I? I drive an Escalade. No need for me to be seen riding around in this."

"Some people consider it a classic."

"Yeah. A classic piece of shit."

"I know it needs some work, but not everyone can have cars given to them."

Murdoc looks over to Jai, attempting to discern whether he is being mocked. Jai quickly puts his mind at ease.

"Not that you didn't deserve it."

"You're goddamned right I deserved it," Murdoc snaps.

"I consider it an honor to take you home," Jai says, and this time Murdoc is sure he is being mocked, but he doesn't care. He's on his way home.

The road is empty. Jai gently steps on the gas. The car is traveling at sixty miles per hour.

"Do you even know where I live?" Murdoc asks.

"That was a tough game tonight," Jai says, ignoring Murdoc's question altogether.

"What?"

"The game," Jai repeats. "It must have been tough losing it like that after winning all the others. Now you don't have a perfect season."

"Shut up, Noodle," Murdoc shouts. Jai slowly steps down upon the gas pedal more. It is so subtle that the increase in speed is unnoticed. The car is now traveling at sixty-five miles per hour.

"Noodle," Jai says.

"Yeah," Murdoc says.

"Why do you guys call me that?"

"Why do you think we call you that?"

"I guess," Jai begins, "'cause I do everything you guys tell me to."

"Yeah," Murdoc responds smugly. "Weak ass."

"That's not my name, either," Jai says under his breath. Jai then steps on the gas a bit more. Murdoc doesn't notice, but the car is now going seventy miles per hour in the darkness.

"What did you say?" Murdoc asks. Jai turns to him, momentarily taking his eyes from the road.

"I said, that's not my name, either. Weak ass." Jai turns back to the road and accelerates. "My name is not Noodle." The car is now going seventy-five miles per hour. Murdoc is suddenly aware of the rate of speed the conversation is occurring at. "And my name is not weak ass, either."

"Slow down," Murdoc commands.

"What?" Jai smiles.

"I said, slow down."

"Don't you want to get home?"

"Slow down!" Murdoc yells. Jai chooses to accelerate even more. The car is now traveling in the dark at eighty miles per hour.

"Oops," Jai feigns. "I think I went up instead of down."

"Noodle, if you don't slow this car down, I swear I'm gonna-"

"You're gonna do what?" Jai interrupts as he turns once again to Murdoc. "If you do anything, you're gonna crash the car. So I think you're gonna sit there and do nothing."

Jai accelerates more. The car is now traveling at eighty-five miles per hour. Jai turns to Murdoc. "Now who's the weak ass?" Murdoc does not respond. Jai turns his eyes back to the road.

"It's funny. You guys have called me Noodle for so long I wonder if you remember what my real name is?"

"Jai. It's Jai," Murdoc says somewhat desperately. "Now slow the car down."

"Jai's my first name," Jai says, focusing intently on the road. "I mean my full name."

"Full name?" Murdoc asks as if he has just been asked an algebra question, not realizing the question will actually be tougher.

"Yeah. Full name. As in first, middle and last."

"How the hell am I supposed to know that?" Murdoc snaps.

"Because you've known me for twelve years. We went to school together for twelve years. You must have heard my name called a thousand times during class. I know yours. Murdoc. Murdoc Calvin James." Jai turns back to Murdoc, taking his eyes from the road and looking into Murdoc's frightened own. "See. Now it's your turn."

"I give up. I don't know. What is it?"

"You haven't even tried," Jai taunts.

"I don't know it!"

"That's not good, Murdoc Calvin James," Jai intones as he accelerates. The car is now traveling at ninety miles per hour. The darkness is whipping by so fast there is almost an incandescent glow that lights it.

"Tell you what," Jai begins. "Because I'm such a nice guy I'll give you my middle name."

Murdoc braces one arm around the back headrest of his seat as he faces Jai; his other arm is extended to the dash, where his right hand grips the edge of it in anticipation of an impact.

"Cool! Cool! What is it?"

"Thelonius," Jai answers. "As in Thelonius Monk. He was a jazz pianist. Pretty famous, too. I'm surprised you couldn't remember that. I guess you're not a jazz fan."

"Thelonius."

"Yeah. Thelonius. Only one name to go."

There is silence in the car, save the sound of the road beneath tires that beg for a collision.

"Well?" Jai asks. Murdoc says nothing. "If I go faster, will that help your memory?"

"No. No …"

"I'm not so sure it won't. Why don't we see," Jai offers as he accelerates even more.

The car is now traveling at ninety-five miles per hour. Jai turns to Murdoc. "For a piece of shit, this thing really hauls ass, doesn't it?"

"Jones? Is it Jones?" Murdoc desperately guesses.

"Jai Jones? That doesn't even sound right. Do I need to go faster?"

"Jackson! It's Jackson!" Murdoc panics.

"You're stuck in the Js. Get out, man. Get out," Jai says with an almost maniacal grin.

"Lawrence. Smith. Williams. Jones."

"You said Jones already."

Jai accelerates. The car is now traveling in excess of one hundred miles per hour.

"I don't know what it is! I don't know. Now slow the car down before you kill us both!"

"I wish I could, but I promised to take you home," Jai says as he floors the gas and the car begins accelerating beyond realms of sense or safety. There is terror in Murdoc's eyes; there is the search for redemption in Jai's.

"When we get to hell," Jai tells Murdoc with a smile, "make sure you tell the devil I drove us there."

The speedometer has redlined. The car struggles to maintain a straight line, and the tires are separating from the road as it becomes airborne, almost attempting to divorce itself from the fate the road wishes to marry it to. The car slowed momentarily, as if by a wind traveling twice as fast in the opposite direction. Jai looks out of his driver's side window and sees Gabriel standing on the side of the road. Their eyes lock as the car passes Gabriel. Jai slams on the brakes but is traveling so fast that the car skids for another hundred yards, the length of a football field, before coming to a halt. Both Jai's and Murdoc's bodies jerk forward, then back as if they were crossing over to the other side but then were told, not yet.

"I'm gonna kill you," are the words Murdoc says even as he came closer than those 14 letters to death himself. Murdoc reaches for Jai, but before he can put a hand upon him, he himself is pulled through the passenger side window by the hand of Gabriel.

Gabriel throws Murdoc down onto the side of the road as Jai exits the car.

Gabriel moves with deliberate steps toward Murdoc, who scampers on the ground like a scorpion walking backward.

"Stay away from me," Murdoc begs as he stops and looks up from the ground.

"But we haven't had our drink yet," Gabriel says as he stops and towers over Murdoc.

"I don't want a drink."

"Neither did I."

"I don't know what you're talking about," Murdoc lies. He has yet to understand the nature of things before him. Gabriel remains silent. "I didn't," Murdoc cries.

As Murdoc looks up at Gabriel, the sky behind Gabriel, vast and black, makes it seem as if he is standing at the gates of purgatory. How long Murdoc remains there depends upon his ability to find the truth within himself.

"Who are you?" Murdoc asks.

Gabriel stares at Murdoc with an intensity that slowly reminds Murdoc that he has seen this stare once before, beneath a pool of water that reflected all his sins.

"No. No. It can't be," Murdoc pleads.

"Nothing can be until it is," Gabriel says. "Nothing is until you allow it." Gabriel kneels before Murdoc. They are now eye to eye. "You allowed this."

"I don't even know you."

"You never did," Gabriel says. "But your actions bound us like brothers. And I was reborn with the blood you spilled. Blood that is brother to the blood on your hands. I am the consequence of your actions. I am the personification of the guilt you should feel. I am the revelation from which you cannot turn away."

"No," Murdoc cries, but Gabriel is not done.

"Your eyes will burn in the fire of truth and only my forgiveness can wash away your tears."

Gabriel rises. Murdoc looks up at him as if he were looking into the eyes of his creator even though it is his creation that looks back at him.

"You're should be dead."

"If you can see the dead," Gabriel tells him, "then they can see you. What are you going to do to make them forget your name?"

"Tell me?" Murdoc begs. "Tell me what to do."

Gabriel extends his hand down to Murdoc. Murdoc stares at it as his own hand trembles like a leaf upon a restless branch.

"Take my hand," Gabriel commands. "I need you to do something for me."

Murdoc takes Gabriel's hand and is lifted to his feet. He takes a fearful step backward. "What if I don't want to?" he asks.

"Then you will continue to see dead people, until it haunts you so much that you forget you're alive."

At long last there is understanding in Murdoc's eyes. "What do you want me to do?"

Gabriel leans in and whispers something into Murdoc's ear. Murdoc's expression dances from confusion to fear and then back to confusion, like a dancer doing an unsteady twirl in front of a mirror.

Gabriel steps back when he is done.

"Where will I get what I need?" Murdoc asks.

"It's already there. It's waiting for you," Gabriel says.

Murdoc looks at Gabriel, then slowly turns and looks at Jai, who stands but a few feet away.

"Davis," Jai says. "My last name is Davis."

"Yeah," Murdoc says. "I remember now."

Murdoc turns back to Gabriel. Gabriel hands Murdoc the keys to his motorcycle.

"Go," Gabriel tells Murdoc. "You have things that must be done."

That which Defies the Fire

I am inside the abandoned church. This will be the last time I ever come. At the moment I am looking up at the sky through the wounds of the roof. I watch as the clouds in the sky slowly vanish and the stars give light to the night. Is someone attempting to watch me unobscured? Am I in danger? No. I have never felt safer as I sit upon one of the few pews whose wood defied the fire. I have come not to say goodbye to Brandon, but to Gabriel. Brandon will always be around me as long as the things that make up this world remain. I see his smile in the sun. I hear his voice in the wind. A child's laughter will recall his heart, so innocent, so pure and so strong. I will be unable to watch a bird take flight without thinking of his ambition. When I look out across the ocean, I will think of his soul, that which sustains life. If I ride across the sands, I will be reminded of how we held time in our hands. I will not hear music without wanting to dance with him. I will not see a sunset without wanting his kiss to make it more brilliant... Gabriel, if he does exist, and I did not dream him out of necessity or madness, I doubt that I will see again. The portion of his existence that might belong to Brandon I think can now rest. I think it is also time to let the portion that is Brandon find sleep, as well.

"Has he come yet?" I hear. I then turn around at the sound of a voice I once heard every day and I last heard telling me not to speak. Mrs. Green stands off to the side of me.

"Mrs. Green," I say. She slides into the row of pews and takes a seat beside me.

"Have you seen him?" she asks.

"Who?"

"Gabriel?" she says, then quickly corrects herself. "I mean Brandon. Did I miss him?"

"No," I tell her. "No one is here."

I am not sure why she now refers to Gabriel as Brandon given our last conversation, but she quickly volunteers why.

"I believe you," she says.

"About what?" I ask.

"Gabriel," she answers. "I believe you that he's Brandon. That Brandon came back."

"I don't know that he's Brandon, Mrs. Green," I correct her.

"Why don't you believe anymore?"

"I didn't say that…"

"I was there at the game," she tells me. "I'm not sure why I went, but I think it was partly because of the things you said, and the things I heard."

"What things?"

"Horrible things," she answers. "Things about Christen and things about Brandon. I know you've heard the whispers around town. They almost always have your name in them. Brandon was a good swimmer. He was an excellent swimmer. And he didn't drink. I understand power and influence. And I understand this town well enough now that I am sorry I ever moved my son here. Everyone in it is consumed by one thing, and they consume anyone that isn't like them. So when I saw—" Mrs. Green stops.

"Saw what?" I ask. "What did you see?"

"The same thing you saw," Mrs. Green tells me.

"What?" I beg.

"I saw Christian lifted from the ground," she says, and now I am beginning to understand.

"You saw it, right?" she asks.

"Yes," I say. "I saw it happen, too."

Mrs. Green embraces me as if I were Brandon. I can feel the wetness of her tears upon the side of my face and they almost compel me to weep. I sometimes forget that there is someone that had Brandon's heart first. That there is someone he loved before me and who returned that love. I forget that there is someone who understands my loss because theirs is greater. Now I am crying, too.

"I'm sorry I didn't believe you," Mrs. Green says as she breaks the embrace. "I wanted to, but—" I interrupt her.

"I know. But it's hard, because if you're wrong, it's like losing him all over again. I still don't know what to believe, Mrs. Green. I only know what I want to."

Mrs. Green looks around the remains of the church. Even in the darkness I can see her eyes, still shimmering with tears, fill with remembrance.

"It makes sense that he would come here. Even though it's the last place I ever wanted to come back to," Mrs. Green says. "You look around at what remains and it looks as if God abandoned this town, but the truth is, they ran him out, then set fire to this place so he would have no reason to ever come back."

"I can't tell you that Gabriel will come back here for you to talk to him, Mrs. Green. There may be no reason for him to. He may be gone for good."

"Did he say goodbye to you?"

"No," I say. "He didn't."

"Then I think he will come back. Maybe not here, maybe not now, but I know my Brandon and if he came back to you, he's not going to leave again without telling you goodbye." I wipe away my tears at the thought, at the hope. "If he does," she continues, "tell him I love him."

"I will," I tell her. And then I ask, "How did you know that I would be here?"

"Your mother told me," she answers. "She was also the one that told me that if you believed something, I should believe that it's true."

The Necessary Darkness

I am home for the first time since the end of tonight's game. I at first have trouble navigating my way through the house because it is completely dark save for the glow of a lamp that leads me towards the living room. Why do I not turn on another light to guide me? I knew when I stepped in there was a reason for the grayness of space. The atmosphere seemed purposeful. The dark seemed necessary. I wanted to find out why before I disturbed it.

I step into the living room, where my mother sits, reading beneath the light of the lamp that, though small, illuminates the entire room.

"You're home," my mother says to me as she looks up from her book.

"Yes," I say.

"Did you see Gabriel?"

"No."

"I'm sorry, sweetheart," my mother says. I step into the living room and stand directly in front of her. She looks up at me. It seems as if this one room is the world around us, and within the glow of fluorescence, we are the only two that exist. I stare down at my mom. "What's wrong?" she asks me.

"I want things to go back to how they were."

"What things?" she asks me.

"Everything, Mom."

"I don't understand," she says.

"I want Dad to be back with us. I want you two to be together again. I want Brandon back. I want him to be alive. I want to be the girl I was before—" I stop. I'm not sure why.

"Before what?" my mom asks.

"I want my life back before everything started to fall apart piece by piece. I want to be whole again."

"You are whole, Olivia," my mother says as she puts the book down upon the table that holds the lamp. "Things constantly change around us, but that doesn't mean you're changed."

"I am," I say, my voice rising in volume and emotion. "It's impossible not to be. How can you remain the same when everything around you changes?"

"Who you are inside only changes if you allow it to. I'm not different because your father isn't here anymore. Only the situation is."

"I don't care, Mom," I yell. "It's not what I was born into! It's not what I want! I didn't want Brandon to die! I don't want to have to move because he did! All of this change is pulling away pieces of me and I don't know who I am when I look in the mirror anymore. There isn't some seventeen-year-old girl staring back at me. I feel like I'm a hundred years old and I should be dead!"

My mother rises. "Don't say that, Olivia!"

"But it's how I feel," I cry. "Everything that's falling apart is pulling me apart and I just want to die because it hurts so bad."

My mother opens her arms to me, somehow sensing I was about to collapse towards her, and I do. She wraps her arms around me and stands there as a deluge of tears finally force themselves from my eyes.

"You can't die, Olivia. You can't," my mom says to me. "That would change me. Forever. I couldn't live without you."

"Then how am I supposed to live without Brandon?"

"Because you're stronger than me," my mother says. "Every child should be stronger than their parents and every parent should do everything they can to make sure they are."

"I don't think I am."

"Olivia. You're the strongest person I know. Your heart beats so fierce! I've dealt with so many people that have wasted the gift of life and you embrace it so much people believe you bring back the dead."

I pull my head from my mother's shoulder.

"Why does so much bad happen?"

"I don't know," my mother tells me. "When we're born to die, then maybe bad is our destiny. Maybe sometimes that destiny doesn't realize you're still alive, or maybe sometimes it's supposed to remind you that you are so when you finally do reach it, it doesn't appear so bad."

"I don't want you to hate me. I don't want you not to like the person I may become."

"Hate you?" my mother says with a tear in her eye that glistens in the necessary dark. "My love for you would never allow that."

I don't think I want to leave my mother. I don't think that I can.

Every Time I Am at Your Grave
a Piano Plays

I think the loneliest sound made by an instrument may be the single note played on a piano. Which note it is does not matter. The residency of the despair is in every key. Is there any other instrument that has a piano's ability to elicit disparate sounds from voices so closely together? The strings of a guitar have the space of torn lovers between them, but the keys of a piano are so closely related, the press of one gives sigh to the other. The single note of a piano is cold. The longer the note is held, the more ice is formed around it. The single note of a piano is the perfect bell to a eulogy. It is the last word spoken before the coffin is closed. It is the tear you shed every time you mourn.

If you put six lonely people in a room together, how many will remain lonely?

The curious thing about the sound of a single note played upon the piano is that, if you take that same lonely note and play five equally desperate notes after it, one after the other, the notes lose their ache and, though sadness remains, you are compelled to feel better by it. This is the dynamics of need. You feel less sad because what you needed was something to express your hurt. What the notes needed was someone's hurt to justify their sadness.

If you put six lonely people in a room and no one speaks, are they dead?

"Hi, Brandon…"

I do not feel sad standing alone at the foot of Brandon's grave. Though I suppose one is never alone in a cemetery. I would imagine that is when the souls of the departed are most restless, stirred by the presence above, thoughts of lying with their loved ones instead of alone, beneath the earth, probably ache the most. Do the dead sleep at all? Do they dream? And if they dream, how do they wake? Is that death, to dream of being someplace other than where you are but then never being able to awaken from the torture of knowing it's not true? Is the false happiness of a dream worse than the knowledge of a reality without any? Maybe it would be best if I came to his grave once a week and told him different stories. Stories about things we talked about doing or things we both know we wanted to do. Yes. I like that thought. That way he doesn't have to be stuck in one moment. He doesn't have to dream one dream. I will lead the dream, and my voice as I tell it will guide him to me. Once a week we will go anywhere other than here.

If you put six lonely people in a room and one of them wanted out, would the other five want him to stay?

"I wanted to tell you that I am not leaving. I'm going to stay here and finish out the year. I talked to my mom and things are going to be better between us…"

There are no lonely keys on a piano. They are all lonely. It is the ones you choose, and the succession in which you choose them, that determines whether the melody will bleed. I think that defines people, as well. The keys of a piano must be struck, we are struck every day, and it is the manner in which we are struck and the events that occur after that that decide whether we will bleed or simply play on.

"Your mother wanted me to tell you that she loved you. She misses you, too. I don't know if that will make you feel better where you are, or make it more difficult, but I know she would feel better knowing she got the chance to tell you."

Is it possible to say the wrong thing to the dead? Or do you think they would just be happy to have someone to speak to? What if they don't know they are dead until someone acknowledges it? Some people don't know they're alive until that happens. Is that the difference between the dead and those that are alive, the number of people who acknowledge them?

If you put six lonely people in a room and they begin to talk to each other, will they disappear from the room one by one?

"I hope it's OK if I come and see you once a week. I hope you like that. You don't have to do anything. I will do all the talking. You always told me I liked to talk. Remember? I hope you remember all the things we talked about doing. I do. And I will make sure we do them all. I even know some things you wanted to do that you don't know I know. We will do those, too. Maybe somehow you can tell me what day. Any day but Sunday."

There are notes from a piano that always resonate in my ears, and the sounds they make are continually sad, but the space that they need to occupy pushes out the grief to make room so I allow their melody. Nothing can fully remove sadness, but if you understand that, then you have already begun to rid yourself of grieving and that will enable you to go on living.

"Hi, Liv."

I know that voice… especially in the dark. Christian stands behind me.

If you put six lonely people in a room, and then you tell the devil where they are, how long before there are seven people in the room, and how soon before only one remains?

When the Dead Realize

I should expect to find monsters in graveyards, but I am still surprised when I turn around.

"Is he here?" Christian asks.

"Is who here?" I ask back.

"A graveyard is no place for games," he says to me with a presence in his eyes that swings back and forth like a pendulum between madness and rage. The difference is difficult to discern in the dark. "Brandon," Christian continues. "That's why you're here, right? You're going to meet Brandon and laugh about how he cost me the game. Am I right?"

I don't answer. I don't want to. I don't have to.

"I said, am I right?" Christian yells. I look in his eyes as the pendulum stops on rage.

"Why are you here?" I ask instead of answering.

"Because I knew you would be here. And I'm hoping your dearly departed boyfriend who likes to pretend he's other people will be here, too."

"Why?"

"Why?" Christian repeats.

"Yes," I say. "Why? What are you going to do? Will you try and kill him again?"

I should not have said that. The pendulum in Christian's eyes swings over to madness. I am unsure why, but I felt safer when they were inhabited by rage.

"Kill him again?" he asks. "That's an interesting idea. Is that possible? How would one go about doing that? In all the books you've ever read, has anyone ever killed someone twice?"

I say nothing.

"Well?" Christian persists. "I'm sure everyone here is dying to know."

Again I say nothing.

"Tell me!"

The rage is back. But there is no comfort in it for me this time.

"*The Iliad*," I say. "I think in *The Iliad*."

"The Iliad?"

"Yes."

"That's a book?"

"Yes. It's an epic poem. I think there are instances of characters that die twice."

"How?" Christian asks.

"I'm not sure," I tell him. "It's been so long since I read it."

"You read everything, don't you?" he asks.

"No. Not everything."

"*The Iliad?*" he repeats.

"Yes."

"Would I like it?"

"I don't know, Christian."

He steps closer to me. "Take a guess," he says. The pendulum in his eyes is uneasily still. I think it's best I answer. I don't like the manner in which his stare hovers.

"I think you would," I say.

"Why?"

"Because."

"Because why?"

"In Greek," I tell him, "the first word of the Iliad is *anger.*"

"That does sound like something I would like. Why were you unsure at first?"

"I don't know. I just was."

"Because it has poems?"

"It is a poem."

Christian steps closer to me. "I'm sorry," he says. "Because it is a poem. Is that better?"

"It's fine."

"Did you ever know I wrote you a poem?" he says. I am waiting for one of the deceased that surround me to realize one of their own has escaped. I am waiting for the dead to arise and take Christian back with them.

"No, Christian. I didn't know that."

"That's because I never told you."

"Why?"

"It was no good," he answers.

"How do you know that? You should have let me read it."

"Trust me," he says as his eyes swing back to madness. "It was no good."

Christian then does the oddest thing. He turns and begins slowly walking away from me. I remain silent, afraid that any sound might startle him from madness back to rage and he might realize he is leaving me. It doesn't matter. When he is about thirty feet away from me he stops and turns back around.

"I did, however, write you another one."

"Maybe," I say slowly, "one day I can read this one."

Christian smiles. I am not sure whether it contains rage or madness.

"Why don't I just recite it to you now?"

Christian begins reciting his poem as he simultaneously takes a step closer to me.

"I am standing amongst the dead

they surround me

they are all around me..."

He slowly walks towards me as he continues, but his pace is slower than when he was walking away from me.

"Dead people..."

Christian stops walking as he also stops reciting. He looks at me from across the distance and darkness.

"How do you like it so far?" he asks.

"I don't," I say.

"Maybe you have to hear more. Where was I? Oh yeah, dead people..."

Christian begins again, both reciting and walking closer to me at a threateningly slow pace.

"There's a pretty girl in the distance

why are you so far away pretty girl?

Are you afraid I'm going to hurt you?

I'd think you would be more afraid of dead people."

"I don't want to hear anymore," I tell Christian. He stops.

"I thought you liked poems."

"This isn't a nice one. I want to go home."

"You can't go home again. Didn't someone famous say that? I'm sure I heard that somewhere. Who was it?"

"I don't want to do this again, Christian. I just want to go home."

"Liv..." Christian says, drawing out my name like a threat that cannot find you.

"Thomas Wolfe," I say.

"I knew you would know," Christian says. "I think you're so smart. I wish I was as smart as you. OK. Only a few more verses, then I'm done."

I swallow and it stops midway down my throat.

"Smile," Christian says. "It gets nicer."

I complete the swallow. Christian begins walking toward me again. I know he will not stop this time until he has reached me.

"Do not be afraid pretty girl
I'm not going to hurt you
I need you
to help me lure a ghost
back from the dead
so I can kill him again
and then I'm going to kiss the pretty girl…
Whether she wants me to or not."

Christian is now standing directly in front of me. There is no more pendulum sway in his eyes. It lays dead center between rage and madness.

"See," he says. "I told you it gets nicer."

Lovers Can Only Get to Hades
in a Pickup Truck

I look at the cemetery from the side-view mirror as we pull away. The farther away the truck gets from the dead, the less safe I feel. Gabriel never came. I never heard Brandon's voice. And those who lie in the sleep eternal never realized that one of their own had managed to wake and escape.

Christian sits beside me in the driver's seat of his pickup truck. His eyes are fixed upon the road before us. Or should I say the road before him. I am but a passenger.

Christian remains silent the entire drive, but it doesn't matter; I can hear his thoughts. They are horrible thoughts.

I can tell where we are by the things that we pass. I think that statement probably holds true about life, that you can tell where you are headed by the things that you pass. The skulls of dead animals line the road. I can also hear their thoughts. They are sad for me, even though they are the ones that lie dead.

As I pass them I look into the cavities where their eyes once were, but I have to look away, because I know they are also looking into mine. What am I afraid they will see? Or is it that I'm afraid they will recognize me? I have been down this road before. I feel like they are shaking their heads at me, judging me, disappointed in me. For a moment, as I continue into the night, I feel like I am one of them, a skull on the side of the road looking at me as I pass by, wanting to shed a tear for me, but unable to because I have no eyes.

I shut my eyes for the remainder of the drive. After a while I feel the pickup stop. I hear the familiar sound of gates opening. I think we are at Christian's home. I can tell by the locking sound that the gates are now completely open, so why is the car not moving forward? I open my eyes. I now know we are at Christian's home. Someone has taken red paint and painted the word *hell* over the doors of the entrance.

I close my eyes again… for I know I shall be entering soon.

The Brave Surrender

I have decided to be brave… What an interesting word, *brave*. It is such a short word for describing something so big. It only has one syllable, yet its definition requires many things. Brave. The word itself is very similar to *grave*. How many people have died not realizing this? I will be brave because I will not surrender, though it is somewhat ironic, because in this same place I was once brave by surrendering. This I now know of surrender … There are some surrenders that can happen only once. That is because surrender takes; it never gives. Some surrenders demand that you give all and that is the surrender you give. You may never be able to surrender again. If you do, then it becomes compliance. Once compliance becomes a part of your soul, that soul is no longer yours. I have decided to be brave… so I do not surrender my soul.

Christian turns on the light to his pool house. The entire space has been prepared. A long table holds a buffet of fresh fruits, meats and drinks. There is a bar with bottles of both liquor and champagne. Balloons and streamers adorn the chairs and walls. It is a reception bereft of joy. It is a banquet for the damned. A feast for the dead.

"Why did you do this?" I turn to Christian and ask.

"It's a welcome home party."

"For who?"

"For Brandon. Who else?"

"Christian," I say.

"Come in," he tells me. "Make yourself at home. I'm sure he'll be here soon."

I walk in. I have no choice. I stop at the end of the buffet table. Christian walks down to the other end before turning back around to me with the smile befitting a gracious host.

"Do you like?" he inquires.

"Where are your parents?" I ask.

"My dad had a trip planned for us right after the game. It was going to be a celebration gift. You know, for winning the championship. He and my mom went without me. That's why I had so much time to prepare all of this."

"I'm sorry, Christian."

"I didn't ask for you to be sorry," he says.

"I know," I tell him. "But I am anyway. They shouldn't have left you."

"Don't you fucking talk bad about my parents!" Christian explodes.

"That's not what I was doing," I quickly defend myself. "I was just saying a parent should never leave a child."

"Didn't your father leave you?"

"No. He didn't," I correct him. "He left my mother."

"Same thing, isn't it?" Christian says to me. "I mean, either way, he's not there. Right?"

I have decided to be brave...

"No, Christian," I say. "You're wrong. My father didn't leave me. He and my mother separated. It had nothing to do with me. My father loved me and always will. He would never do what your parents did." I look Christian dead in his eyes as I continue. "He would never leave me."

The smirk on Christian's face is momentarily gone. I do something I never thought I would be capable of. I rejoice in his presence.

"Why don't you sit down and have something to eat while we wait?" Christian says, deflecting the attention away from his wound.

"I don't know what we're supposed to be waiting for," I tell him.

"I told you. We're waiting for Brandon."

"Brandon's dead, Christian," I say with a coldness that competes with the room.

"You keep saying that."

"That's because he is."

The smirk is back upon Christian's face.

"Yeah. That's what I thought, too. But you and I know that's not true, right?"

I have decided to be brave...

"The only thing I know is that you killed him."

"Really?" he asks. "And how do you know that?"

"Because if you didn't kill him, you wouldn't be so afraid that he wasn't dead."

Christian takes his hand, the hand that could not win him the championship game, and pushes food from his banquet table to the floor.

"Sit down!" he roars.

I have decided to be brave...

"No! I won't do anything you ask me to!"

Christian walked toward me, stopping when he had closed half the distance between us. Because I stand unafraid.

"You're not afraid of me?" he asks.

"You don't have Murdoc and Russel with you."

"I don't need Murdoc and Russel," he tells me.

"And I am still not afraid of you," I say. "You've already violated my body and mind. You forced me to give you everything you wanted. I am not giving you anything else. And that includes my emotions. Not even hate." I pause, only so he knows that I am in control. "I look at you and the only thing I see is something to be pitied. But I refuse to even give you that. So that means when I look at you, I see nothing. And it's impossible to be afraid of nothing."

Christian walks toward me. I have decided to be brave...

The Dead Aware into Every
Stare Familiar

Jai drives while landscape fills Gabriel's eyes as it passes by. There is a familiarity to the way the both of them sit side by side. There is a body language, an unspoken language, a secret language that would take years to develop, the language of best friends that they seem to posses.

"Can I ask you something?" Jai asks. Gabriel turns to Jai, indicating that he may indeed ask him anything. "Are you Brandon?"

Gabriel remains silent, though he continues to look at Jai. Jai stares into Gabriel's eyes, searching for the answer that may lie in the familiarity of a stare. He turns back to the road with no greater awareness.

"Why do you think Brandon would come back?" Gabriel asks.

"To make things right," Jai answers.

"It's up to the living to make things right," Gabriel responds.

"What if they can't make it right on their own? Isn't that why people believe in God? Isn't that why they felt the need to create him?"

"Some people believe in God not because they want him to make things right, but because they want him to give them the strength to do it themselves."

"I don't know that I can make the things I've done right. I don't think even God could." Again, Gabriel remains silent. Jai speaks while keeping his eyes upon the road. "If you're Brandon, I just want you to know that I'm sorry. I want you to know that what I did lives with me every day. It never leaves me, not even when I sleep."

"Do you think the sky created the ground?" Gabriel asks.

Jai turns to Gabriel. "I don't know what you mean?"

"In order for the sky to be the sky it needs something beneath it," Gabriel elaborates. "The same is true for the ground. Without anything above or below it, it's just an undefined plane."

"I don't understand," Jai says.

"Look at it as the order of the universe. Everything is connected by something unacknowledged. The sky doesn't acknowledge the ground any more than the sun acknowledges the moon. But the living always acknowledge the dead. Why do you think that is?"

"I don't know," Jai admits. "Why?"

"Because the living must share awareness with the dead in order for them both to exist. The awareness connects them so the dead are not forgotten and also so the living understand that they're alive. If you are really sorry for the things that you did to Brandon, if it's in your heart, then Brandon knows, because that's where your memory of him resides. Your awareness... His awareness."

Jai pulls up to the entrance of Christian's house. He stops the car as he reads the word *hell* painted across the entrance. Jai turns to Gabriel. Gabriel smiles.

"It's OK. They're expecting me."

Icarus Wept

Christian has forced me to sit at one end of the table he has set up, while he sits at the other. I have not taken a single bite of the food before me for fear it is as poisoned as the mind that prepared it. That mind, Christian's, will not let me know what it is thinking. He has not uttered a word in the last twenty minutes. He has sat there, as have I, as still as the surface of the water in the pool, awash in the echo of apprehension.

I am unaware that Gabriel has entered the pool house until I see Christian's head turn and a smile draw upon his face.

"Welcome," Christian says as he rises from the table. "I'm so happy you could make it."

"I'm sorry it took me a while." Gabriel smiles. "I had to come from a very long way away."

I leap from my chair. If gravity had a heart, I would be in Gabriel's arms.

"Sit down!" Christian commands. I look at Christian, then back over to Gabriel. I sit down only because Gabriel's eyes beg me to, not because Christian's threaten me. Christian turns his attention back to Gabriel. "I bet it was."

"I've come to take you back with me," Gabriel tells Christian.

"I don't think so," Christian responds.

"You don't understand. You don't have a choice. That's how it is sometimes."

"Bullshit!" Christian cries. "I don't believe in ghosts!"

"It doesn't matter," Gabriel responds. "If they believe in you."

Gabriel takes a step toward me. I rise from my chair once again to run towards him. Christian picks up a revolver from the table and points it at me.

"I said, sit down!" he yells, pulling back the hammer of the gun for emphasis. I have no choice but to comply. Christian swings the gun in the direction of Gabriel. "Do ghosts believe in bullets?" Christian asks.

Gabriel turns to me and smiles in reassurance, the same way in which Brandon would smile at me when he was killing a bug I was afraid of. He then turns back to Christian.

"Your father's gun," Gabriel says, though I have no idea how he knows, and from the shock that washes across Christian's face, neither does he.

"How did you know?"

"Because. Everything you have is your father's." I can see the comprehension flood Christian's eyes like a tidal wave of awareness. "But that doesn't give you absolution for your sins."

"Fuck you," Christian spits. "And fuck absolution." Christian walks toward Gabriel. He never stops pointing the gun at him as he nears. "You like words, right? Quotes? Here's one. I learned it just for this occasion. 'Through me you enter into the city of woes, through me you enter into eternal pain, through me you enter the population of loss.'" Christian is now standing directly in front of Gabriel. The gun is but inches away from Gabriel's face. Christian finishes the quote. "'Abandon all hope, you who enter here.'" Christian then turns his head around to me and looks me in the eyes. "God," he says. "You are so fucking hot!"

Christian turns back to Gabriel, turns the gun on himself and fires.

I am the particle that drifts through the air, unseen, until the light from an apathetic sun pulls my existence into your view. I will be forever changed. Once I have been betrayed by the random refraction of light, I will never be able to hide from you again. And you will never allow me to remain what I was, as I floated along, hidden in the safety of the shadows.

Christian falls to the floor. Revenge doesn't weep. Redemption does not awake.

That Portion which Is Not Eternal
yet Still Remains

A shroud of white linen descends at the rate of reverence, as if gravity leads the funeral procession. A body beneath swims in blood, spilled not by remorse, but retreat. In moments as the sheet Gabriel lays across the body of Christian falls upon him, innocence will be forever stained by the consequence of evil. The blood will never come out, no matter how many times the sheet is washed. A portion of it will always remain. I cannot mourn that which has caused mourning. I cannot shed a tear for one that has caused a deluge to flow. I will not pray for one that has preyed. Amen.

I rush into Gabriel's arms, and he locks them around me. I hope that he loses the key. "I knew you would come," I say to him. "I knew you wouldn't let Christian hurt me."

"Your strength prevented that. Not me."

"But that's why you came back, isn't it, to protect me? And that's why you have to stay."

"No, Liv. That's not why I came back. And as much as my heart desires, it doesn't beat here anymore, so I cannot stay."

I break the embrace and look into Gabriel's eyes, searching for the reasons he keeps from me. "Then why did you come?"

"I left something," he tells me.

"What?"

"Your heart."

Gabriel looks over to the pool, and I follow his eyes. There, beneath the blue of the water, I see it. Only a portion is visible, but I can clearly see it. It is a clasp, caught between the openings of the pool drain, preventing it from being pulled away into the nothing. I look up at Gabriel. "Brandon," I say to him.

"It fell from my neck," he says softly. "I didn't want to go away without it."

He turns away from me, towards the pool. I turn him back. "No!"

"No?" Gabriel asks with confusion in his eyes.

"No," I tell him again. "I don't want you to get it. Let it stay down there."

"Why?" Gabriel asks.

"Because once you have it, you'll leave me. Let it stay there. Forever."

"I have to leave with or without it, Liv. I don't belong here anymore."

"You belong with me! You always have!" I wrap my arms around him. I wish for the strength of a hundred men. I am not going to let him dive into the pool. I repeat over and over in my mind, I have decided to be strong, I have decided to be strong, I have decided to be strong.

"Liv," he begs.

"Just leave it!" I cry. "Leave it."

My arms are not as strong as my realization that I will never be able to keep him here. I slide down his body and collapse to the surface of the deck at his feet.

Gabriel slowly kneels down beside me. He places one hand upon my back. It feels like my father's touch. I break down as tears fall to the floor.

"Don't," I plead. "Please don't."

"Liv," I hear again. Gabriel then takes his other hand and with his fingers gently lifts my head. I take hold of that hand and bring it to my lips. I press my lips against them as if I am dying of thirst and they are water. Gabriel looks into my eyes and then recites the last poem Brandon ever wrote for me.

"There is a place where you know my touch
it is beyond where flesh is allowed
it is deeper than where feelings dwell
you have but to whisper my name..."

I look back into Gabriel's eyes and begin reciting where he left off.

"You have but to whisper my name
and everyone that has ever been in love falls silent
they would dare not interrupt my answer
they would dare not come between our love
the space they listen from is around us
eternal is the place that surrounds us."

Gabriel takes my hand with his and lifts me from the floor. He steps to the edge of the pool. "Don't worry," he tells me. "I'll be right back."

I immediately think back to when he was in the pool at my house. Something was wrong. Something about water. He almost drowned then. "No," I say. "The water."

Gabriel touches the side of my face, reassuring me. "It's OK. Everything is wonderful."

I watch Gabriel as he, with the grace of a bird taking flight from a cliff's top, dives into the water of the pool. His body barely causes a ripple as he breaks the surface.

I hold my breath waiting for him to surface. I wonder how long can he hold his? What if the clasp slips from his grasp? Will that mean he must stay or does that mean he must follow it down never to resurface? I want to dive in after him. I step to the edge of the pool. Has it been one minute or has it been ten?

I watch as he seems to struggle with the drain, attempting to remove it so that he can retrieve the necklace. His body shakes back and forth in a violent rhythm and the surface of the water reacts nervously.

"Brandon!" I scream.

He has been down there too long. Bubble of air rise to the surface and release his cry for more.

"Brandon!"

I can wait no longer. I dive into the pool, disappearing beneath the water and swimming around to him. He has freed the catch and the necklace is in his hand, but he is not breathing. I drag his body to the surface as I struggle to pull my own above the threat of drowning. I manage to get us both to the edge of the pool, but only I am breathing. I get myself from the pool first, and then with every fiber of strength that has ever resided in my body, I pull Gabriel from the pool and his body collapses onto the deck. He gasps in air, and I feel the breath being pulled from my body as if I am breathing for the both of us. When he releases that air, I feel as if a kiss has rushed past my lips.

"Breathe, Brandon!" I cry. "Breathe!"

He is having difficulty. I don't understand it. Why is he choking? Was he underneath too long? Has he been here too long? Was he never supposed to be here? If the guardian of the dead has awakened to discover Brandon gone, if he has somehow found him and is attempting to take him back, then he will have to take me with him.

"Breathe!" I cry. I look down at Gabriel's right hand. He is clutching my chain and pendant even as his lungs struggle to breathe. I have to do something. I press my lips up to his to give him my own air. I can feel him pulling breath from inside me and now I am suffocating. "Let me breathe for you," I say as I pull away from his mouth and draw in more breath for him.

I lean back over him and breathe the air I have just taken in into his mouth. His lungs pull the air in as if drunk with the taste. My body wants to fight back, but I will not allow it. I will not allow him to die a second death. And if there is not enough air in my body to sustain him, then I want to go with him. He is a vampire sucking the last drops of blood from willing veins that ache to be dry like his.

"I will breathe for you. I will be your air," I think because I do not have the air to speak.

"No!" Gabriel says just as I feel my body embracing an eternal sleep. "That's enough, Liv." Gabriel now breathes on his own. "That's enough."

Gabriel takes his hand and pulls me into him. Both our bodies are soaked as we collapse into one another's arms.

"What were you doing, Liv?"

"I was trying to save you."

"You did, Liv," Gabriel says to me. "You did."

We rise from the floor, both still struggling to clear our lungs completely of water. Gabriel stands directly before me and hands me the necklace. I take it with my cold and trembling hands and gently place it around Gabriel's neck. I feel the clasp lock with my fingers, so I know it is safe. The heart-shaped pendant lies upon Gabriel's chest just above his own heart. He leans in and softly kisses me. I close my eyes and I feel a rush across my body as if I have been moved. I open my eyes and I no longer see Gabriel but Brandon. We are now in the desert in the same space we were when we last kissed.

"I love you," Brandon says to me.

"I love you, too, Brandon. I love you, eternal..."

Sunday

It is Sunday. Sunday. Sunday is my favorite day. Sunday. Sunday is the day that I spend with my father. Sunday. Just my father and I. Sunday. Sunday may be the only day I recognize.

There is often eloquence to things imagined, especially when imagined to soften the reality of how things really may be... Or how they were... Or how they are. Reality cannot be escaped, but it can be politely disregarded, like a prisoner that refuses to see bars. Eventually the bars can no longer see him.

I am driving to the beach today with my father. We are on a long ride that I want to go on forever but I keep fearing will be done in an instant. It is the same relationship of fun and fear that takes up residence in the core of my stomach every time I do something with him.

The top of the Mustang is down, and the sun takes full advantage by soaking us in its rays, as if dared to follow us. I am wearing my father's sunglasses to protect my eyes. My father wears none, because he gave me his, to protect his daughter's eyes. I look over at him and he looks back at me and smiles.

"Dad," I say, drawing out the word with feigned temper because I know he is smiling at the playful way the wind creates a maelstrom of hair atop my head. I struggle in vain to keep my hair in place, much in the same manner I attempt in vain to contain my father's laughter. He loves when my hair is messy. He says it's my true me. He thinks deep inside I am a jumble of thoughts and ideas and feelings that constantly collide. I think he likes my hair messy because his is always so. I don't care what his reasons are. And I don't care that he laughs at me. I love my father's laugh, and the only reason I would ever try and contain it is so I could take it with me everywhere.

I turn back to the road. My father and I are the only two upon it. The road is so beautiful. The road is so vast. My eyes cannot see an end even though my heart knows we are approaching one.

"Dad," I say as I turn to him in the car. "We should be at the beach soon." My dad simply smiles.

I love my father. That is why I visit his grave every Sunday. Sunday. Sunday is our day. Sunday. The day I imagine things for us to do and places for us to go. We are always the only two there, and I always want the adventure to go on forever, but it always feels like it is done in an instant.

Some of the things we do or places I choose for us to go are based on talks we had, and some are from the journals he left for me to read. Journals in which he wrote down places he wanted to go with me and experiences he wanted to share from the moment my mother told him she was pregnant. We had been to the beach once before with my mother, but in his journals, he wrote of how he wanted to go with me one day when I was older. He wanted to take an incredibly long ride on an impossibly sunny day and absorb the world uninterrupted through my eyes. That is what we are doing today.

I can see the ocean from the road. It is equally as vast. Waves roll gently onto the shore and it reminds me of the rush of waves my body felt when I was little and my father would take my hand.

My father died shortly after he and my mother decided that the road they were upon was splitting into two and each had to take a separate path if they were to avoid a catastrophic collision. The coroner's report read that the cause of death was acute alcohol poisoning, but I know it was from a sense of loneliness that remained with him no matter who he was with. The world did not kill my father, but it could not contain him.

The last time I visited my father's grave it was not a Sunday, it was a Thursday, and I told him about my rape. I imagined how he would comfort me and what he would say from the things I knew of him and things he had already said. His voice inside my head gave me strength, and my tongue could taste the lemonade he used to make as I talked about him making it. It makes me smile. And that makes me think of my father's smile. And then my heart writes him a poem.

> *"You are my father*
> *I am the portion of you you chose to release*
> *But I am the portion that will always return*
> *for I am the portion of you, eternal."*

I love you, Dad. Happy Sunday.

Epilogue
Zippo

Click. Click.

I flip the top of my father's Zippo lighter open and closed. It fits in my hand as if it were designed while its makers stared at a picture of my fingers. How else would they have known my thumb is so tiny and therefore made the front of the top so narrow that it almost fits within the grooves of my fingerprints, so that it slides up so effortlessly when I yearn for flame? How else would it never fail to light knowing I always yearn for flame?

Click. Click.

I sit on the hood of my '65 powder-blue Mustang. The sun is in my eyes, but its brilliance no longer impresses me. I have seen darker things that burn more intensely and I have touched brighter light that did not burn at all. The desert surrounds me like an undisturbed dream. I know that beneath the dream, souls that both haunted and protected me share an uneasy sleep, awakened by every footstep that I take. I try and walk lightly wherever I go.

Click. Click.

A click might be the most powerful sound in the world. Whether it is the click from the hammer of a gun announcing evil's entrance, the click of a briefcase whose contents plead for or try to avoid your future, or the click of a door-lock informing you that you cannot leave.

Click. Click.

A breeze blows past my body. Uh-oh. A ghost must be opening his eyes. I don't think I walked lightly enough. It's OK. The breeze feels good. It hasn't rained in the desert in months. When Gabriel first came, it seemed as if the rain never stopped. Maybe because Brandon died in the water, he could only return during its presence. Maybe what kills you never completely leaves you. Even if you are a ghost.

Click. Click.

It has also been months since I have seen Jai. It is he for whom I am waiting now. He is on his way to meet me. He is coming because I asked him to. I know that I said I would never speak to him again, but if Brandon could come back from the dead to avenge me, I could drive out to the desert to forgive Jai. Are vengeance and forgiveness not related? Are they not brothers separated only by intent?

Click. Click.

Other things have happened in the last months. My mother rejected a plea offer for Lucas Dunagan. He is going to stand trial. She convinced the victim to testify. She did it by promising that if she did, Lucas would never see the desert sun again, but every remaining day of his life, he would feel as if he were lying on its surface.

Click.

Murdoc never went on to play college ball. He was offered scholarships by no less than six different schools, but instead he chose to remain in Lago. He formed a group for troubled boys and their first project is to tear down and rebuild the abandoned church. Christian's father is paying for the entire project. No one but Murdoc is certain why, but I would assume it had something to do with the conversation Murdoc and he are said to have had in private.

Click.

I see Jai's car approaching in the distance. It disrupts sand and dust as if death sneezed and everyone waits to see what settles and what does not. I want to tell you one more thing before he arrives. I ran into Danielle the other day. She smiled and I looked into her eyes and they smiled, as well. She asked me if I had seen the new Zooey Deschanel movie. I told her I hadn't. She said we should see it together. I told her that would be great. I have seen enough ghosts; I think seeing Zooey would be nice.

Click.

The breeze has stopped. The ghost is back asleep. Maybe he was never fully awake. Maybe his eyes opened momentarily because even the dead become restless... like a fire in a desert. I hold the Zippo up. The top is open. My thumb pulls the flint wheel down, which ignites the flame. I have no cigarette. There is nothing for the flame to burn. I will not extinguish it though. I will allow it to remain. That is the beauty of fire... that even without purpose, it is able to consume you. I think the same can be said about love.

Chapter 1 - The Eternity of Ghosts - Locust

The worst part of death is that there is no worst part. The stages of dying come at you like a swarm. A swarm that allows momentary glimpses of hope as you attempt to peer through the horrific motion of a million wings fluttering. But ultimately the density and rapidity of the nature of swarming is too much for that hope to penetrate.

Not every swarm is the same, but then, not every death is important. My mother's death was important, not because she was my mother, but because I was forced to witness it. Like a car crash, while the car was being designed, before it had ever been built, and my mother had ever turned the key. That's how long it seemed it took for her to die.

Are you aware that locusts are typically solitary? The primary difference between them and other grasshoppers that make of the Acrididae family is that they have a swarming phase. For reasons truly known only to themselves they alter their habits, becoming gregarious in nature. The sole purpose of this once solitary creature then is to become part of something larger and effect devastation upon the landscape that once granted it solitude.

I wonder if cancer can reside within a single cell. And if it can, what is it waiting for? Does it know its purpose? Does it care? And if it did, would it remain alone to prevent the devastation of its own congregation?

I think mothers die stronger than fathers do. Even though my father did not hide the fact that he was dying one glass at a time, he sort of romanticized his demise. I used to think it was because he thought there would never be a last glass. That he thought he was invincible. Watching my mother struggle just to smile when I could not I understood that my father's bravado was actually fear. He did not have the strength to battle his alcoholism. And because he was so afraid of dying the only way to cope was to embrace death it as if it were his lover.

My mother never embraced death. But neither did she fear it. If you fear something you always have one eye upon it and she wanted to take in everything and everyone every time as if it were her last. She would however have daily conversations with death, almost as if she thought she might talk it to its own end. She did this with every treatment, every statement, every breath. And when it was death's turn to have the final word, she politely allowed it. Mothers die stronger than fathers do because the cycle of life is within them. They understand it better.

You know what the worst part of cancer is? That it allows the answer to every question except the one that really matters: Why me?

The last words my mother spoke to me were, "Don't be afraid... It's a harmless moon." She smiled with her eyes and then she closed them.

I don't dream of ghosts. I do believe in them. But this you already know. Ghosts are not good or bad. They are both. Which manifestations appear before you depends upon why they felt you requested them. That's the thing about ghosts. They don't appear unless you ask them to. I don't dream of ghosts. Ghosts dream of me.

Do you know what the worst part of love is? That sometimes it comes at you like locusts. And when it does, you understand why God used them to frighten mankind when his voice no longer did.

But by then it's too late.

About the Author

Maurice Jovan Billington was born in Chicago, Illinois and currently resides in the Tampa with his wife and three children. Known as A Cat Named Mo for his radio show on 102.5 The Bone, Maurice is working on the second novel in his "Eternal Trilogy" to be titled "The Eternity of Ghosts." He is an accomplished screenwriter, with his screenplay "9" winning the Fade In Screenwriting Award for Best Thriller. Also a poet and director of multiple short films, Maurice hopes to eventually write a movie for "A Portion of the Eternal."

www.ingramcontent.com/pod-product-compliance
Lightning Source LLC
Chambersburg PA
CBHW050035030726
47506CB00001B/282

* 9 7 8 1 9 4 5 8 1 2 1 6 3 *